Members of the Over 50's Singles Night

BJ FRANKLIN (FOUNDER): She'll do anything to get her sister out of her house, including humiliating herself by letting the folks at temple think *she's* on the market for a boyfriend.

IRIS MEYERHOFF: Widowed for a year, she's actually quite happy being single. She just wishes her sister BJ would let her be. And no, she's not going to have any more plastic surgery—well, maybe just a little Botox.

HARVEY SUSSMAN: This retired optometrist only attends as a favor to BJ...and she owes him. Big-time.

FRED SHULMAN: Seeing that Fred isn't in the market for a *girl*friend, we're really not sure why he's a regular.

ARNOLD LIEBERMAN: He's got the hots for Iris. Too bad his ill-fitting toupee keeps getting in his way.

MOLLY GERBER: Is just there for the food.

Ellyn Bache

Ellyn Bache began writing freelance newspaper articles
when her four children were small. As they got older
and gave her more time, she turned her hand to short
stories. It took her six years to get her first one published.
Then, for many years, her fiction appeared in a wide
variety of women's magazines and literary journals and
was published in a collection that won the Willa Cather
Fiction Prize. Ellyn began her first novel, *Safe Passage*,
the year her youngest son went to school full-time. That
book was later made into a film starring Susan Sarandon,
and Ellyn went on to write other novels for women, a
novel for teens, a children's picture book and many more
stories and articles. There's more on her Web site,
www.ellynbache.com.

Ellyn Bache

OVER 50'S
SINGLES NIGHT

OVER 50'S SINGLES NIGHT

copyright © 2006 by Ellyn Bache

isbn 0373880871

TheNextNovel.com

 HARLEQUIN®

PRINTED IN U.S.A.

From the Author

Dear Reader,

It's been a privilege for me to write this lighthearted story about two not-so-young widows whose lives move in surprising new directions. A few years ago, when my husband of more than thirty years passed away, it was hard to imagine getting beyond those first heavy months of pain and grief, much less ever "moving on." Like countless other women before me, I discovered that the loss of a spouse is something to get "through" rather than "over"—but I also realized that you really *do* laugh again, and that some of the old sayings really are true: the other side of loss is freedom; the other side of sorrow, joy; the other side of tears, laughter.

BJ and Iris are widowed sisters learning to embrace their freedom (whether they want to or not)…startling themselves by feeling joyful (even in the midst of the domestic mayhem that rules their lives)…and daring to move on.

I hope you'll enjoy them. I hope they'll make you smile.

Ellyn Bache

CHAPTER 1

"So now BJ Fradkin has the brilliant idea to start an over-fifty singles night? Of all people!"

Oh yes, BJ knew what they'd say. This would be Sarah Kline, nosy and nasal.

"Why not? David died six, seven years ago. Maybe she wants companionship." This would be—who? Amy Friedman, head of the bereavement committee? "Maybe she needs money," Amy would whisper.

"Pfft. David left her plenty, and what BJ makes from that advertiser rag she runs, she has more money than she knows what to do with." Sarah would tug at a skirt far too short for a woman of sixty—a fact she might have known if she'd shut up long enough to listen. "And that house! If BJ minded rattling around so much, she'd have found a companion years ago. Or sold it."

Amy would consider this.

"She's not looking for sex, either," Sarah would continue. "She once said her interest in sex was over, kaput, done with, thirty years ago after Janelle was born."

This was an out-and-out lie.

Would Sarah actually *say* such a thing?

Get a grip, what difference did it make? At the Temple of Israel there was always plenty of gossip. You ignored it and did what you had to. At the moment, an over-fifty singles night was the best idea BJ had.

She mentioned it first to Rabbi Seidman, who said, "An over-fifty singles night? Sure. Why not? Just clear it with the board."

BJ wrote a little proposal. She'd served three terms on the board, back when she'd been building her business. She knew what to emphasize. The more activities the temple offered, the better the chance of signing up new members, who helped fill the treasury. There was never enough money. Tactfully, BJ noted that over-fifties were generally richer and more likely to make donations than, say, new families with preschoolers and an expensive sitter.

Kay, the temple's longtime secretary, had an untreated cataract no one ever mentioned, even when her notices went out rife with errors. But when Kay nearly sent out an e-mail announcing an Over-Fifty Singles *Club*, BJ couldn't remain silent. "Singles *night*, not singles club. Call it a club and people will think they're making another commitment, the last thing anyone wants."

BJ didn't want another commitment, herself. What she wanted was a new husband for her sister Iris, who had been widowed nearly a year and a half ago. To BJ it seemed like forever. Iris had spent the past two months sleeping in BJ's guest room and showing no inclination to leave. Iris walked BJ's dog, Randolph. Iris exhausted whole bottles of Windex wiping streaks and paw prints from sliding-glass doors that had been dirty for years. Iris shopped for groceries and wouldn't let BJ pay. After work BJ's den smelled like Lemon Pledge and her kitchen smelled like the stuffed cabbage their mother used to make. It was pleasant enough, but BJ was worried. Iris was only fifty-five, seven years younger than BJ, and BJ had always looked out for her. Much as she loved Iris, she knew her sister did not need another woman, even a sibling, to cook and clean for. Iris needed a man.

"I know what you're doing," Iris said on the afternoon before the first Singles Night Out. She had wrapped ice in a towel and was applying it to her left temple, claiming a headache. "You're trying to cheer me up, get me out of the house."

"I'm trying to provide a nice social environment for people who enjoy a weekday evening out that isn't a business meeting," BJ replied. "But in the event that my motive *was* to cheer you up, why would that be so terrible?"

"Because I'm not depressed." With dramatic nonchalance, Iris sank into the oversize cushions of the couch, practicing the artful, slow-motion collapse she had perfected in second grade. "I'm not lonely. I don't need companionship. I just have a headache." She hunkered deeper into the cushions. "But if you need me so desperately to make your project a success, I'll make every effort to recover."

BJ studied her sister. In her purple Ralph Lauren sweatpants and matching sweatshirt, Iris looked stylish and not the least bit sick. Slender except for her big bust, long limbed for a woman who stood only five-three, Iris could have risen from the couch and gone to the dinner without changing clothes or touching up her makeup, and still have been the most put-together person at the table. Even her hair, held back from the top and sides with combs and left to its natural curl in the back, looked presentable except for the dye job that always left it far too patent-leather-black.

At fifty-five, Iris also had a firm, taut jawline with no trace of a double chin. She had no bags under her eyes and no sagging above them. If BJ had once been critical of Iris for responding with cosmetic surgery to each of her husband Sheldon's dalliances, now she thought her sister had had the right idea. The new man, whoever he turned out to be, would appreciate Iris's youthful face. Except, possibly, for her nose. Iris's nose, reshaped more than once, sloped to a short, perky point that in other circumstances might have been lovely. But in combination with the black hair and luminous, almond-shaped black eyes and smooth olive skin, it gave Iris more than a passing facial resemblance to Michael Jackson. The likeness was eerie. BJ was always amazed how many people thought Iris reminded them of someone but never made the connection.

"Why are you staring at me?" Iris opened her eyes and struggled to sit up among the bulky cushions that engulfed her. "You think I look older, don't you?"

"No, of course not. I wasn't staring. I was thinking."

"I do look older. After the death of a spouse, people age." She ran a manicured hand across her cheek. "You're thinking I should probably have a little more work done."

"Don't be ridiculous. What work could possibly be left? You look fine."

"You think I ought to go for another consultation."

"I don't think any such thing. When did you get to be such an expert on what I'm thinking? Besides, I thought you gave it up." Shortly before Sheldon's untimely demise, Iris had read that deep general anesthesia could leave patients cognitively impaired. Frightened more by the prospect of early dementia than by wrinkles, she declared a moratorium on any procedure too painful to be numbed by a shot of lidocaine. As far as BJ knew, her sister had limited herself thereafter to Botox and dermabrasion and the occasional blue peel.

"Well, think whatever you want to, but I'm finished with surgery even if I turn into a hag," Iris said.

"Honey, your face is gorgeous. Your bosom is high. Your stomach is flat. How many other women over fifty can say that?"

"Thank you, but the key term here is 'over fifty'," Iris said. "I know when I'm being referred to as old."

"Iris, listen to me. I've been looking at you since the day you were born, and even now, fifty-five years later, the sight doesn't make me gag or throw up."

"Very comforting. Very reassuring." Iris tried in earnest to release herself from the clutch of the pillows. She looked like someone treading water.

"Anyway, you can fix yourself all you want to, but someday the backs of your hands will break out in age spots or you'll get arthritis that makes you walk with a limp."

Horrified, Iris catapulted herself off the couch into a standing position. She examined a flawless hand and flexed an arthritis-free knee. "I wish you wouldn't say those things," she said.

"Come on, Iris. Come to the dinner with me. How could it hurt you?"

"It could make me fat," Iris asserted, and headed in the direction of her room.

This turned out to be just as well. The Over-Fifty Singles Night was still a work in progress. Although BJ had chosen Pepper's Restaurant and Sports Bar because it was a favorite with local men, five females showed up, all of them closer to seventy than fifty, and only one male, Fred Shulman, who was gay.

"So why are you here, Fred?" BJ asked over a glass of merlot. "You still miss Tommy?"

"Well, sure. I'll always miss Tommy. You don't miss David?"

"After six years, not so much."

"Mainly, I came because I get tired of eating alone," Fred said.

"Not me," piped the reedy voice of Molly Gerber, age eighty-seven, a resident at Manorhouse Retirement Home. "You're never alone in the dining room over there. But the food! Don't ask."

One of the two other women she'd brought nodded in vigorous agreement. "No salt. No nothing." She waved dismissively. "Pap."

They had just given the waiter their orders when another man approached the table. He was BJ's age, early sixties. Pleasant face, deep tan, really terrible toupee.

"Oh, good. You came," Fred said. "Everybody, this is Arnold Lieberman."

"You belong to the temple?" Molly Gerber asked.

"No. Unaffiliated." Arnold sat down next to Fred.

"Gay?" BJ had never been one to mince words.

"Straight," Arnold growled.

She thought, lose the rug and he's not bad for an old geezer.

Arnold was probably thinking, what a bitch.

It was not an auspicious beginning.

Iris's husband, Sheldon Meyerhoff, hadn't died immediately. BJ believed it would have been better if he had. After collapsing onto the plushly carpeted floor of the restaurant where he was lunching with thirty-something Dee Dee Adams, Sheldon had responded to CPR administered by the bartender, and spent a week in cardiac care before succumbing to a second massive heart attack. During that week, he had apologized to Iris repeatedly, in a pathetic thin voice that had no doubt won her heart. At the funeral, Iris's daughter, Diane, and Diane's husband, Wes, walked on either side of Iris to hold her up. In BJ's view, Iris displayed a grief Sheldon didn't deserve.

Despite the standard admonition to do nothing the first year, Iris had put her house up for sale almost at once. Both Diane and BJ tried to talk her out of it. "What's the hurry? Why not wait? You don't need the cash." Sheldon, who at various times had been a salesman of everything from automobiles to vinyl siding, had never been well-off, but he had provided handsomely for his widow. During a brief stint with a life-insurance company, he had been his own best customer. Iris would not have to work another day in her life.

"It's not just about the money," Iris said. "I can barely live in this house another minute, never mind another year."

"Okay, but I want to be clear on this," BJ said. "Are you moving because of what the neighbors might be thinking? Or because you don't want to spend any more time than you have to where that stinking, womanizing piece of slime sometimes slept?"

Iris averted her eyes and said nothing, unable even now to acknowledge the fitness of BJ's candid descriptions.

Iris's house languished on the market for months.

Iris seemed too busy to notice. When Diane, pregnant with her second son, Noah, was put on bed rest for a month, Iris spent most of her time cooking meals and helping with two-year-old Jonah. When Noah was born in June, Iris spent another month helping Diane and her husband cope with a newborn and a toddler. Then Diane went back to work, leaving the children in the care of their so-called nanny, Patti Ann. Iris turned her attention to the details of Sheldon's estate. She also sold most of the furniture she'd lived with for nearly thirty years. After giving Diane her good dishes and silver, Iris spent part of each day packing house-hold items into cartons and taking them to Goodwill. At night she returned home, sat on the single foot-stool left in her family room, and watched a television perched atop a cardboard moving box. When at last a buyer made a lowball offer for her house, Iris accepted without further negotiations. She cleared out all the rest of her possessions. She had spent her entire first year of widowhood being busy. The only thing she was not busy doing was finding another place to live.

BJ discovered this only two weeks before the settle-ment. She assumed Iris would take an apartment while she looked for a smaller, more suitable house than the one she'd shared with Sheldon. She guessed Iris would eventually buy one of the new condos around the corner from Diane's subdivision. None of that turned out to be true. What Iris wanted was "time to think."

What Iris wanted was to spend a little time at her sister's. At a time like that, how could BJ say no?

The week after her first attempt to create a congenial social environment for Iris, BJ's notice in the congregational e-mail read, Tired of Eating Alone? Come to the Over-Fifty Singles Night Out. If Fred Shulman wasn't exactly eligible, at least he was male, and if he'd been willing to eat with a bunch of old ladies just for the company, no doubt others would be, too.

On the afternoon before the event, BJ said, "Iris. Please. How could it hurt you to have a nice dinner out with me? To offer me some moral support?"

"Believe me, I want to. But Diane and Wes both have meetings and I promised to babysit the boys."

BJ was annoyed. She knew Patti Ann was always willing to extend her babysitting hours if it meant extra cash. Next time, BJ would hint to Iris that a person living in her sister's home, off her sister's largesse, had an obligation to come to dinner if her sister asked. She would do this tactfully.

That second night, all the retirement-home ladies showed up again, along with doddering Lou Green, who took five minutes to get from the front door to the table, inching his way along with the help of his cane. He sat beside Fred, the only other male. Arnold, the man with the terrible toupee, had not returned. BJ looked for support to her friend, Resa Taub, whose husband had recently left, and who—

unlike Iris—had responded to BJ's request by actually showing up.

In the middle of the meal, Molly Gerber choked. When BJ and Resa leaped up and slapped her on the back, a wad of half-chewed chicken fajita flew out of her mouth and onto her plate, along with Molly's full set of dentures. BJ and Resa offered soothing words, wiped off the chicken-laden dentures with a wet napkin and helped Molly put them back in her mouth. The other retirement-home women stayed seated and observed the drama calmly, as if this happened all the time. It probably did.

Iris was sitting in the family room when BJ got home. "I thought you were babysitting."

"Diane got home early. She's still nursing the baby."

"I know that, but so what?" Diane's powerful electric breast pump could extract a full day's supply of milk in half an hour. She bottled it every night so Patti Ann could feed it to Noah the next day. When Diane went on a week-long business trip, she overnighted ice-packed breast milk to the house. It was a new world. A woman did not need to rush home to feed her child when she had breast pumps and FedEx.

"I know what you're thinking," Iris said. "You're thinking I wasn't babysitting. That I was making up an excuse not to go to the singles night."

"That's ridiculous." BJ hated when her sister read her mind.

"So how was it?" Iris asked. "The dinner?"

"I felt like I was running a geriatrics ward." BJ gave a few details. She did not add that Fred had practically had to drag Lou Green to the men's room after he announced loudly, "I gotta poop. *Right now*." Nor did she describe the lump of Molly Gerber's half-chewed food sitting atop the rest of her uneaten chicken fajita, or mention that, as she replaced the old woman's dentures, the slick, saliva feel of Molly's mouth nearly made her gag. BJ and Iris had known Molly Gerber all their lives, first as their religious school principal and later as president of the Sisterhood before she grew old and started shrinking. They had always admired Molly. In view of that, BJ decided there were a few things Iris didn't have to know.

But more details were not going to be necessary. Iris's expression had already softened. She had forgiven BJ for entertaining the notion that she was not, in fact, babysitting. In return, BJ felt compelled to forgive her sister for not coming to the dinner, although she would have been justified in holding the grudge a little longer, as they both knew.

"I'll go next time," Iris said, reading BJ's mind again. "Next time, I promise."

CHAPTER 2

Two days later, Iris burst into BJ's bedroom without knocking, something she never did. It was a little like Kramer flinging himself into Jerry's apartment on the reruns of *Seinfeld*. Like Kramer, Iris stopped short and smoothed her hair to compose herself. In her outstretched hand was a soft-cushioned child's potty seat, emblazoned with bright cartoon figures, which she was waving at the window. She took a deep breath and said in the unnaturally calm tone she reserved for times of crisis, "There's a man outside with a weapon in his hand. Don't get upset. There's still time to call nine-one-one."

The intrusion jolted BJ out of her midafternoon haze. Having changed clothes after a boring chamber of commerce lunch, she had been eyeing with jealousy her dog, Randolph, sound asleep on the floor. Iris's entrance did not faze Randolph, who snored on. Cautiously, BJ moved toward the window.

Her second-floor bedroom overlooked the front yard. Below her, she saw a man's clean-swept bald pate, half-hidden beneath the colorful leaves of a Chinese tallow tree. He advanced toward the house with a long pole slung over his shoulder, attached at the top to a sharp blade swaying precariously above his head. Held aloft like that, the cutting edge seemed more likely to decapitate the man himself than any intended victim.

Iris picked up the bedside phone.

"Put that down, it's just Harvey Sussman," BJ said. "He doesn't have a weapon. He has an edger."

Iris stared at BJ blankly. She clutched both the receiver and the potty seat to her chest.

"A *garden* tool," BJ explained. "To make a neat line at the edge of the lawn. When was the last time you took a good look at the guys who do yards?"

Iris put down the phone.

The front doorbell rang. Randolph opened an eye and looked startled. As if recalling his duties, he got reluctantly to his feet and began to bark. By this time a murderer could have been in the house and up the stairs, slitting their throats.

After a few seconds, Randolph warmed to his role. He was a watchdog! There was work to be done! He practically knocked BJ over as he raced from the room and bounded down the stairs. He wagged his tail riotously. His barking reached a crescendo. When BJ opened the door, he jumped onto Harvey as if onto a long-lost friend, his nails digging at the waist of the visitor's cutoff jeans.

"Hey buddy, howya doing, buddy," Harvey said as the dog attempted to climb him.

"Get down, Randolph."

"It's okay." Harvey set the edger on the porch and scratched the dog behind the ears. Randolph stretched and luxuriated. After a while Harvey stopped rubbing. "Hey, buddy, time to calm down. Calm down, buddy."

Randolph ignored him. His pink tongue lolled out of his mouth as he panted and jumped.

"This is crazy. The Boston Strangler could come to your door and Buddy here would try to lick him to death," Harvey said.

BJ disliked Iris echoing her thoughts, but when a casual acquaintance like Harvey did it, it was alarming. "I think they caught the Boston Strangler a couple of decades ago. Besides, Randolph knows you."

Harvey's gaze traveled upward from the dog to the landing of the stairs, where Iris stood, trim in her black slacks and a red sweater that fit snugly across her bust. Taking a step in their direction, Iris held gracefully to the banister with one hand and let the bright potty seat dangle from the other. BJ thought she detected a glimmer of admiration in Harvey's glance.

"Harvey, you know my sister, don't you? Iris, this is Harvey Sussman."

"Pleasure," Harvey said.

Iris took in Harvey's grass-stained cutoffs and T-shirt. She nodded with noncommittal politeness.

"Grandchildren?" Harvey pointed to the potty seat. Iris glanced at it, as if just realizing it was in her hand. "Oh. Yes. Two. I'm on my way to take this over there. Jonah's two and a half. The nanny's trying to train him," she babbled. "But it's hard, with a baby. Sibling rivalry. Noah's only four months old."

"Ah. The waterboys." Harvey smiled.

Iris looked blank.

"Jonah and Noah. Jonah was swallowed by a whale. Noah built the ark."

"Oh. Sure." Understanding and embarrassment dueled for control of Iris's well-preserved face. "The waterboys. The Bible," she said as a slight flush infused her reinforced cheeks. Anyone could see how much she hated not to get it the first time. "Well, if you'll excuse me, I promised to be there." She came down the steps and edged past Harvey out the door.

Randolph, seeing that he was going to get no more special attention, flopped down in the tiled entryway. Without being invited, Harvey picked up the edger and stepped inside. Any other neighbor would have left the implement on the porch. A sprinkling of dark soil landed on the tile. BJ glanced down to show her distaste. Harvey did not seem to notice.

"To what do I owe the pleasure of this visit?" BJ asked.

"My lawn mower's in the shop. Lend me yours and I'll edge your lawn. Which needs it, by the way. You've got grass creeping halfway across your sidewalk."

Although this was true, in some people candor was not a good quality—as when, years before, Harvey had heard BJ's name for the first time and said, "BJ? I hate people with just initials. Why BJ? Why not Betty Jo or Barbara Jane?"

"If your name was Beulah Jeannette, you'd be BJ, too," she'd replied.

"You got a point," he'd said bluntly. "Beulah? Wasn't that some overweight housekeeper on early TV?"

She'd never cared for Harvey much, after that. It was a particular mystery that for years he'd picked on her, and not some friendlier neighbor, to lend him garden tools when his were in the shop or on the blink.

Harvey set down the edger, then seemed to realize he was inside the house. He snatched it off the floor, leaving behind the dirt but no obvious scratches. "So? The lawn mower?" he said.

Having sold ads for twenty years, BJ was always aware of her bargaining position. It was true she'd neglected her yard since Iris had arrived. She'd spent her spare time with her sister. It was also true that, in spite of her inattention, her yard looked better than Harvey's. BJ's landscape was dominated by the warm-season grasses that thrived in Fern Hollow but grew more slowly as summer faded into fall. Only the annual rye that stayed green all winter grew rampantly now, while the weather was still mild. It wouldn't slow down until a serious freeze. BJ hated the stuff. Harvey always planted a ton of it. Even in January and February his front yard would look like an out-of-place patch of springtime wedged between the neighbors' brown, dormant lawns. Right now, if BJ remembered correctly,

Harvey's yard was becoming an unruly mat of emerald-green rye, clashing with the fall colors.

Recalling the interest that had flickered in Harvey's eyes at the sight of Iris, and his passion for a well-trimmed lawn, BJ said agreeably, "Sure, you can edge my yard in exchange for borrowing the lawn mower. As long as you agree to one other thing."

Harvey was not a tall man, but he had a rather large and dignified face, with brown eyes that flashed with sudden suspicion behind his wire-rimmed glasses. "One other thing?"

"Come to the temple's next Over-Fifty Singles Night. You've probably read about it in your e-mail."

"What does that mean, exactly—'Over-Fifty Singles Club'?" When he frowned, Harvey's sternness was imposing.

"It's not a 'club,' it's just a 'night.' Dinner at a restaurant with a bunch of other people. Good company. Food and drink. It'll be fun."

Harvey retreated onto the porch, edger in hand.

"Don't look so worried. Nobody's going to ask you to serve on committees. All we do is eat and talk. Who knows? You might meet the woman of your dreams."

"At an over-fifty function? Not likely. At an under-forty function, maybe."

"Then you're in for a long and lonely old age. And very tall grass."

Harvey paused for a long beat. BJ could almost feel the tug-of-war going on in his head between the stooped, gray-haired women he imagined would surround him at the singles night, and the scraggly, overgrown lawn that would declare him unfit for another Fern Hollow Neighborhood Award of the Month. "What restaurant?" he finally asked.

"Pepper's."

"Just this once."

"Fine." BJ closed the door behind her. A minute later she heard the edger start up.

As often happened when people lived a few doors away for many years, the Fradkins and the Sussmans had never known each other well. Harvey was an optometrist who had moved into his house about ten years ago, after he and his first wife divorced. The rumor in temple was that the marriage had never been happy, and finally the wife had served separation papers and moved out of state. Hordes of females swarmed Harvey almost at once. Within a year he was married again, to a much-younger woman who worked as a receptionist in his office. Like most men, Harvey Sussman thought with his dick, not his brain.

But no. That wasn't quite fair. BJ would never have started the Over-Fifty Singles Night if she'd thought no man wanted a woman over forty. Wives provided many valuable services, and not just sex. They cooked, or at least sat across from their husbands at the table. They kept them company in front of the TV, even when the show was *The Simpsons* or Monday night football. They sorted bills while listening with one ear to the status of laundry in the wash and the other to the lament of a troubled friend on the phone. Women could multi-task. Men could not. This was why a man required a wife at all stages of his life, while an independent single woman or divorcee or widow like BJ, with enough money and reasonably good health, could function per-fectly well on her own. When it came to providing services, experienced women often said to themselves, *been there, done that*—with the result that they were not always available. The man who could find an attrac-tive, seasoned wife (like Iris, for example) was lucky indeed. Such a wife would watch his cholesterol, save him from having to go alone to parties and help him plan vacations with the verve and expertise of someone who had either been there—or wanted to be. During her years of financial strife, Iris had studied travel catalogs (as well as those for clothing and other goods) with the dedication of a Rhodes scholar, and was now well qualified to put her knowledge to use.

BJ recalled that vacations must have been a partic-ular interest of Harvey Sussman's second wife, also. Within a month of their wedding she had convinced him to retire from his optometry practice, though he was only in his mid-fifties at the time and (it was rumored) not really ready to stop working. The newly-weds went on a couple of cruises and finally an around-the-world tour. BJ remembered this because the new wife had queried all the neighbors about dog-sitting for her yappy miniature poodle, so she wouldn't have to board the creature. BJ had not volunteered. Ten minutes after the world tour ended, or so it seemed, the wife and poodle were gone.

Ever since, Harvey had shown up at services on the High Holidays and spent the rest of his time working in his yard. There was rarely a day he wasn't out there, even in July during Fern Hollow's famous heat. The year his wife left, he pulled out every foundation planting surrounding his house and single-handedly enlarged all the beds, using shovels and hoes and pieces of equipment from A-1 Rental. He bought a pickup truck and hauled new plants in from Ott's Nursery, replacing every bush and shrub. In the fall he put in hundreds of bulbs and small perennials. In the spring, he added flowering annuals: marigolds, petunias, impatience, zinnias. All summer, he could be seen outdoors at sunrise, cutting off spent flower heads. He edged and pruned and mulched and weeded. He created great piles of compost and spread them for fertilizer. Once, without asking anyone for help, he had moved a spiny six-foot holly tree from the front yard to the back. Harvey Sussman was the only person BJ had ever known for whom gardening was a form of anger management.

A woman like Iris, BJ told herself, might be just what he needed. The interest on Harvey's face as he had looked at her was unmistakable. Iris was nothing if not pleasing and soothing. She would calm him down, tamp his fury into good-natured enthusiasm. In return, Harvey would protect and admire her. They would be good for each other. She would love the bouquets of flowers he'd bring her, and make a fuss over the vegetable plot of tomatoes and squash and green beans he'd add, to provide fresh produce for her famous vegetable medley casserole. Iris was just the sort of woman to convince the editors at *Southern Living* to come to Fern Hollow and write a feature on Harvey's garden. He would be thrilled. They might spend the rest of their lives gardening together in Harvey's yard just down the street.

Except that Iris would never ruin a manicure by plunging her hands into damp soil.

Well, that was just a detail. She didn't have to *dig* in the garden. She just had to appreciate it.

Back upstairs, BJ went into her bedroom to put away the clothes she hadn't had time to hang up earlier. Randolph followed. He flopped onto the floor with a grunt, as if to express annoyance at being interrupted from his nap and gratitude to be back to it. BJ began to have second thoughts. What was she *thinking*? Trying to set up Iris with a man who had bypassed dozens of age-appropriate women in order to marry a bimbo? It would be like Sheldon Meyerhoff all over again.

On the other hand, Harvey and the bimbo had parted years ago, and BJ had never seen him with *any* woman since then, let alone a younger one. He must have learned his lesson.

Still, Harvey had said he'd never find a woman at an over-fifty event, only an under-forty one.

He had probably been joking.

A man who had devoted his professional life to tending people's eyes, and his retirement to nurturing plants—how bad could he be?

BJ looked in the mirror and pretended to talk to someone just out of her line of sight. She gestured with either hand to indicate where people were standing. "This is my sister, Iris Sussman," she practiced. "And my brother-in-law, Harvey."

It didn't sound so terribly far-fetched.

CHAPTER 3

Iris took the same route to Diane's house at least three times a week, so she didn't understand why her heart was beating quite so fast and frighteningly today.

Well, of course she understood. Who was she kidding?

If she was having a heart attack like Sheldon's, she probably deserved it.

No. She'd done nothing wrong.

You didn't have heart attacks over a potty seat. No one did.

In her effort not to get more agitated than she already was, Iris often turned her mind to the one thing she knew would calm her down—remembering all the people she loved. In times of stress, this was the essential thing to hold on to.

She loved her daughter, Diane. She loved Diane's husband, Wes. She loved her sister, BJ, despite a betrayal for which she'd forgiven BJ years ago. Most of all she loved her grandsons—Jonah, who at two and a half had become an interesting little person, and Noah, who at four months was beginning to look less like a turtle than he had at birth.

Iris also loved her husband, Sheldon, even though he was an adulterer and dead. This was problematic. The memory of his youthful handsomeness before he gained all that weight, especially the way his thick blond eyelashes caught the light, could still bring tears to her eyes no matter how much she told herself it shouldn't. She'd been twenty when she met him. She'd lived with him more than thirty years. The first time he came home smelling like another woman, two-year-old Diane had run to him, all bouncing dark hair and laughter, and he'd lifted her into his treacherous arms. They'd looked so happy that Iris hadn't been able to utter a word. She'd simply watched, her spirit cowering in some dark corner of herself, while one thought formed clear as a voice inside her head: *Decide*.

In the space of a heartbeat, she'd decided to stay.

Maybe that was a mistake. She would never know. For a long time she'd thought she'd done the right thing by making sure Diane never lived in a broken home. Even after Diane was grown and married, Iris had believed that. But after Sheldon died, Iris had felt an urgent need to start a new life and throw the old one away. She guessed she hadn't gotten very far, unless you called selling your house progress, and moving in with your duty-bound and probably still guilt-ridden sister. At least she had this litany of people she loved: her daughter, her grandsons, her sister, her husband. Even her son-in-law. How many women could say *that*?

The person Iris did not love was Patti Ann, the nanny.

It comforted her as she sat at the endless light in front of the mall to remember that BJ did not love Patti Ann, either.

"What makes her a nanny instead of a sitter?" BJ had asked two years ago when the woman had been hired to care for Jonah so Diane could go back to work. "Nannies are twenty-three. Or Hispanic. Or from some island in the Caribbean or somewhere. Not gray-haired white women of fifty."

"They hired her through some service," Iris had explained. "I think she went to nanny school."

"Is that where they taught her always to carry Diane's phone around so she can call nine-one-one?"

Iris tried not to smile.

"Nanny, my ass," BJ concluded. "She looks like a sitter to me."

In the two years since, Iris had kept BJ's assessment in mind. She kept it in mind now as she drove the thirty minutes across town, determined to confront Patti Ann while Diane and Wes were still at work, to settle the matter of the potty seat before it kept her awake another night.

"Take him to the bathroom before you go," Patti Ann had commanded the other day when Iris was leaving with Jonah for Barnes & Noble, where he could play with the train set in the children's department. It was his favorite outing, and they were halfway out the door. Patti Ann didn't care. Ever since Noah had arrived, she'd transferred her unjudgmental affection to the baby the way a mother might but a nanny shouldn't, and she'd been hell bent on toilet training poor Jonah, no matter what.

"We're leaving right now," Iris had called.

Patti Ann, overweight and huffing as she lumbered toward them with Noah slung over her shoulder, said, "Oh no, we put him on the potty every forty-five minutes." Using the royal plural. "Come on, Jonah." With her free hand, she reached out to grab him. Jonah darted behind Iris and clung to her leg. "We're leaving," Iris repeated, and dragged him out the door.

When they returned an hour later, Patti Ann gave them an absentminded wave while cooing to Noah with a big smile. Jonah, in a move so quick that Iris had no time to respond, pulled down his pants and said gleefully, "Look, Patti Ann," and peed all over the floor.

Iris rushed to clean it up, though it would have been smarter, and perfectly appropriate, to hold the baby instead. *This is not my job*, she thought as she sprayed Resolve onto the carpet. Much as she loved her grandchildren, at this stage of her life she did not want to do toilet training or clean up after the lapses. She didn't *need* to. Patti Ann was the hired help.

All the same, she scrubbed and said nothing. She seethed but remained polite. She let Patti Ann gloat, no doubt thinking, *well, Granny, you might have won the battle, but look who won the war*. When Iris was ready to go home, Patti Ann had thrust the red-and-orange-and-blue potty seat into her hands. "Here. This is an extra one. You can use it when Jonah visits you." As if the two of them were now in cahoots about getting him trained. But they weren't in cahoots, or even in agreement. If Jonah's behavior didn't prove that a child with a new little brother had enough on his mind without being hounded into the bathroom once an hour, what did?

Yet Iris had taken the potty seat to BJ's without saying a word.

Now, with the accusatory bright ring on the seat beside her, Iris let her foot settle heavily on the gas as she rehearsed once again how she would say, in a calm but authoritative voice, "Patti Ann, I appreciate that you're trying to train Jonah, but I'm his grandma and want him to get positive reinforcement from me, especially now when it's difficult for him, with his brother taking up so much attention." She would hand back the potty seat with a show of magnanimous good humor. "For right now, any time I'm in charge of him," she would say, "I'll just let him wear diapers."

Patti Ann would not be expecting this ambush, because Iris often came over in midafternoon to take Jonah outside after his nap, into the leafy yard any other nanny would love but Patti Ann regarded as essentially hostile. Earthworms and ants and garden toads were not objects of interest to Patti Ann, but potential sources of bites or allergic reactions or worse. Dirt carried disease. Snakes hid in sandboxes and flower beds, waiting to strike. For safety's sake, Patti Ann would plop Jonah in front of the TV even on the most beautiful days, and turn on *Sesame Street*, which Jonah to his great credit would ignore in order to play with his toys. She would say to Iris, "See? He likes his shows, but he doesn't watch them nonstop like some kids do." To which Iris would squelch her temptation to reply, "He's two! He doesn't *have* shows. What's wrong with you?"

On one picture-perfect day last week, Iris had finally cajoled Patti Ann out into the yard with Noah while she herself pushed Jonah on the swing. You'd have thought she was torturing the poor woman. Patti Ann pulled a baseball cap over her gray curls and slathered sunblock over every inch of Jonah and Noah's olive-skinned arms and faces before offering the tube to Iris, who refused it. Outside, she'd dragged a lawn chair close to the swing, eased her bulk into it, plunked the baby down in her lap, and regarded the glorious October sky with dismay.

"If my doctor knew I was out here, he'd have a fit," she muttered.

He wouldn't give the first damn, Iris thought. Aloud, she said mildly, "Have a fit? Why?"

"I'm not supposed to get any sun. I had a skin cancer taken off a few years ago." Patti Ann pulled up her sleeve to reveal a thick, pasty forearm that looked as if it hadn't seen daylight for decades. The woman probably had a Vitamin D deficiency.

"Oh?"

"Yes," Patti Ann said. "You wouldn't have thought it was anything, just looking at it. Nothing but a little, rough, pink spot on my arm. But it was a cancer. It could have killed me! They burned it off with this spray from a spray gun."

"Liquid nitrogen, you mean?"

"That sounds right. Liquid nitrogen."

"They don't burn cancers off with liquid nitrogen," Iris said. "They cut them out. What you had was probably an actinic keratosis. Sun damage. A precancer. Sheldon had dozens of them."

"Oh, it was a cancer, all right."

But Iris knew what she knew. The nonexistent cancer was an excuse to keep her grandsons locked up in the house after their naps instead of out in the bright world.

"Higher!" Jonah had shouted as she pushed.

"If you go much higher, you'll bump into the moon!" Iris had teased. *Look how happy he is*, she'd wanted to say. *Look!*

Now, approaching Diane's street armed with the potty seat and what she hoped was the appropriate attitude, Iris noted the bevy of children and young mothers out in their yards, and reminded herself that, like Diane, they all felt safe enough to leave their doors unlocked during the day. Iris did the same when she was babysitting, and so did Patti Ann—unless, of course, she knew Iris was coming. Then she demonstrated her concern for the children's security by locking the house up tight as a tomb. Mentally, Iris tried to prepare herself for this. She tried to prepare herself for everything.

Iris had many theories about life, among them that each life was a journey toward love, with some people much farther along the path than others—Mother Teresa, say, as opposed to Osama Bin Laden. You worked your way toward being more and more loving, which explained why older people were often said to have mellowed. But much as you tried, you were never as loving as you aspired to be because life threw certain obstacles and challenges at you, which it was your task to overcome, such as Sheldon's infidelities and Patti Ann's quick fingers on the dead bolt. The paradox was that while you needed to be loving, you also had to be firm and command respect so that others didn't take advantage of you. It was a delicate balance. Iris parked the car, tucked the potty seat under her arm and dug out Diane's extra key as she prepared to charge the fortress.

But Patti Ann flung open the door before Iris was halfway up the walk. "Hi, Grandma! We've been waiting for you!" She shifted Noah in her arms and raised one of his little hands to wave at her, then held him out so Iris had no choice but to take him and give Patti Ann the potty seat in trade. Noah looked up at her and opened his mouth in a toothless smile. "See? He knows his grandma!" Patti Ann exclaimed. "The only other one he smiles at like that is Diane." All this friendliness was disconcerting.

Iris trailed Patti Ann's swaying mass up the walk, her

eyes on the other woman's voluminous plaid shirt above her elastic-waist jeans with Diane's phone hooked onto them. Sensing the indignation she'd felt in the car begin to drain, Iris told herself that if Patti Ann actually needed the phone for an emergency, it would be because she'd tripped over something she couldn't see because of her combined bulk and the weight of little Noah, who was almost always in her arms, and she would probably crush the baby in the process.

Frightening as this was, Iris didn't actually believe it would happen.

In the den, Jonah was moving a convoy of miniature heavy equipment across the floor toward a tower of plastic blocks.

"Gamma!" he shouted, and ran to her just long enough for her to kiss the top of his head. Then he toppled his tower by ramming it simultaneously with the bulldozer and a crane. "I building," he told her.

"Demolishing, sweetie. You're demolishing."

Jonah beamed. "I love you, Gamma," he said.

Patti Ann set the potty seat on an end table without comment. She chattered on about what a good lunch Jonah had eaten, her idea of a healthful meal being sugar-sweetened yogurt, sugar-sweetened fruit cups (God forbid she should cut up an actual apple) and anything she could warm in the microwave. As Patti Ann spoke, she popped into her mouth one and then another of the caramel-flavored candies she kept in a plastic bag and snacked on all day. Jonah knew they were "nanny food" and no longer asked for them, but Patti Ann offered the bag to Iris, who refused. Patti Ann had much to learn about good nutrition—she could stand to lose fifty pounds—but this wasn't the time. Iris mustn't forget what she'd come here to discuss. On days like these, when Patti Ann greeted her like this, so good-natured and full of news, it was easy to be distracted. They had a common interest: Iris's grandchildren. After all, how many people loved these children? How many other people cared what they did? It was hard to sustain a constant level of irritation and dislike.

"My tower broken," Jonah announced. "I fix it." He began to rummage through his toolbox, selecting appropriate plastic implements. Already he knew the difference between a flat-head screwdriver and a Phillips, pliers and a wrench, a tin snip and needle-nosed pliers, distinctions Iris herself hadn't made until she was an adult. Proud as this made her, it was a bit daunting. She hoped she lived long enough for her grandson to come over and do all her house repairs—providing she ever *had* a house again, other than BJ's.

Iris noticed then that the TV was on, as usual—or rather, that hateful *Baby Mozart* tape. A few bright windup toys in primary colors marched across the screen in time to a Mozart piano piece that sounded like fast, difficult scales. Jonah, stacking blocks and poking resolutely at them with his tools, paid no attention. But Noah, sitting on Iris's lap, seemed rapt.

"Look at him. Why does he like this so much? A bunch of windup toys?"

"I think it's the colors," Patti Ann said. "They say the music, too, but I don't know. That piano. It isn't very tuneful."

"No. I don't get it. It sounds more like counting than music."

"Counting?" Patti Ann cocked her head and considered this. She nodded thoughtfully. "I guess so. Yes. I see what you mean."

The two women sat in companionable agreement, listening. Iris liked most classical music, but not Mozart or Bach, which reminded her of math, in which she had never excelled. To Iris, Mozart sounded like fractions, multiplication tables and equations. It gave her a headache.

"Of course, Diane likes all this Baby Einstein stuff," Patti Ann said. "It's supposed to make them smart. She likes me to play it, so I do." She shrugged, the dutiful employee following her mistress's instructions.

Transfixed, Noah hadn't taken his eyes off the screen. This couldn't be good for him. Hadn't Iris read an article saying television could impair brain development in a child under two? She lifted him from her lap and put him in his vibrating baby seat. She seized the remote and turned off the TV. Her indignation rushed back in an unpleasant whoosh.

"I wanted to talk to you," she said to Patti Ann, all at once summoning exactly the right tone. She would be firm but pleasant, handling this in such a way that she and Patti Ann could continue, in harmony, their mutual job of seeing to her grandsons' well-being. She gestured toward the potty seat.

At that moment—Iris wasn't even surprised by this—the phone began to ring.

Patti Ann stood, lifted the tail of her shirt to reveal a few inches of pale belly fat, and unclipped the receiver from the elastic waistband of her pants. "Hello?" A brief silence. "Oh, yes, sure. I'll get it and call you back." She hung up. As she moved the phone back toward her waist, her arm paused in midair, then went limp. The phone clattered to the floor. Patti Ann flopped back into her chair and cupped her head in her hands.

"You okay?" Iris asked.

"The woozies," Patti Ann said. "I'll be okay in a minute."

"You sure?" Iris didn't actually believe in the woozies, which Patti Ann had on a regular basis, but only when she wanted something. Well—too bad. If Patti Ann wanted to avoid discussing the potty seat today, she'd have to pass out cold.

Iris bent to retrieve the phone. "Is there something I can get you?"

"Maybe a glass of water," Patti Ann mewed as she took one of her candies from a pocket and popped it into her mouth.

In the kitchen, Iris replaced the phone on its base

and turned on the spigot. Patti Ann appeared behind her. "I just needed a minute," she said. "I'm fine now." She snatched the phone from its resting place, clipped it back onto her pants and took the glass Iris offered.

"Who called before?" Iris asked.

"Wes. I said I'd get him Larry Sherman's phone number." Patti Ann gulped her water and set the glass beside the sink, then clutched the edge of the counter-top for effect. "If you'll watch the kids for a minute, I'll get the number and then put a load of laundry in," she said.

"Don't be silly. If you're not feeling well, you should go home and rest. I can get Wes the phone number. The laundry can wait."

"Oh, I'm fine," Patti Ann insisted.

"You'll be even better at home," Iris felt compelled to say. "I was planning to stay here for a while, anyway." She wasn't about to leave her grandchildren alone with a newly woozied nanny, malingerer or not. "Diane will be here in an hour."

"Well, maybe I should." Patti Ann let her voice go weak.

Iris didn't notice the potty seat again, still resting on the end table, until long after Patti Ann was gone.

Once more, she had let the other person get away with it.

The story of her life.

At least she'd brought the potty back to Diane's, she told herself. At least it was not at BJ's house anymore, reminding her of her cowardice every time she looked at it. Surely that was something.

But Iris fumed all afternoon, and was still furious as she drove herself home. When she walked into BJ's house, her sister took one look at her and said, "It's the sitter, isn't it? And—no. Let me guess. It's not the sitter you're mad at. You're mad at yourself."

Iris told her the story.

"So did you tell Diane?" BJ asked. "About the woozies?"

"No. Of course not. I didn't want to worry her."

"Worry her! Maybe she *should* worry. A person who pegs your people-meter like that deserves a little extra worry."

"Patti Ann doesn't peg my people-meter, for heaven's sake!" The family acted as if Iris's famous "people-meter" were one of those carnival games where you pounded a lever and tried to propel a ball high enough to ring a bell. But it had never been like that, except the time Iris worked in a clinic where one of the nurses gave her the creeps so bad she couldn't stay in the same room with her. It came out later that the woman had poisoned two patients, though neither of them had died. Most of the time Iris's people-meter was only a vague uneasiness. "You give me too much credit," she told BJ. "Sheldon didn't peg my people-meter, either."

"That was different. You were young. It's different when sex is involved."

Iris ignored that. "Believe me, if Patti Ann tripped my people-meter, she wouldn't get within ten feet of those boys."

"She's still a jerk," BJ said decisively.

This is what Iris most admired about her sister. While Iris was relieved that Patti Ann didn't trip her people-meter, BJ was offended. BJ had the ability Iris lacked to focus on a person's failings. To hold a grudge. To get things done. Being seven years younger, Iris had thought when they were children that her sister was effective simply because she was bigger and stronger. But later she realized it wasn't a matter of age, or even of strength: it was a matter of character. BJ had a low but booming voice; people listened to her. Iris trilled and no one cared. BJ was tough. Iris was tender. Even when Iris got angry for good reason, she couldn't hold on to it. In no time at all, she would get over it and revert to her usual state of mildness. It was a sign of weakness.

Now that she was an older woman on her own, she needed to remedy that. It was the only way she could get control of her life and feel secure. It was the only way she could allow herself to be loving.

She needed to practice being meaner.

CHAPTER 4

BJ was thrilled. The big, round, Over-Fifty Singles table was full, and six of the eight occupants were under seventy. Arnold Lieberman had returned, his hairpiece slightly askew, as well as Fred Shulman and BJ's friend, Resa Taub. Molly Gerber and Lou Green arrived from the retirement home in a cab. They seemed to be a couple. Best of all, Harvey Sussman walked in just as BJ was herding everyone toward the table. In gray trousers, burgundy shirt and a dark tie, he was more presentable than she'd seen him since Yom Kippur.

"Well, you cleaned up nice," she told him.

"Just a coincidence. I came right from a board meeting for Eyes to the Future."

"Eyes to the Future?" BJ knew all about it—a volunteer program to check the vision of all the elementary-school kids in the county.

"Why should that surprise you? In my former life I was an optometrist. An eye doctor. Vision screening is a natural interest."

"I thought you were retired."

"Does that mean I have to shut down my brain entirely?"

"No. Of course not. I just thought you refocused it on the vegetable rather than the animal kingdom."

"Only partially," Harvey said.

BJ pointed him to a seat next to Iris, with Arnold Lieberman on her other side. Surrounded by men. Excellent. Tapping Iris on the shoulder, BJ said, "Did you know Harvey was involved in Eyes for the Future?" Here was something the two of them could discuss. Iris had spent mornings at various schools for nearly a month, pointing to letters on the eye charts set up in the cafeteria.

"Oh?" Iris looked blank, as if the project meant nothing to her. BJ signaled the waiter for a glass of merlot.

The others followed. Iris and Resa ordered Chardonnay. All the men had Bud Light except Lou Green, who said he couldn't handle alcohol anymore, hadn't been able to since the night of his eightieth birthday when he'd gotten so sick he'd remembered every detail this whole five years, though most events nowadays sifted through his head like air. He chuckled and ordered a Coke. Unaccountably, this story seemed to put everyone at ease. Conversation flowed. BJ luxuriated in the rise and fall of voices: bass, treble, bass, an opera of the genders. Iris's soprano seemed a little harsher than usual. She was probably nervous. Well, of course she was. When was the last time she'd been in a mixed group, socially?

"What I mean is, why did you call her dog Buddy?" Iris asked Harvey. As if for emphasis, she tapped the table with a long fingernail. "His name is Randolph. You've lived down the street from BJ—what? Ten years? You borrow her lawn mower, for heaven's sake! Don't you know her dog's name?"

"Iris," BJ cautioned. This wasn't like her sister.

Molly Gerber reached across the table and placed her spotted, wrinkled fingers atop Iris's smooth, manicured ones, causing Iris to stop her tapping. "It's all right, dear. All men call dogs Buddy. They can't help it. It's just something they *do*."

Iris blinked.

"Tell me, Iris," Molly added quickly, "what are you doing these days? I heard you moved in with BJ while you look for a smaller house."

"I see my grandchildren a lot."

"Grandchildren! They're wonderful, but I remember with Ruby, all I could think of was, what do I do with a two-year-old, and by the time I figured it out, she was thirteen. Or else they live three thousand miles away and before you know it they vanish into thin air." Molly winked at BJ, in deference to BJ's own distant grandson, Eli, who lived on the West Coast. The rest of the table laughed.

Ignoring that, Iris cleared her throat and spoke to the group in general. "My point is, when you live down the street from someone as long as Harvey has, it's only polite to learn the actual name of your neighbor's dog."

When Harvey didn't respond, Iris said, "Randolph. *Randolph*," as if he were too dim-witted to remember.

"Oh, it doesn't matter what Harvey calls him," BJ intervened—soothingly, she hoped. "The dog loves him. Always has."

"The dog loves everybody," Harvey said. "Not necessarily a good trait."

Murmurs of assent vibrated around the table. Conversation gradually resumed its former harmonious melody. Food orders were given. The salads came. Harvey bent his head toward Iris and spoke in a low tone. This was good. He poured dressing over his greens. He began to gesture with his fork. This went on for several minutes. Iris frowned.

"Like I said, it's manners," she asserted, her voice rising again above the general hum. "Just manners and common decency!"

"That's exactly my point," Harvey said. "The dogs aren't trained, just the people. They think it's 'manners' but it's brainwashing. It makes no sense."

Interested, the others turned in his direction.

"I've seen you do it yourself," he said to Iris. "You walk down the block with little Buddy—whoops, *Randolph*—on his leash, proper as can be, holding a plastic grocery bag in your hand. It's usually a white bag, for some reason. Everybody favors white bags, they look more sanitary. They let the dog sniff and investigate a little, and they reel him in if he wanders an inch too far. Finally he finds a nice place to poop, and the minute he's finished they bend over and pick it up in the bag, no matter how soft and runny it is, because God forbid it should litter somebody's lawn."

"And you don't think that's only considerate?"

"Dog poop is *fertilizer*," Harvey said.

"On the contrary, it can burn the grass," put in Arnold Lieberman from Iris's left. "Too much of a good thing."

Iris shot Arnold a look of gratitude. He tipped his head, and his lopsided toupee seemed about to slide off, but it didn't.

"All I can say," Harvey continued, "is that ten years ago when I moved to my house, nobody walked around with a plastic grocery bag. They weren't expected to be such good little robots. And I'm here to tell you, every dog in the neighborhood used my lawn as a bathroom one time or another, and I never had burn spots, only the greenest grass on the block." He shoved a forkful of lettuce into his mouth. He had rested his case.

Arnold Lieberman waited out the awkward silence that followed, then said to Iris in an oily, confidential tone, "So. You like living with your sister?"

BJ tuned out the rest of it. She noted that Molly Gerber had wisely ordered the spaghetti BJ had suggested earlier. The noodles were soft and pliable, unlike the chunks of chicken fajita she had choked on last time. Molly did not lose her dentures. Fred Shulman told Resa he was thinking of buying a rental property. Resa was in real estate. Lou Green did not have to be rushed to the bathroom. On balance, the evening was a success.

"So what happened back there?" she asked Iris on the way home. "What made you set Harvey Sussman off like that?"

"What made *me* set him off? I think he got going all by himself. You didn't hear the half of it."

"There was more than fertilizer and trash bags?"

"Harvey doesn't think a dog ought to be subjected to walking at the end of a leash all the time. Oh, no, too restrictive. He thinks they're entitled to run free. He thinks— Actually I don't know what he thinks. I think he was just trying to be abrasive."

"He had a dog himself once, years ago. He walked it on a leash like everybody else."

"So why did he say all that?"

"Oh, honey, I think he was putting you on."

"Why? He hardly even knows me."

"Because you embarrassed him about calling my dog Buddy. The whole table heard. He was trying to save face."

"Well, he should have known Randolph's name."

"I know, sweetie. But it was a small crime. I was surprised at you. Usually you're so tactful."

For a long beat Iris considered this. "You know what I think? I think I need to speak my mind more often instead of keeping my mouth shut. *You* say what you think. Harvey Sussman certainly does. I should be more assertive. I should tell people the truth."

"If that was the goal, why not tell Arnold his wig was on crooked?"

"Assertive is different from mean."

"I was kidding, honey. It was a joke."

"I know that." But it was clear Iris didn't. BJ had been teasing her sister all her life, and all her life Iris had been pretending she got it, but in some deep-down, visceral way, she never did. She was slow on the uptake; she always had been. But mainly Iris always seemed befuddled by one simple question: Why would people be mean to each other, even in jest?

"I always admired your tact," BJ told her. "I always figured if I had half your tact, I could have sold twice as many ads and made twice as much money."

"You'd have been out of business within a year." Iris sounded perfectly serious. She wasn't usually the weepy type, but as they drove down the long block toward BJ's house, Iris blinked a lot and studied the clasp of the purse in her lap. "I was just practicing," she whispered finally, which seemed to mean, *This is something I'm not going to be good at, either.*

BJ felt terrible. After a life of diplomacy and gentleness, there was only one reason Iris would think she needed to be assertive. Because she didn't have a man.

She just wished Iris hadn't decided to practice on Harvey.

Two hours later, Iris was in bed sleeping and BJ was sitting at her kitchen table, wide-awake, drinking Drambuie. Randolph, who had dutifully followed her downstairs, settled on the floor by the stove and regarded her with sleepy forbearance. "I have insomnia," she told him. "I can't help it." She took another sip of her drink.

She didn't even like Drambuie. It was too sweet, and left an odd, fizzy sensation on the tip of her tongue. David was the one who'd always bought it. He was never much of a drinker, but sometimes late in the evening when he couldn't shake work out of his mind, he would pour an inch of Drambuie into a brandy snifter, swirl it around like someone in a movie and sip it until it calmed him down.

Why, six years after his death, BJ still kept the treacly stuff in the house and felt compelled to drink it now and then, she had no idea. She drank a little more.

BJ was not used to failure. She was not used to matchmaking, period. She had counted on Harvey Sussman to capture Iris's interest, not her enmity. She wasn't even sure what had gone wrong. She had no background to prepare her for this.

If someone had asked her, ten years ago, what she and Iris would be doing today, she would have said, "Iris will be divorced, and I'll be preparing to spend my old age with David." She had always assumed that Iris would someday tire of Sheldon's lies and move on. Sheldon would never leave *her*, because he had too good a deal. Her departure would leave him desolate. Iris would have her sweet revenge.

Beyond that, she hadn't really thought it through. She'd assumed Iris would remarry. Compared to

Sheldon, almost anybody would be an improvement. Certainly Harvey Sussman was.

Or maybe not. As she'd already reminded herself, Harvey had opted for youth instead of excellence when he chose a second wife. Maybe Iris's people-meter had warned her off. But BJ also kept in mind that the unfortunate marriage had ended years ago and Harvey hadn't made the same mistake twice. Despite her people-meter, Iris was not always a great judge of character. BJ's gut told her that, at some basic level, Harvey was probably all right.

Then again, any dalliance with a man at this late date was fraught with danger.

Distracted, BJ took another swallow of her drink. It burned all the way down.

"Jesus!" she said aloud.

Randolph opened a suspicious eye.

Was it really fair to subject Iris to a latter-day romance? BJ wasn't planning to have one herself, and her own marriage, compared to Iris's, had been an idyll.

Unlike Iris, BJ hadn't been young and stupid when she married. She'd been twenty-five and educated. She knew lots of women who liked the idea of being married but weren't crazy about their husbands. *She*, by contrast, hadn't cared about the domestic trappings but had truly loved David.

Even so, she wouldn't have predicted that, after Janelle was born two years later, David would want her to become a full-time mom. "I'm a dentist. I can support you. Give me a chance to provide you with this luxury," he'd said.

He was so sweet about it that BJ would have done it if she could. She stayed home for a year. It was awful. Then BJ's aunt left her a small inheritance, and she used it to buy the advertiser, *Ads Unlimited*. She renamed it *The Scene* and added editorial content as well as ads—not much, just enough to make it look more respectable—and set out to meet every business owner in town. She made money. She liked it. David had never understood her need for a career once she had a family. He never saw that her success didn't make her love her husband or daughter less. They talked about this for years—softly, so as not to hurt each other any more than they had to—until finally they had ground it to such a fine powder between them that there was nothing left to say. Outwardly, David always supported BJ's work, especially after Janelle was in school and it was clear there wouldn't be another child, not for lack of trying. By then David had developed a reputation as a pioneer in the field of dental implants. In addition to his clinical practice, he wrote papers and traveled to give lectures. If BJ had not been tied to *The Scene*, she might have gone with him. He would have liked that. Their years together played out against this subtext.

Then David got what at first seemed like a flu that wouldn't go away. It turned out to be non-Hodgkin's lymphoma. Janelle, working at a dream job in

Seattle, had also been in the first flush of her romance with Luke, so happy they hated to worry her. They sketched David's condition for her in rough outline, holding back the scary details. His illness became a secret between them. More than at any time before, in the last year of David's life they worked as a team.

After nearly thirty years of staunchly defining herself as a career woman, being with David was all BJ wanted. She drove him to every doctor appointment. She sat beside him while chemicals were dripped into his veins. The young couple who worked for *The Scene* had been wanting to buy the paper for a year. BJ sold it to them without a second thought, agreeing to stay on, as much as she could, to sell ads. But for the duration of David's illness, BJ wasn't in the office more than a few hours a week. Instead, she and David went to dozens of movies, all comedies and all matinees, because he was too tired to go out at night. She cooked special dishes he liked, until he had no appetite. It was the most wrenching year of their lives. But in some ways, also the best.

For a year after he died, she could barely look at the color turquoise. It was, in a way, "their" color, the way other couples had a special restaurant or song. With her dark hair and pale complexion, BJ had never thought she could wear turquoise until David gave her a silk blouse that became one of her favorites. She'd worn the color often until the morning of David's funeral—but not since then, and not to this day, which always struck her as strange (though it didn't change anything), because she had never been sentimental.

Back in the summer, on the way home from Sheldon's unveiling, Iris had whispered to BJ in the car, "I never would have thought this. But it's true. Just because one of you dies, it doesn't mean you're not still married."

"Oh, honey, of course it does. Think of your wedding vows—Till death do you part."

"Yes," Iris had whispered. "But you know what I mean."

BJ did. During her marriage, she had often teased David by saying, "If you ever leave me, that's it for me and men. No more. Too much trouble." She'd thought it was a joke, but maybe not. If she hadn't married David, she might have been too independent to marry at all—too keen on earning her own money, making her own rules. David was trouble, yes, but he'd been worth it. They'd worked it out. If she was finished with men now, it wasn't just because they were trouble, but because the term, "till death do you part" seemed meaningless when it referred to someone you kept loving even though they were gone. She had neither the energy nor the need to replace him.

She drank the last of the Drambuie in one punishing gulp, waited for the fire in her throat to go out, and put the glass in the sink.

But if BJ didn't need a man, Iris still did, for so many reasons. She needed someone to boost her confidence, relish the meals she took such delight in cooking, help her make decisions. And if not Harvey Sussman, then who? Arnold Lieberman? Any man who wore his hairpiece askew struck BJ as untrustworthy, insufficiently attentive to detail. Lou Green? He was eighty-five and enamored of Molly Gerber. Fred Shulman was gay. This might take longer than she expected. It was time to formulate Plan B.

BJ had always loved her house. Even earlier tonight, approaching it from the street, thinking how she had left way too many lights on, the place had looked so cheerful and welcoming that she didn't care. She and David had found it when Janelle was two, a big four-bedroom Colonial of handsome red brick, with green shutters and an imposing paneled front door, set on a generous wooded lot perfect for play equipment and cookouts. Back then, with Janelle growing up and so many people coming in and out, the house had seemed just the right size. Now BJ's friends asked, "Don't you rattle around in that big place?" so often that she had to stop and think, "Well? Do I?"

The answer was no.

Even in the grief-swollen, turbulent months after David's death, she had felt more peaceful here, inside the house they had shared for so long, than she did anywhere else. It wasn't at all a matter of "rattling around." It was more like being embraced by large, comforting arms.

Did Iris feel that way, too? Did BJ's house offer her the same sense of being sheltered and protected? For the past two months, ever since she'd moved in with

BJ, Iris had made it plain that she was in no hurry to leave. Now and then she said she was going out to look at a house, but the account of her day she gave later was always about Jonah or Noah or Patti Ann, not real estate, so that BJ understood her sister hadn't been house-hunting, only playing with her grandchildren.

Probably Iris had simply been waiting for BJ to issue her an invitation to stay.

Certainly the house was big enough for both of them. There was even an old wooden swing set in the yard from when Janelle was a child. It wouldn't take much to fix it up. Jonah could play on it when he came for visits.

The truth was, he already did.

How hard could it be to live with your own sister, someone you'd known all your life, who cleaned and cooked meals and walked your dog? It would be an adjustment, but everything was. A few ground rules, and everything would be settled.

It was pure selfishness that she hated the idea so much.

CHAPTER 5

"About your lawn mower." Harvey Sussman stood at BJ's front door, arms crossed over his chest in a not-wanting-to-admit-he-was-cold posture, huddling into a sweatshirt far too thin for the raw day. Beneath his usual cutoffs, his legs were covered with goose bumps. The sudden cold snap after weeks of warm sun made it feel even chillier than it was. The sky was gray. "Come inside," BJ told him. "You look like you're freezing."

"No, I'm fine. Listen—" Randolph, fresh from doing God-knows-what upstairs at the far end of the house, produced a belated chorus of barks and howls, and reached the bottom of the steps in what seemed like a single bound. Harvey dropped his arms just in time to fend off the assault.

"About your lawn mower," Harvey said again as he rubbed the dog's neck. He cast his eyes toward the living room and then up the staircase. Was he looking for Iris, even after their ill-fated Singles Night? BJ certainly hoped so.

"About my lawn mower?" she prodded. Harvey had

probably returned it to her shed, where she would find it next spring.

"I took it to the shop. You know, for an oil change, a new blade. Drain the gas for the winter."

"You took it to the shop?" This struck BJ as highly unusual.

"It should go in every year. Prolongs the life of the equipment."

"Right." Still puzzled, BJ nodded cautiously. "You can bring me the bill."

"My treat. Think of it as an apology." Harvey shuffled his feet as if to pound feeling into them. BJ could hardly stand to watch it—a grown man, acting like a teenager trying to be macho. Exasperated, she pulled the door open wider.

"Come *inside*," she demanded. "It's too cold for shorts. You're going to make yourself sick." She sounded like his mother. "You took my lawn mower in as an apology for what?"

"For not being nicer to Iris." He shook his leg again and stepped into the foyer. "I know Iris is your sister. I know I owed you to go to the restaurant. I didn't mean to let her get on my nerves."

"Seems to me you were the one who got on *her* nerves."

Harvey shut the door behind him, his dark eyes behind his glasses registering shock that he, not Iris, might be considered the irritant.

BJ led him into the kitchen. "I just made some coffee." She pointed to a chair with such authority that

Harvey immediately sat down, more obedient than Randolph. The dog, having finished his sound-and-motion medley, followed them and flopped onto the floor.

"I know Iris has been through a lot," Harvey said. "I knew Sheldon. Over the years he probably tried to sell me ten different things. He was a schmuck."

"Yes, and don't think it didn't take great decency and sacrifice for Iris to put up with him. She never wanted her daughter to know what he was like. She was very loyal." BJ poured steaming liquid from the coffeemaker into mugs, clunked one down in front of Harvey and set her own across the table from him. "But if Sheldon gave Iris anything in return, I still haven't figured out what it was."

"Even a schmuck is a warm body," he said.

"Not if he's dead."

"True." Harvey wrapped both his hands around his mug as if to warm his own chilled body. It occurred to BJ that she should have offered sugar or milk. Maybe even a bagel. Finally Harvey lifted the cup and tasted the coffee. "Not bad."

"What did you expect? Mud?"

He drank a little more. "I guess I was cold," he said. "It's true what they say about your blood thinning when you move south. When I lived in Pittsburgh this would have been a nice fall day."

"I didn't know you lived in Pittsburgh."

"For nearly forty years. Then I got the offer down

here and Karen—that was my first wife—wanted to come. She hated it before we were here ten minutes. But for me, it was an opportunity. I had a nice practice, and we started selling the glasses as a value-added feature, so people wouldn't have to go somewhere else. You'd be surprised how often patients come back wearing the wrong prescription they got at one of those one-hour places. Even when you send out for lenses yourself, they come back wrong half the time. This way I could check them before they left the office. I liked having control."

He had grown so animated, BJ almost felt sorry for him. All these years later, he probably still regretted that he'd retired.

She felt stingy for not offering him something to eat. Holding up a finger to signal him to wait, she went to the pantry for the coffee cake Iris had made yesterday. She put a slice on a plate for Harvey and set the rest on the table. He tasted it and nodded approval. "Good."

"Iris made it. Eat and feel guilty."

"I said I was sorry. I really am. I got carried away."

"You mean when you told her dogs shouldn't be leashed but ought to be able to run free?"

"That might have been a little extreme." Harvey forked up more cake. "But about the electric fences, I was serious."

"She didn't tell me you discussed electric fences."

"They're barbaric. What kind of person imprisons an

animal by putting a collar around its neck that jolts it practically to kingdom come if it strays over the wire? People go all gaga over their pets, but they don't think twice about electric fences. I asked Iris how would she like one of those collars herself. It didn't go over well."

BJ bit back a smile.

Harvey concentrated on his plate, washing down cake with sips of coffee. "I wouldn't have an electric fence," he finally said. "That's why I don't have a dog anymore. I'm out in the yard all the time. It wouldn't be fair to leave an animal inside. But I don't want to be chasing it around the neighborhood, either. Or worrying that it's going to bite some child."

"If you ever feel deprived, you can borrow Randolph. He doesn't bite children. He just knocks them to the ground and licks them into traumatic shock."

Hearing his name, Randolph glanced at them with a jaundiced eye.

"Very generous, but I'll pass," Harvey said. He forked up more cake and scanned the kitchen, checked out the adjacent den, looked through the doorway toward the dining room. Hoping Iris would pop out of one of the cabinets or closets? After the other night, who would have expected this?

Yet why else would he have taken the lawn mower to the shop, except as an excuse to come over?

"She's out," BJ said.

"Pardon?"

"Iris. She went out."

"Oh." He nodded and ate the last bite of cake.

Considering Harvey's obvious interest, maybe she should talk to Iris, urge her to give him another chance. Even in his ratty gardening clothes, Harvey looked healthy. He was slender. He looked like he might last a while. Most men over fifty were paunchy, or even fat, like Sheldon Meyerhoff in the adulterous days before his demise. Screwing around did not build muscle the way yard work did. And for someone who downed his cake so fast, Harvey seemed to be relishing it rather than shoveling it in. Sheldon, on the other hand, had always looked like he was gulping his last meal—which eventually, in a rare instance of poetic justice, he had.

Without asking, BJ slid another piece of cake onto Harvey's plate and refilled his coffee.

"You said something the other night about being on the Eyes to the Future board," she said. "Did you know Iris was involved in that, too?"

"You told me at the singles dinner." He did not stop eating.

"Last month she was at the schools testing kids almost every morning. She knows a lot about it. You know—how the children react to certain testers. What to do. What not to. If you talked to her, I bet she'd be useful on one of your committees."

Harvey didn't speak until he'd swallowed. "I'm not really involved with the committees. They keep me on the board because my company provides some of the glasses for the indigent kids. It's a good program."

"But I thought you were retired."

"Retired from the practice, yes. But I kept a share of the frame-and-lens business. Like I said, I like being able to double-check the prescriptions. And the money is good. So I kept part of the business, just like you kept yours."

"I didn't keep mine. I sold it lock, stock and barrel."

"You sold it?"

"A long time ago. Seven years. I work for the people who bought it."

Harvey put down his fork. The light that hit his glasses seemed to reflect a twinkle in his eye.

"Why are you smiling?" BJ asked.

"Nobody knows, do they?"

"Pardon?"

"People think you still own the paper. You don't tell them different."

"It's easier to sell ads if they think you're the owner."

Harvey uttered a rough guffaw, then let it stretch out into a long laugh. BJ felt like a kid who'd been caught pilfering cookies. "It's that funny?"

"It is."

BJ bristled. "Did anyone ever tell you it isn't polite to come into a person's house and bray at them like a damned donkey?"

"Okay. I'm sorry." Harvey composed himself. "You're a sneaky broad, Beulah Jeanette. I like that in a person."

"If you think I'm flattered, don't. And don't call me Beulah Jeanette."

"Okay. I'm sorry," he said again. He pushed his plate away. He patted his stomach. "Thanks."

Again he was surveying the scene. He perused the kitchen, examined the archway that led into the dining room, peered out the bay window that overlooked the backyard. He rose from his chair and walked into the den as if he had every right to be there, examining the molding and the woodwork. He nodded. "Big house."

"I like it," she said before he could ask her if she didn't rattle around.

"Nice. I've never been inside before."

"No?" She supposed he hadn't.

"How many bedrooms?"

"Four."

"Mine has three." He raised an index finger in the air. "Wait. Let me guess. People always ask you if you don't rattle around in here."

BJ glared at him.

"That's what they always ask me. 'Don't you rattle around in that big house, Harvey?' It's really not even that big. And never mind that they know how much time I spend in the yard—that maybe I'm staying there for the yard. No, if I have two inches to spare in any direction, I must be rattling around." Unashamed, he lowered himself into a wing chair as if she'd invited him to, and pushed his glasses up on his nose. "I guess I was just asking for a second opinion."

BJ was so surprised that she thought, okay, he asked

for it, what the hell. She sat down on the couch. "Of course they ask me if I rattle around," she said. "And here's why I think they do it. Because they're lonely. It's the human condition, even if they have six kids and two jobs and a live-in aunt. They want to think being married gives them some kind of protection, but secretly they know it doesn't. Seeing me in this big place only rubs it in. It makes them think, uh-oh, this could happen to me, and then I'll be even lonelier. They want to put me in some tiny, one-person box where I won't scare them so much. Poor bastards, they have no idea how nice it can be to come home from work and not have to think about what somebody else wants for dinner."

Harvey raised an eyebrow.

"Well, you asked, and now you have it—BJ Fradkin's Theory of the Big House. People like to think, oh, she's so lonely, she's rattling around in that big house, but I'm not rattling around—I'm just alone."

"Except for Iris."

"Well, yes. Except for Iris." As engrossed as BJ was in her theory, this mention did not escape her.

"All day long I talk to people," she said, "either in person or on the phone, trying to sell them ads. You know when I'm lonely? When some client goes into a long dissertation about how his kid got picked for some traveling soccer team I don't give a damn about, and I have to listen because he's a dermatologist who goes from one fancy new laser treatment to another, and I figure he'll be buying ads for years. That's when I'm lonely. Not when I'm in my house."

"Me, too." Harvey smiled, and BJ imagined all the traveling soccer teams *he* must have heard about, in a career of checking eyes.

Then she was embarrassed. She got up. "This was a very odd conversation," she said.

"It was," Harvey agreed.

They walked together into the foyer, Randolph at their heels. Harvey stopped in front of the hall table and picked up a small framed photo. "Yours?"

BJ shook her head. She kept her own kiddie-photos upstairs, where she could see them from her bed. This one was a baby picture of Noah. Iris must have put it there. She was taking over the place. "Iris's," she said.

"Cute little guy." Harvey put the picture down.

"She'll be back sometime this afternoon," BJ told him. "Around four or five, I think." BJ opened the door. A brisk breeze blew in. Harvey lifted a hand to shield the bald top of his head.

"When it's windy like this, a bald man should wear a hat." She sounded like his mother again.

He dropped his hand from his head like a rock. "When it gets below freezing, this bald man does wear a hat."

"Good." She hadn't meant to insult him. Most men Harvey's age fretted about hair loss to the point of the ridiculous. Sheldon had combed his remaining long blond strands across his crown like Donald Trump. Arnold Lieberman had chosen a wig you could spot half a block away—not just ill fitting, but a solid chestnut color, without a strand of gray, which couldn't have been his natural color even when he was younger. BJ hoped to hell Iris wouldn't end up with Arnold. By contrast, Harvey's sleek head with its *au naturel* white fringe around his ears and the back was dignified and attractive.

"Well, thanks for the cake," he said. "Now I'm warm. Now I can face the day."

"And as a further gesture of apology to the woman whose homemade baked goods you've just wolfed down, you can come to the next Over-Fifty Singles Night."

Harvey grimaced. "I wouldn't miss it for the world."

BJ could tell he was grimacing just for effect. With a little matchmaking finesse, she reasoned, she might be able to pull this off. She might be able to put off asking Iris to move in with her, indefinitely.

"Oh—and thanks for the deep thoughts," he said.

"Just so you'll know, I don't generally do deep thoughts."

"Neither do I."

He was almost out the door when he stopped and turned to face her. "One more thing. About your sister."

BJ arched an eyebrow.

"She looks like Michael Jackson," he said.

CHAPTER 6

What amazed Iris most was this: the way Diane came in from her ten-hour workday looking as fresh as if she'd just emerged from a long nap, kissed Jonah and Noah, dismissed Patti Ann with a regal grace Iris had been trying to develop all her life, shed her elegant suit for sweats, and settled onto the couch with Noah at her breast, still with a smile on her face. Imagine: Iris's own daughter born to the dual role of executive and mother. Such energy, such competence, such brains. Where did Diane get all that? Not from Iris, that was for sure.

Iris didn't think she'd gotten it from Sheldon, either.

"Can you help me on Wednesday, Mom?" Diane stroked the baby's arm and then brushed a lock of fluffy-but-not-messy dark hair off her forehead, hair Iris had been thankful for every day of her daughter's life, considering the unruly stuff she and BJ had inherited, BJ especially.

"Sure, honey. Wednesday or any other day. I live to serve." Noting the ease with which Jonah mediated a dispute between a toy dump truck and a tractor, Iris decided the boy also showed some of his mother's promise.

"Well, I'm going to give you a choice of tasks," Diane said, "though I already know which one you'll choose."

"So that's it? I'm as transparent as glass? I used to be a woman of mystery."

"I'm sure you still are, Mom. But I'm taking a long lunch because Noah has his checkup. Either you or Patti Ann can meet me at the doctor's—" the pediatrician was two blocks from Diane's office "—and the other one can pick up Jonah."

"No contest. No doctors' offices," Iris agreed. Jonah's two-mornings-a-week preschool let out at noon. She would take him to lunch, diaper bag at the ready, free of Patti Ann.

"What I never understood, Mom, was how you can't watch a child get a shot but you don't mind being shot up yourself. All those operations. That Botox."

"Oh, Diane, I'm finished with all that. Well, maybe I still do Botox. But no more surgery. I just hope you won't follow my bad example. I was lucky I didn't get one of those horrible infections."

"But to do it for all those years, and still be so squeamish when someone else is in the doctor's office."

"I used to think of it like labor pains. You can stand a lot of discomfort if you're going to get something wonderful in return, like a baby or a better chin. But to watch a doctor stick a needle in a helpless child—" Iris shuddered.

"He gets lifelong immunity from measles, mumps, chicken pox, diphtheria, whooping cough—"

"Yes, but it's nothing you can see. Keep in mind that I was always one of those shallow people who went for the quick fix." She winked at her daughter, then strode over to Jonah and tickled him under the ribs. "Now for the *culinary* quick fix… Sweetie, how about after school next time, you and I go out for chicken and fries? Just you and grandma."

Jonah giggled, interested. "Me and Gamma? Chicken and fries?"

So there she was, with two hours of Wednesday morning to fill before she had to pick up her grandson, standing at the entrance to the mall, determined to buy BJ the perfect gift if it killed her.

Which it very well might.

For two months, BJ had refused to let Iris pay a penny of rent. For two months, BJ had refrained from asking Iris about her plans. For two months, BJ had reluctantly allowed Iris to tend her house and dog (BJ pretended not to be reluctant, but Iris knew). For two months, BJ had fretted over Iris's fragile mental state, ignoring Iris's assurances that she was fine. But when Iris finally said, "If you won't let me pay, at least let me *get* you something," BJ wasn't even nice about it.

"Don't even think about it! This house is already so full of stuff that it's about to smother me."

"Oh, BJ. *Now* whose mental state is fragile?"

"I'm serious, Iris. The minute I put away whatever household gadget Janelle sends for Chanukah, the whole kitchen will probably sink under its own weight and collapse into the crawl space."

"You love those do-dads!" Iris said.

"Remember how good you felt when you took all your stuff to Goodwill? Sometimes I think I ought to do the same thing."

"You do not!" When Sheldon had died and Iris was struck with the need to sell her house and get rid of her possessions, that was something else entirely. Shedding thirty years of objects that, for all she knew, *some other woman might have touched* made Iris feel light, as if she'd gone on a diet. But on the rare occasions when Iris lost weight (she was never very fat, anyway), she always knew she'd gain it back, just as she knew she'd accumulate more possessions to fill the new space and new life she'd build for herself when she got around to it. When BJ talked about getting rid of things (and why *would* she?), she sounded like she meant it for good.

"*Stuff* is the spice of life," Iris said. "An expression of your personality. There's nothing wrong with it."

"In moderation," BJ sniffed. As if Iris's desire to buy her a present—and maybe Iris's own love for clothes and knickknacks—was some kind of crime. Well, Iris couldn't help it, and she wasn't ashamed. She loved decorative pillows, fancy luggage, coffee-table books with attractive covers. For years she'd pored over mail-order catalogs and filled out order forms for clothes from stores as affordable as Chadwick's and pricey as Neiman Marcus. She'd chosen kitchenware from the

Chef's Catalog and Williams-Sonoma. She'd selected whole itineraries for trips to Israel and China and the islands of Greece. The only thing she didn't do was send in the orders because she couldn't afford them. But she learned to be a skilled and clever shopper. At T.J. Maxx, the special, remarkable sale item jammed onto the racks would jump right out at her. She could tell without opening the morning paper that this was the day the extra twenty-percent-off coupon from Belk would be inside. She dressed her family stylishly and decorated her home in the best of taste. If she paid half what anyone else did for almost everything she owned, who had to know? Her limited savings went into her cosmetic surgery fund. And now, if she had to shed a few possessions in order to move on with her life, it wasn't for lack of appreciating the comfort they could bring. BJ's attitude made no sense at all.

"If it weren't for Janelle's apple corers and pepper mills and egg slicers," she told her sister, "your kitchen would be dull."

"It would be *clean*," BJ insisted. But Iris knew what she knew. Janelle's kitchen-themed gifts went a long way toward making up for the fact that she was rarely there in person. BJ prized her collection of wine corks and refrigerator magnets as much as she did the fancy coffeemaker Janelle had sent in a moment of financial security. And that wasn't all. David's torn and tattered leather recliner, still in its prominent place in the den six years after his death, made the house look as if he'd walk in and sit down at any moment. In BJ's bedroom, a framed photo sat on the bureau of Janelle holding her little son Eli, before she divorced and voluntarily gave up custody to the boy's father, claiming she wasn't ready for single motherhood just yet. BJ could see her grandson's photo the moment she sat up in bed. And BJ never walked past the table in her foyer without lightly touching the colorful Murano glass candy dish David had brought from his last trip to Venice, after receiving some fancy dental award.

The real reason BJ didn't want more *stuff*, Iris believed, was because she was afraid she might get another gift that meant something to her, and it would only add to the burden of tenderness she pretended did not exist inside her heart.

Ordinarily, Iris understood and sympathized, but today BJ's pretense was only irritating. "Did it ever occur to you," she asked, "that telling me not to buy anything is inconsiderate?"

"That's crazy." BJ plucked a ripe peach from the fruit bowl, held it up, squeezed it for firmness. "Peaches in October?"

"They were on sale. Stop changing the subject! I'm telling you that not letting me pay rent or buy you anything makes me feel like a leech."

"You're not a leech. You're my sister."

"Your sister, the leech."

BJ dropped the peach back into the bowl. "Fine! Get me something, then! Just make sure it's not—clutter."

"Oh. Let me write that down." Iris pretended to scribble on her palm. "No clutter." She discarded her imaginary pen. "Something intangible, then? Don't think I haven't thought about it. Gym membership? You already have one. Concert tickets? Whoops, you've got a season pass. Movies? You hate them."

"No I don't. Not *all* movies."

"Oh—here's an idea. A gift certificate for a manicure." BJ had always claimed polish smothered her nails, which needed air and light in order to thrive.

"I've *had* my manicure," BJ said.

"It wasn't a regular manicure. It was tips. And if you'd asked me, I could have told you they were way too long before you nearly jabbed your eye out trying to put in your contact lenses." This had happened just before BJ left for Janelle's wedding in Seattle. The minute the event was over, BJ had peeled off the tips, leaving her nails so shredded they took six months to recover.

"Okay. No manicure. Maybe a cut and color at some trendy new hair salon."

"Don't even go there, Iris."

"Heaven forbid." BJ's hair had always been much more wiry and kinky than Iris's, and completely out of control. Even at ten or eleven, she'd worn it with ballsy fearlessness in a short, unruly white-person's Afro that framed her face and dared anyone to criticize, which no one ever did. When she was about twenty, her hair began to go gray in odd streaks and patches—a phenomenon Iris assumed BJ would correct if someone just pointed it out. "It's pretty unusual looking," she finally got up the nerve to say. "Have you ever thought of coloring it?"

"Ask me what I want to do with my life—dye my hair or become a marketing magnate. I'll give you one guess," BJ had growled. "Once you color your hair, you're into it forever." Forty years later, the modified Afro persisted, as did the gray.

"Okay," Iris said now. "Manicure—out. Hair—out. Lavish vacation to the tropics—out."

"Lavish vacation to the tropics actually sounds pretty interesting." BJ spoke lightly, but the bones in her face looked frozen. It was the closest they'd come in years, Iris thought, to actually having a fight.

Which made it all the more critical, now that Iris stood at the entrance to the mall, to choose exactly the right thing.

She started at JCPenney where the smorgasbord of merchandise might give her some ideas. Towels, no. Kitchenware, no, that was Janelle's domain. Jewelry, no, and not because the usual sale wasn't really a sale (no one bought jewelry in there at full price, Iris had learned long ago), but because BJ wouldn't wear it. It weighted her down even more than nail polish, she claimed—except for the tiny gold hoop earrings she'd worn ever since the two of them had had their ears pierced when Iris was fourteen and BJ was already twenty-one. As a preteen, Janelle had bought her mother the kind of heavy, dangly earrings the girl herself wished for, and BJ's struggles to endure them were truly heroic. Ditto for her wedding ring, which she took off the minute she came into the house. The only concession she made was to an expansion-band Timex watch she wore because she couldn't stand not to know what time it was. She replaced the watch with an identical one each time the battery quit for good, claiming it was the only style that didn't bother her wrist.

Clothes were out, too. For work, BJ wore the same uniform every day: dressy black or gray slacks and a blouse or pullover, topped in cool weather by a blazer in a limited variety of shades. Her closet was full, but her wardrobe was predictable. Anything outside BJ's narrow set of parameters would sit in a drawer forever.

JCPenney proved uninspiring. Twenty minutes later, Iris was out in the middle of the mall, despondent and—insult of insults—having a hot flash. She was sure she'd been beyond menopause before the hormone scare convinced her to eschew estrogen, but she'd been having hot flashes ever since. They didn't come all the time, thankfully, only when she was aggravated about something. Today, she blamed BJ.

How did you buy for someone so set in her ways?

Really, it was impossible.

A new clothing store next to the vitamin shop was having a grand opening sale on winter outerwear, which seemed pointless since winters this far south didn't begin until January and were often so mild you didn't put on your heavy coat at all. Fanning her face with a hand, Iris wandered into the store and flipped through a rack of toboggans like the ones BJ favored, but with fake fur trim that made them a bit more stylish. Iris picked one up, not for a "present," just something to slip into the coat closet, where BJ would never know it hadn't been there for years. Besides, it made her feel better to buy something. Anything.

She handed the sales girl a twenty. The cash register opened, and a screen showed how much change Iris was due. No brains needed at all. *It wasn't always that way*, she wanted to say. At her own first job cashiering in a shoe store, Iris had been on the verge of tears by the time BJ arrived to pick her up at closing time. "I don't see why they don't give you more pencils and paper for this!" she had blurted as she completed her final sale.

"For what, honey?" BJ asked.

Lifting the tiny scratch pad she'd been using all day, she showed BJ pages so dotted with calculations that you could hardly read them. "To figure out how much change to give," Iris said.

"What do you mean?"

"Like, if the sale is six dollars and thirty-three cents and she gives you a ten. A scratch pad to write down ten dollars and subtract six thirty-three. I can't do it in my head."

"Oh, *honey*. You don't have to do the math at all. Didn't anyone ever teach you to count change?" BJ sounded so hurt, you'd have thought Iris slapped her.

Then, seeing the tears well in Iris's eyes, BJ had said brightly, "Come on. Let's get out of here. I'll buy you a Coke and show you something amazing."

Sitting in the drugstore, BJ had taught Iris the art of making change. "Okay. The sale is six dollars and thirty-three cents and she gives you a ten." BJ dumped all the money from her wallet onto the table between them. "You put the ten in front of you so you won't forget what the customer gave you," BJ instructed. "And then you count *up* from the amount of the sale to the amount she gave you. Watch." She dropped two pennies into Iris's hand. "The sale is six thirty-three, right? So this makes six thirty-four, six-thirty five." Then BJ picked up nickels, a dime, quarters. "Six-forty, six-fifty, six seventy-five, seven dollars. You count it out aloud and put it in her hand. Then you give her the bills—eight, nine, ten." She put the bills into Iris's palm. "That's all there is to it. See?"

Iris was a little confused at first, but after a few more times she understood. "All you have to do is count," BJ stressed. "You don't have to add or subtract or do any kind of calculations on paper. You don't have to be good in math."

From anyone else, this would have been the worst kind of insult. But BJ was only trying to help—and of course Iris had been able to make change ever since, even though she'd learned a little late.

Looking at the hat as the clerk slipped it into its little plastic bag, Iris thought: Why, the real reason I want to get her something isn't even because she's been putting me up all these months. It's because she taught me to count change.

And like a light going on, she knew just what to do. BJ might be a little loony, but the truth was, if she really didn't *want* more things for herself, she'd just tolerate whatever Iris got her. BJ's being nice about it would be like BJ shelling out more charity.

But what if Iris bought something for Randolph? A toy, and maybe some of those expensive liver treats. It wasn't that Randolph needed anything. It was more that getting something for him was like getting something for BJ by proxy. She would be flattered in the same way Iris would be flattered if BJ bought something for Noah or Jonah, to show she cared for them, or at least that she cared for Iris enough to know how much Iris valued her grandsons. BJ would not resent anything Iris bought for her dog.

Slinging her purse strap over her shoulder, Iris headed in a speed-walk toward the pet store at the opposite end of the mall. She knew the place very well. Next to playing with the trains at Barnes & Noble, checking out the fish and birds and puppies was Jonah's favorite excursion. Today, the display window featured a pair of bunnies, probably soon to become a whole community. Inside the store, the usual bored young mothers blocked the aisles with their strollers or oohed and aahed with their preschoolers over the caged puppies, which Iris tried not to look at since she always felt sorry for them and wondered what would happen to the ones nobody bought before they lost their cuteness.

Edging past the strollers to the dog-toy section, she picked out a rag doll that squeaked if you pressed its middle and had long floppy limbs Randolph would enjoy pulling on. She picked out a ball with a jingle-bell inside. Around the corner, she was just about to reach for a box of the much-loved liver treats when she caught sight of a familiar figure standing some ten feet away, near the circular Plexiglas corral that served as a cage for the parakeets.

The familiar figure was Patti Ann, holding Noah in her arms.

"Look, angel-boy," Iris heard her saying. "See the birdies?" There was no top to the cage—the birds' wings must have been clipped to keep them from flying, though they didn't look mutilated, thank goodness. Patti Ann stood close and held the baby aloft over the sea of activity.

The sight gave Iris a little shiver of alarm. Was she going to *drop* him?

But no. Patti Ann was only trying to give Noah a better view. The birds were a rainbow of colors, some eating seeds from the feeders or drinking water or chewing on cuttle bone, others sleeping with their heads under one wing, two or three chattering and snapping at each other with their beaks. Jonah liked to point at the different birds and ask Iris which one was her favorite, but anyone could see Noah was too young to be interested—although he was being pleasant about it, as Noah always was.

"See? That's a yel-low birdie," Patti Ann said, pronouncing the syllables distinctly. "Yel-low. And that one is blue."

Iris stayed where she was, packages in hand, not wanting to interrupt but poised to sprint forward if things got out of control. Did Patti Ann really think a four-month-old cared about being shown around a pet shop? It certainly wouldn't have occurred to Iris to come here just with the baby. It made no sense.

"See, angel-boy," Patti Ann pointed again. "These birdies are called parakeets. Par-a-keets."

Noah smiled, not at the birds but at Patti Ann's pointing fingers. The nanny's face reflected such relief that she might have been rescued from drowning at the bottom of a well. She sighed and put Noah back in his stroller.

Then Iris understood. She remembered why she'd agreed to pick up Jonah from preschool. She remembered what day this was. Of course.

Patti Ann hadn't come here with malice in her heart. She'd come because she cared for Noah and wanted him to have at least a little bit of fun before his doctor appointment and his shot.

It was odd, but it was okay.

Wasn't it?

How could you argue with love?

CHAPTER 7

*Y*our sister looks like Michael Jackson. What the *hell* did that mean?

For two weeks BJ had been toying with these words that had dropped from Harvey Sussman's lips, and it infuriated her that she was still none the wiser.

Your sister looks like Michael Jackson, but she's a lovely woman anyway and I'm interested?

Your sister looks like an aging male pop star, and although I can't help looking around your house to catch a curious glimpse, basically the idea disgusts me?

This morning BJ was worrying this question over as she swam her three-days-a-week laps at the Y. She went religiously at eight in the morning, every Monday, Wednesday and Friday, because if she didn't get it over with, she wouldn't do it at all. She swam eighteen laps, half a mile, breast stroke in one direction and a slow crawl in the other. Once she got into the water, she enjoyed it, though not so much today because her goggles were leaking. She needed new ones and kept forgetting to buy them. Stupid. She always wore one contact lens in her right eye so she could see when she came up for air, and counted on the goggles to keep them dry. She'd put in the left lens later.

So was Harvey interested, or not?

Impossible to say.

The week before, Singles Night Out had been canceled because everyone had plans for Halloween. Then, when the group finally got together again, it was as if each member had stored up critical business that had to be dealt with immediately. Resa Taub and Fred Shulman launched into a detailed analysis of a property Resa was trying to sell him. Two women from the retirement home pestered everyone to buy raffle tickets for an afghan one of them had made, proceeds to go to the Manorhouse Recreation Fund. When Harvey Sussman arrived, BJ thought he was about to save the day by sitting down next to Iris and starting a normal, social conversation, but then Lou Green grabbed his arm and drew him away. "Sit here, Harvey. There's something I want to ask you about." They'd spent the rest of the evening discussing Lou's macular degeneration. Was it the wet or the dry type? What had the doctor said? Harvey reassured Lou, with surprising patience and gentleness, that it didn't sound like a worst-case scenario at all. He itemized a few self-help tips. He turned over the paper placemat and began drawing diagrams and writing out the definitions of medical terms Lou's doctor had used in their discussions but never explained. Molly Gerber, sitting on Harvey's other side, leaned close and nodded in agreement.

It was the most bizarre Singles Night so far. Even the retirement-home ladies kept talking business long after they'd finished tallying the receipts from their raffle tickets, pitting the merits of silent auctions against the certainty of greeting-card sales. Only Iris and Arnold Lieberman seemed engaged in normal chitchat—though BJ cringed when she overheard her sister telling Arnold how worried Diane was that little Noah hadn't turned over onto his stomach yet. "By the end of the fourth month, I guess most of them do," Iris lamented. At that, the usually-admiring Arnold patted his toupee and got a glazed, faraway expression on his face. BJ made a mental note to warn Iris, tactfully, that when you were a doting grandmother, it was best not to let anyone else know.

She felt a sharp twinge of guilt as soon as she formulated this thought. After all, what right had she to hold her sister in such little esteem? Iris, who by necessity had held dozens of jobs over the years, had never valued any of them very much, keeping the best of herself for her family: Diane primarily, but also Sheldon (who didn't deserve it) and now her grandsons. *Don't begrudge her that,* BJ told herself. Under other circumstances, she might have been just as insufferable about little Eli. The first time she'd laid eyes on him, she'd taken note of the coolness between Janelle and her husband, Luke, and instinctively pulled back from the impulse to love the baby completely. *This child will not be part of your life,* something had told her. Sure enough, within a year Luke and Janelle had filed for divorce, and Luke got custody of the boy because Janelle decided she wasn't ready to raise a son alone. BJ had hidden her disappointment, both in her daughter and in her loss of easy access to her grandson. Eli was four now. BJ had not seen him in a year.

Across the table, Iris chattered on like a happy child while the retirement-home ladies, finished with their calculations, giggled merrily. Their outburst went unnoticed by Fred and Resa, who were deep into an amortization schedule. It went unnoticed by Lou and Molly, who focused on Harvey's fingers as he sketched what looked like the cross section of an eye. BJ was the sole observer, shipwrecked on the island of her own awareness. For a moment, such a dizzying sense of isolation filled her that she had to hold to the edge of the table until it subsided. She took a breath. She forced herself back to the business at hand. *Your sister looks like Michael Jackson.* For the next twenty minutes, as she made her silent way through a plate of linguine Alfredo, she kept asking herself, *What the hell does looking like Michael Jackson* mean?

Now, blinking away the chlorinated water beneath her right contact lens, she stroked dutifully across the pool and turned again to her memory of Harvey's words, coupled with his behavior at Singles Night Out, and tried to come up with a scenario that had him secretly casting admiring looks at Iris as he outlined treatment options for Lou. Who was she kidding? The truth was, once they'd all paid their bills, she and Iris had gone together to the ladies' room, and when they'd come out, Harvey was gone.

At the end of the pool, BJ snatched off her goggles, poured out the water and set them back on her head. No matter how she adjusted the strap, the goggles wouldn't stay dry. BJ gutted her way through her full eighteen laps.

Her right eye was pink and teary when she finally climbed from the pool. In the dressing room, she raised her face into the full force of the shower, letting it rinse the chlorine out of her eye. By the time she'd gotten dressed, the irritation was nearly gone. She had to meet Iris in an hour to shop for the *oneg* they were hosting at temple, but if she didn't get a new pair of goggles *this minute*, she'd find herself still struggling with the old ones two days from now. She finger-dried her hair and headed out to her car.

Shulman's Sporting Goods was not really big enough for all the equipment it carried, but at first glance customers often thought it was. Fred had created an intricate pattern of crisscrossing aisles that somehow made it seem perfectly logical to find shin guards between the baseball bats and swim trunks, and swim goggles all the way across the store next to the women's running shorts. The place had once been a clothing store belonging to Fred's father, who would have sold it if Fred hadn't returned to town just as Wal-Mart and Target and Old Navy were buying up properties nearby. Fred and his mother had left Fern Hollow during Fred's formative years—which is to say when it became obvious he was homosexual and not inclined to lie about it. By the time he returned he was a handsome, middle-aged man who favored expensive, colorful silk shirts that brought out the intense blue of his eyes, and about whom heterosexual women were inclined to sigh, "It's such a shame," while at the same time hiring Fred's devoted partner, Tommy, to decorate their homes. Fred, always a fine athlete and a cross-country skier during his years up North, had remodeled the defunct clothing store into a sports emporium that had flourished ever since. Whenever anyone in the temple needed anything sports-related, they always came to Fred.

Even so, BJ didn't expect to find him personally rearranging shelves when she walked in, and probably wouldn't have except that she arrived the minute the doors opened, before he had time to escape to his office.

"BJ. Don't tell me. You had a hard workout." Fred waved vaguely in the direction of her damp hair. "I have just the thing." He plucked a bottle of blue-tinted sports drink from a shelf, unscrewed the top and thrust it in her direction.

She shook her head. "Not a hard enough workout to make me drink Windex. I just need some swim goggles."

"I didn't realize you swam."

"Eighteen laps, three times a week. Which takes me forty minutes. The other swimmers race by me and snicker. If *you* snicker, I'm off to Wal-Mart."

"Fine. But keep in mind that their goggles are made in the Far East by slaves chained to their benches." Fred took a swig of the sports drink and made a face. "You're right. Windex. But listen. I wouldn't laugh at you no matter how slowly you swam. Forty minutes in the pool is healthier than forty minutes in bed. Depending, of course, on what you're doing in bed."

"Sleeping. Tossing and turning. Worrying. Nothing interesting."

"Ah. Too bad." He motioned her to follow him and plucked a pair of goggles off a rack. "Nice and soft against your face, but completely waterproof. Just what you need." He took her credit card, and when she'd signed the slip, he checked his watch. "If you've got a minute, come into my lair and I'll give you a cup of coffee."

"Your lair? I'm flattered. I've never been invited to your lair. If I knew you had a lair I probably would have tried to sell you bigger ads. But I have to pick up Iris."

"Ah. The little sister."

Having forgotten Iris for a full twenty minutes, BJ was dismayed to feel the renewed niggle of worry dig a crater of lines between her brows. "Well, yes. The little sister." As long as she was here, she might as well also dig for a little information. Or confirmation. Or something. "She seems to enjoy Singles Night Out, don't you think? You, too. Better than you expected?"

"I'm thinking of buying a rental property Resa has listed. I'm like you, BJ. A person who believes in networking."

"And if the group spawns a little romance here and there, that's not so bad, either," BJ said.

"I think Lou Green and Molly got together at the retirement home," Fred told her. "I don't think Singles Night had anything to do with it."

"I didn't mean Lou," BJ said. "I meant Harvey Sussman. I think he's interested in Iris."

Fred registered mild surprise. "You do?"

"Don't you?"

Fred stared at her for a long beat, long enough for her to say she was joking, which she did not. Then he slipped the goggles into a plastic bag and pushed it absently across the counter. "You mean Harvey is interested in her theories about remembering the names of people's dogs? Or interested in Iris herself, personally?"

"I wouldn't put too much stock in all that talk about the dogs," BJ said. "I think they were just trying to impress each other."

Fred shook his head. "I think he's more interested in *me*, BJ. And I don't think he's gay."

BJ noted Fred's exceptionally fine, high cheekbones. She pictured him beside Iris, two fashion plates looking collectively twenty years younger than their age. She thought, as so many other women had over the years, *what a shame.*

"You're trying to find her a man," Fred stated flatly, joining the legions who regularly read BJ's thoughts.

"Not exactly. It's just that I worry about her. Sometimes she's just so helpless."

"She never struck me that way."

"No?"

"Listen. Everybody knew Sheldon. A woman who puts up with a Sheldon for thirty years has a few resources."

"Well, of course she does. But still. She used to be such a Southern belle."

Fred toyed with the cuff of his crimson shirt as he considered this. "There's no such thing as a Jewish Southern belle," he concluded.

"Of course there is. You didn't know Iris in her prime."

"I guess I didn't."

"And it's hard to think of a Southern belle without a man," BJ told him. "She seems sort of—unfinished."

Fred shook his head. "You really think so? Listen. Iris had Sheldon for thirty years. Now maybe she's better off. No disrespect to your sister, she's a nice woman. But helpless and unfinished? No. A little too put together, maybe. Even when she's in sweats or jeans, she looks a little too put together. And you figure it's probably all neat little boxes inside, too." He tapped his temple. "You know what I mean? She's the kind of person—you always want to mess up her hair."

"Well, that could be an *attractive* quality, couldn't it? To some man?"

"Other than Harvey Sussman?"

"Well, sure. But who else is there? Arnold Lieberman with his toupee?"

"There's Howard Ades."

"Howard Ades!" BJ snatched her bag off the counter. "All three of his wives died of cancer. It would be like setting someone up with Typhoid Mary."

"Now you're being superstitious."

He was right. Next thing she knew, she'd be spitting three times to ward off the evil eye. "I can't help it," she defended. "Iris is my sister. I care about her. I'm going to ask her to move in with me. I certainly don't want her getting cancer!"

Fred laughed. "You don't want to have to nurse her back to health, you mean."

"It isn't funny," BJ sniffed.

"It is," Fred told her. "If you had any perspective you'd see that. Besides, I thought Iris *already* moved in with you."

"Not officially. Officially she's just visiting. It sounds trivial, but there's a difference. I'm going to ask her and make it official."

"And you don't love the idea."

"No. But it's fine. She needs me. It's fine."

"I'd be willing to bet," said Fred, "that she doesn't need you as much as you think."

This comment stayed with BJ the rest of the morning. Was it possible she'd underestimated Iris? If so, where was the house Iris was so sure she was going to buy? Where was her sense of purpose? Why did BJ have such a strong sense that her sister was still languishing?

Of course, at the moment, *languishing* was hardly the word. When they got to the supermarket to buy supplies for the *oneg*, Iris metamorphosed into a dynamo filled with purpose, just as she had done in any kind of retail establishment since she was eight or nine. She held the newspaper ad in one hand and her shopping list in the other. She checked off items as she put them in the cart. People's schedules being what they were, the temple had recently resorted to assigning "*oneg* duty" to its members, rather than waiting for volunteers, so that a different family was obligated to provide after-services refreshments each week. But even if there had been no assignments, Iris would have volunteered once a month as she always had, in order to insure that the Shabbat goodies met her own high standards.

"I'm thinking a pumpkin roll, now that it's November," Iris said, "and the usual cookies for the kids, and of course The Cloggeroo." This was a rich cake they called Chocolate Delight in public but privately termed The Cloggeroo because it contained enough butter and sour cream to clog the healthiest artery. Everyone loved it.

"You're going to be in the kitchen all day," BJ said.

"I don't mind." Although Timmons Bakery offered excellent cakes and pastries, Iris was always disappointed when people didn't make their own. The least a person could do was bake some brownies or a few cookies, even if she used a mix. When they were made in a spirit of love and giving, Iris often said, even mediocre homemade goods tasted better than anything from a store.

"So what else do we need?" BJ asked. "Give me a job."

"Fruit for people who don't eat sugar." Iris turned a page of the ad. "Grapes are on sale, and apples." She pointed BJ in the direction of the produce section. "I'll pick up cheese and some nice crackers."

Twenty minutes later they were in the checkout line with a cart much fuller than BJ had anticipated. Iris had stocked up on broccoli, Romaine lettuce, two-for-a-dollar yogurt, and frozen turkey breast on sale—"Turkey is always a bargain all through November"—while engaging BJ in their annual "discussion" about Iris's desire to have BJ at Diane's house for Thanksgiving dinner, versus BJ's desire to work at the soup kitchen. BJ always chose the soup kitchen because it meant she wouldn't have to feel like an addendum to someone else's family, even if it was her own sister's. "Your own sister *is* your family," Iris maintained. They made their way through Iris's tactful invitation and BJ's tactful refusal only because Iris would not have felt hospitable if she hadn't offered. They loaded their groceries onto the checkout belt. Iris, distracted, began rummaging for something in her purse.

"What are you looking for?"

"My phone." She poked around a little more.

"You should carry a smaller purse," BJ told her.

Actually, the current purse was by no means Iris's largest. She dumped its contents out onto the conveyor belt. There was no phone. "Oh, no," Iris said.

"You think you lost it?"

"I think I left it at Diane's. Diane's forever after me to keep it charged, so I plugged it in when I was there. I'm sure it's right where I left it. Diane has this theory that I should keep the phone on all the time in case she needs me. She's never needed me once."

"Yes, but you're her security blanket." Poor Diane, caught between relying on Iris and relying on Patti Ann. "If you want the phone, we'll run by Diane's and get it."

"You don't mind?" Iris's face bore almost heartrending relief.

"Why should I mind? Am I doing any work, anyway? No. I'm buying sour cream and chocolate chips for The Cloggeroo. I'm insuring that American Jewry eats homemade junk food on Friday night. I'm performing a *mitzvah*. What's another ten minutes?"

"See? I knew you didn't want to spend your day selling ads," Iris said.

Patti Ann opened the door before they rang the bell. The woman probably spent her days staring out the window, hoping something interesting would happen.

"Oh. Too bad. Jonah just went down for an early nap," she said. The trip to the doorway had left her slightly winded. Clutching Noah to her middle, right arm around his waist, she clung to him as if he were a large tumor she had to hold in place.

"So," BJ said, running a finger across the baby's soft cheek. "How's the little loaf of bread?"

Noah gurgled with delight. Patti Ann regarded BJ sternly. "Loaf of bread?"

"A term of endearment," BJ explained. "Solid little guy. Always heavy for his size."

"Personally, I think 'loaf of bread' sounds insulting."

"Staff of life," BJ said amiably, and turned to follow Iris. On the far side of the family room, Iris ran her hands across a chest-high shelf with an outlet above it. "It isn't here," she said.

"What isn't there?" Patti Ann asked.

"My phone. I'm sure I left it here the other day."

"Oh, your *phone*. It's right over there." Patti Ann waddled over to a bookcase by the door, and poked through the mess of items on top. A tangle of keys, a squeak toy shaped like a turtle, a pile of mail, a few charge-card receipts and beneath all that, finally, the phone, still attached to its unplugged charger. Patti Ann dangled it in front of Iris as if it were a snake.

"Thanks." Iris took it more meekly than BJ thought was warranted.

"And my sister was supposed to find her phone there?" BJ asked. "In the pile of stuff where you hid it?"

"We don't plug things in because of Jonah." Patti Ann said. She clutched Noah ever more firmly, as if BJ might otherwise reach out and seize him. "It's my first responsibility as a nanny to keep the children safe."

"Commendable," BJ said. "Understood." She walked over to the shelf where Iris had originally left the phone. "But Jonah would have to stand on a chair to reach this outlet. If he wants to electrocute himself, why go to so much trouble?" She pointed to an outlet low on the wall. "Why not just plug in a hairpin right there along with the TV and that lamp?"

"It's okay, BJ," Iris pleaded. Peace at any price.

Patti Ann cut her eyes from one sister to the other, apparently noting the possibility of friction between them, and let the hint of a smile spread across her face.

Give me a break, BJ thought. "Patti Ann," she said carefully, "maybe *we* don't plug things in because of Jonah, but Iris does, and sometimes I do, too. And *we* don't move those things or hide them, because they belong to members of the family, and those members of the family might need them."

"I was just trying to do what I was hired for," Patti Ann said weakly. Bracing Noah against her chest, she flopped heavily into a chair.

BJ knew high drama when she saw it. The best policy was to ignore it, dismiss it out of hand. But it was also true that Patti Ann had gone a little pale, and drops of sweat were beginning to bead on her forehead. "What's wrong? Are you sick?" BJ asked.

"I'm just not used to having people talk to me that way." Clinging to Noah, Patti Ann reached into her pocket and retrieved a hard candy—caramel, it looked like—and popped it into her mouth. "I do the best I can," she whispered.

"Of course you do," Iris reassured.

"I'm careful with the children," Patti Ann said.

"Even if something happened, they'd be safe." She lifted the edge of her blouse to show BJ the phone clipped to her waistband.

"Ah. The ever-ready link to the outside world. And how is that going to help if you clunk your head and knock yourself out?"

"BJ!" Iris exclaimed. "Don't talk like that!"

This was hopeless. "I have to go work," BJ said. "Come on. I'll drop you at home on the way."

"Or I can drive you later, if you want to hang around to say hello to Jonah," Patti Ann added quickly. "He should be up by lunchtime."

Iris looked from Patti Ann to BJ and back again. "Well—" she said uncertainly. Had no one ever taught Iris how to maintain the offensive?

"She can't," BJ snipped. "She has too much baking to do."

"She's right," Iris told Patti Ann apologetically. "If I get a chance, I'll bring you some of the cookies."

BJ sighed. So much for Fred Shulman's theory about Iris's self-sufficiency. No one was going to bail Iris out, least of all Iris herself. It was time to stop procrastinating and ask Iris to move in with her permanently, once and for all, no matter how much she cringed at the idea of a long-term housemate. Time to put someone else first, for a change. Act like a *mensch*. She would ask her tonight.

CHAPTER 8

Sitting in services that evening, Iris reflected on the fact that even though she wasn't very smart, she could take comfort in the fact that there were certain things she understood very well. One was medical information, probably because of having so much surgery. The other was her religion.

Right now, Rabbi Seidman was droning on in a monotone that had lost her completely, but as a child, the first time Iris had heard a sermon about Moses at Sinai, it had been quite a different story. She'd been sitting in temple between her father and mother, with BJ on the other side, because when the two girls had been next to each other—even though BJ was a teenager and not a "girl" anymore—they had been carrying on. Wedged between her parents, Iris had no choice but to pay attention. The rabbi was saying that the covenant between God and the Jews was not just for those gathered at Sinai, but also for those yet to be born, all the Jews who would pass through the world down through the generations. Hearing that, Iris had thought, *yes, of course.* The idea of being a link in a chain that stretched backward to Sinai and forward as far as she could imagine made a shiver of excitement and belonging run down her spine. She had never doubted, from that day to this, that the ancient covenant with God was also a covenant with *her*, Iris Louise Braudes Meyerhoff. It was a central fact of her life.

For that reason, she always had a warm and spiritual relationship with the temple, even though she was never sure about the details of the covenant beyond the Ten Commandments. She did know the men were expected to be circumcised, and both genders were supposed to do *mitzvahs*, which were either good deeds or commandments or both, depending on how the current rabbi explained it. Either way, she tried her best to keep up her part of the bargain.

Over the years she'd co-chaired the Chanukah dinner and the break-the-fast meal after Yom Kippur. She'd helped with the popular "Passover Kitchen" event in the religious school, and co-chaired the Sisterhood program committee with Sarah Kline. She'd been Sisterhood's corresponding secretary, contact person for Interfaith Outreach and liaison for the Sunshine Committee. The only thing she had never been was president of the Sisterhood or chair (rather than co-chair) of any important project. Iris knew this was partly because she'd worked full-time for so many years and partly because people didn't regard her as a leader—but mostly it was because of Sheldon. There was no point putting someone in charge whose husband might have an affair with another committee member and cause the attendant havoc and embarrassment. This had actually happened once. An organization like the temple couldn't afford a repeat. Iris didn't dwell on this often, because she had made her peace with the Sheldon situation and knew it was wise not to second-guess herself. But every once in a while, when the nominating committee named someone other than Iris to run for high office, she would experience a fierce pang of disappointment that, no matter what she did, she couldn't make things right.

Yet, for the most part, she was content. Stronger than any doubts Iris ever had was her certainty that she was playing a role in the holy covenant she was lucky enough to be part of. Tonight, as the congregation stood for the *aleinu*, one of the final prayers, she noted with satisfaction the more-than-respectable crowd in the sanctuary for services. And afterward, when the service had ended and people were oohing and aahing at the laden table she and BJ had created in the social hall, she felt positively *fulfilled*. They had designed a colorful autumn centerpiece of gourds and dried leaves. They had arranged the sweets and fruits and cheese in such a way that everything looked mouthwatering. As usual, The Cloggeroo was a hit. The pumpkin roll was a new recipe, but after both Sue Gordon and Linda Zimmerman asked for it, Iris relaxed. Everything was going perfectly.

Then Arnold Lieberman appeared at Iris's side. It was a bit of a shock. She hadn't spotted him earlier in the sanctuary, and at Singles Night he always seemed proud of not belonging to this or any other temple.

"Arnold. How nice. What brings you here?"

"I thought it was time to check it out. If I'd known there was all this food on a Friday night, I might have joined years ago." He had piled his plate with little cheese-and-crackers sandwiches and so many cut-up pieces of fruit that the lone slice of pumpkin roll seemed about to fall off the side. It was clear he didn't prepare meals for himself at home.

"You can join the temple at any time. Even at this late date," Iris said as she opened the top of the coffee carafe and poured in more decaf. "The treasurer would be thrilled."

Arnold was saying something else, but Iris's attention was diverted by the sight of the ice bucket, which was almost empty. BJ was supposed to keep an eye on it, but she was nowhere in sight. "I have to get something from the kitchen," she said as she picked up the bucket.

"I'll help you."

"Oh, you don't have to. Go ahead and socialize." Iris didn't want help. When she was hosting a party, it was easier to work alone. But Arnold stayed at her side as she moved across the room, even after she quickened her pace. He was nice enough—a retired accountant—but there was something about the total falseness of his toupee, the way it looked like a hat rather than hair, that made her want to pluck it off and say, *Buy something that didn't come from the dollar store, for heaven's sake!* Iris hated being so mean-spirited, even in the privacy of her mind, and the last thing she needed right now was to berate herself all the way to the kitchen, instead of concentrating on the tasks at hand.

But she couldn't stop the sour flow of her thoughts. Arnold was probably ten years older than she was, and he looked it. He might fall apart at any moment. More times than she could count, Iris had watched a fifty-something friend get involved with a sixty-something man who fell sick ten minutes after the relationship got serious, leaving the woman feeling obligated to take care of him, sometimes for years. After what she'd been through with Sheldon, she felt absolved of ever having to tend some other man, as a sex object or a nurse or anything else.

Arnold Lieberman stayed in step with her, walking remarkably fast for someone who was possibly on the verge of collapse. If it wouldn't have been so obvious, and if she hadn't been carrying both a coffee decanter and an ice bucket, Iris would have broken into a run.

To her relief, Sarah Kline suddenly materialized out of the crowd. "Here. Let me introduce you," she said to Arnold.

"Sarah! Meet Arnold Lieberman." Sarah's husband, Manny, had not been to services for a month. Iris was sure this signaled marital troubles Arnold would be happy to soothe. "Arnold comes to Over-Fifty Singles

Night sometimes. He was in finance until he retired."
Okay, accounting.

"Finance?" Sarah looked interested. Iris held up the empty ice bucket, gestured toward the kitchen, and moved off.

She practically ran into BJ. "Where *were* you? I thought you were going to keep track of the ice." Iris shoved the ice bucket at her sister, then smiled as Nancy Goldman approached, gesturing toward the sisters with her fork.

"Iris, this cake is wonderful!" She pointed to a piece of The Cloggeroo on her plate. "Did you make it?"

"Yes. I'm glad you like it," Iris said demurely. "It's an old family recipe." Excusing herself, she shouldered her way through the kitchen door behind BJ.

"Old family recipe, my foot," BJ said. "Mom never made that. Where'd you get the recipe, anyway?"

"Probably *Southern Living*." With its glossy color photos and stunning layouts, *Southern Living* had always been Iris's gold-standard for culinary ideas.

"I'm surprised at you," BJ said. "Although it's heartening to hear you lie not just to be diplomatic, but for the sake of mystery and drama."

"It wasn't a lie. I've had the recipe for years, and I've changed a couple of the ingredients. So in a sense it really is an old family recipe," Iris said.

"You should be ashamed of yourself," BJ told her.

"I know."

* * *

When everyone had finally cleared out, leaving BJ and Iris to clean up, Iris noted with satisfaction that not one piece of pumpkin roll was left on the plate. She wadded up the doily and threw it into the trash.

"Is the coast finally clear?" BJ came out of the kitchen, looked around to make sure there were no stragglers, and then said in a breathless gasp, "You won't believe what happened with Sarah Kline."

Iris hated to disappoint, but not enough to keep her mouth shut. "Sarah approached you about coming to Singles Night?"

"How could you *know* that?" BJ stopped short, hands full of dirty silverware she'd begun to collect from the table. "I can't believe you *knew*."

"Simple deduction."

"Of all people! Sarah never speaks to me if she can avoid it, but there she was, all friendly and charming—and you knew all about it!"

"Not *all*. What exactly did she say?"

"She said, 'I've heard about the Over-Fifty Singles Night, and I'd like to come next time.' Straightforward as that. I said, 'I guess you know it's called Over-Fifty Singles Night because it's mainly for singles,' but Sarah didn't bat an eyelash. She just said, 'Right. That's me. Single. Manny and I are separated.' I nearly dropped my teeth. She said, 'Don't collapse on me, BJ. I'm not looking for a new man. I'm just looking for dinner.' *Don't collapse on me!* When did I ever collapse on anybody?"

"Never, BJ. You're not the type. Here, give me that silverware before you drop it."

But even on the way home, BJ was still going on about Sarah's separation. "Since when do people their age get separated just like that?"

"It happens all the time," Iris said. "This has been in the works for a while. It's been obvious something was going on."

"Not obvious to *me*."

"That's because you don't pay attention. You can always tell what's going on with a couple at services. All you have to do is watch the way they sit."

"How they *sit*? Sitting is the key to their most intimate secrets?"

"I'm serious, BJ. Think about Diane and Wes when they first got married. Or that cute new Katz couple that just joined. When they're new and in love, they always sit close together with their shoulders touching. Like this." Iris unbuckled her seat belt and shifted toward BJ, who swiped her away.

Iris scooted closer. "Sometimes they hold hands, too."

"Touch my hand and you're out on the street."

"But mainly it's the shoulders." Iris leaned in to demonstrate. "Like this, the edge of his jacket against the sleeve of her dress. And every once in a while they'll tip their heads toward each other and whisper into each other's ears." Tipping her head close to BJ's, she whispered, "Like they can't stand not to talk to each other for one more second. Especially during High Holiday services. You've seen it a million times."

"Move over, Iris. Put your seat belt on. What if we wreck?" BJ was doing her best not to smile.

"Then a year or two will pass, and they'll relax away from each other some, but they'll still sit close," Iris said, increasing the distance between them just a smidgen. "Usually that's how they stay from then on. Think about the Feldmans. The Goldbergs. The Weismans."

"Okay. Point taken."

"But when things between them start to go bad, there's a different posture altogether. They both sit up straight and concentrate on the service. They don't lean toward each other or speak." Iris sat up straight, put on her seat belt, looked stern. "The first time, it could be nothing. It could just mean they had a fight. But if you see it week after week, you know they have nothing more to say to each other. Sarah and Manny were like that for months. Then Manny stopped coming to services altogether."

"And you were watching them. All that time."

"You probably were, too. But you didn't notice."

"Sarah hates me. Why should I notice her? I try not to, every chance I get."

"She doesn't hate you. She's just a gossip. That's how she gets attention. Otherwise, who would even know she was there? Look at her. Except for those silly skirts she wears, she's like a boring little old gray mouse."

"Well, that's certainly Sarah. Straight little-gray-mouse hair. Plain little-gray-mouse eyes. Skin with that mousy grayish cast." BJ considered for a minute. "You think she's sick?"

"No, of course not."

"And those little gray skirts three inches above the knee. Probably the same ones she wore forty years ago. You want to say, *oh, sweetie, cover up those varicose veins.*"

"Now you're being mean, BJ." But inwardly, Iris agreed. Sarah had always been proud of her long, thin legs, which in the past few years had deteriorated into stringy old-lady legs the skirts didn't enhance. And even though Sarah's gossip could be wicked, as Iris remembered from her unfaithful-Sheldon days, it was sad that Sarah's husband had left, and sad that she was trying to look younger in clothing so inappropriate and unbecoming that it added a good ten years. "What you want to say to her," Iris instructed, "is, *You know, Sarah, someone with hips as slim as yours would look wonderful in those new pants suits they're showing, with those long, narrow legs that make such a nice silhouette.*"

"Always the diplomat." BJ was grinning. "I still can't believe the way she came right up to me. She must be truly desperate."

"So if she wants to come to Singles Night, we have to be hospitable. Sarah probably gets frustrated because you don't usually give her anything juicy to talk about, but she doesn't dislike you. It's a compliment to you at a time like this that she's looking to you for support."

"If you're trying to get me to feel sorry for Sarah Kline, forget it." BJ shook her head.

"But you do feel a little sorry for her, don't you?" Iris asked. "Admit it. You do."

"Only because you're pestering me."

"See?" Iris said. "I'm right."

At the house, they carried in the trays and serving platters and silently put them away. After the long day, Iris was having trouble keeping her eyes open. "I'm beat," she told BJ. "I'm going up to bed."

"No. Wait." BJ pulled a bottle of Drambuie from the pantry and poured some for each of them. Iris never touched the stuff, and didn't think BJ much cared for it, either. Having no choice, she took the glass BJ offered and followed her into the den. "I know you're tired," BJ said after they'd settled into chairs, "but I promised myself I'd discuss this with you tonight."

"Ah. Always thinking of the other person."

"Well, I'm sorry, but I meant to do it before and didn't." BJ took a swig of her Drambuie and made a face. "I want you to move in with me. I mean, permanently. To make this your home. I don't want you to feel you have to go looking for a house somewhere else. Consider this the formal invitation."

Iris set her glass on the end table, where no doubt it would make a ring. "The formal invitation?"

"Well, yes." BJ set down her own glass with a clunk.

"Oh, honey," Iris said. "This is so nice of you. But you don't have to do this. I know you feel obligated and guilty, but you don't need to. I forgave you everything a long time ago."

"You forgave me *everything?*" BJ looked genuinely puzzled.

"You don't have to pretend anymore, BJ. This is better. Better we finally have it out in the open."

"I have no idea what we're talking about, Iris."

"I've always known, BJ. I knew the night it happened. It doesn't matter anymore."

"*What* doesn't matter?"

"What you did with Sheldon."

BJ stood up, ran her hands through her hair and sat down again. "You want to run that by me slowly? What I did with Sheldon, I mean?"

"The night you had *sex* with him," Iris said tersely. She was surprised at the cold, clipped sound of her words.

"You think I had *sex* with Sheldon?"

"Don't pretend, BJ. There's no point." She crossed her arms in front of her chest.

"Pretend! I never had sex with Sheldon. Half of Fern Hollow had sex with him, but not me. You knew how I felt about him. I thought he was an asshole womanizing *schmuck* who didn't deserve you. Who told you Sheldon and I had sex?"

"Why, he did, of course."

BJ's mouth opened as if she were about to speak, but for a long moment she just stared. Finally she said, "So Sheldon told you I had sex with him." And then more loudly, "And you believed him?"

"Well, yes."

BJ took a breath. "And exactly when was this supposed to have happened? This—*sex* between me and Sheldon."

"At that party David had for all those dentists. The night it started to snow."

"That must have been twenty years ago," BJ said dully, acting as if she could hardly remember. Really!

"You and Sheldon both disappeared for half an hour," Iris said. "When I looked outside, our car was gone. Then both of you came back."

"I see. And Sheldon told you we'd gone off to screw in the romantic snowfall, in the back of your car?"

This was not going well. "Something like that," Iris whispered.

BJ sprang up from the couch. "You know, I can't believe this. I really can't believe it. Your flaky, unfaithful husband who betrays you every ten minutes tells you he screws your sister and you believe it—" she snapped her fingers "—just like that." She paced back and forth across the carpet. "Why didn't you ever ask me, Iris? Why didn't you ever ask *me?*"

A sudden wash of tears stung in Iris's eyes. "I don't know." And the truth was, she didn't. She didn't know.

"Well, *I* know." BJ stopped in front of Iris and looked down like an interrogator. "It's because you were so damned tied to him you couldn't see beyond your own nose. He lied to you twenty times a day, but you didn't want to trust anyone but him. Not your own good judgment. And not your big sister who had no history of lying to you. No history of betraying you. No, quite the opposite. Your big sister was always pretty loyal. Or don't you remember that?"

"Of course I remember. Of course I—"

"And you didn't even ask me!" BJ threw her hands into the air, as if the gesture said it all.

"I'm sorry, BJ. I am." The tears spilled over, down her face, and her sobs came in loud, racking breaths.

"Oh shit," BJ said. "Don't blubber. Don't tell me you're sorry. You believed this for twenty years and you're apologizing *now?*" She put her palms over her ears.

Iris tried to stop crying. She couldn't.

"Well, it's not really your fault, is it?" BJ said with such sarcasm that Iris knew it *was* her fault and she'd been a fool not to know it.

"I always knew Sheldon was a sick bastard, but *this…*" BJ flung her arms heavenward again. "I used to think you were just humoring him. Apparently not. He got you so you were so cut off from everyone else that he was all you could see. Cut off from your family. Cut off from your friends. So isolated it was only his lying mouth you were prepared to believe."

It was true. Iris put her hands over her face. A fistful of tears got caught in her throat, and she couldn't draw air. She gasped.

"Oh, for God's sake. Breathe." BJ came over and put her hand on the back of Iris's head. "Don't hold your breath. *Breathe.*"

Iris gasped once more, and then her lungs filled, as

if with a rush of angry wind. BJ brought her a glass of water. "Drink," she ordered. Iris did.

"Okay, I'll tell you what happened that night." BJ sat down on a footstool beside Iris's chair. Her voice was cold and flat. "Remember when Janelle first got her periods and she had those terrible cramps? That's what happened. She was upstairs watching TV, and called me up there to look for the medicine the doctor had given her. But she'd run out. We had to refill the prescription."

"I don't see what—"

BJ held up her hand to cut Iris off. "Just *listen*, for once. My car was at the top of the driveway, blocked in by about ten other cars. Your car was at the curb. So I asked Sheldon to run out and pick up the medicine. I couldn't ask David, because he was the host. I couldn't ask any of the dentists because I hardly knew them, and I didn't want to ask you because I didn't want you driving on those slick roads. So I asked Sheldon. Even if he was a *schmuck*, he was family. And he got the prescription. And once I gave Janelle her pill, I came back downstairs. End of story."

"Oh, God," Iris sighed.

"And to think of you believing him all these years. Thinking I would do something like that to you. Thinking I would do something like that, period." BJ stood up again. Her face was white. Her hair stood out in spikes. "I can't believe only two hours ago I actually laughed when you lied about the cake being an old family recipe."

"I didn't lie about *this*."

"No? What would you call it?"

"I didn't lie. I just didn't tell you."

"Even worse."

"BJ—" Iris began.

BJ chopped her open palm through the air. "Not now. I don't want to hear another word. Not tonight."

"Do you want me to leave?" Iris whispered.

"No, of course not." BJ drew her brows together. She looked confused. "I just want you to go to bed."

CHAPTER 9

It was Saturday morning, and BJ never swam on weekends, but she figured if she didn't, it might be weeks before she calmed down. If nothing else, she could count on swimming to wear her out.

She slid on her new goggles and started out fast and furious, more energetic than she'd felt since she was thirty-five. Bottle up enough anger and you could go to the senior Olympics, she was sure of it. All you needed was a way to sustain your fury. Not a problem. Iris was *such* an idiot. Angry flashes of light sparked at the edge of BJ's vision as she raised her head to gulp air. Breast stroke in one direction, crawl in the other. After three laps she slowed down to catch her breath for one lazy length, then resumed her mad race.

Amazing how strong she felt, considering that she probably hadn't gotten two hours of sleep. Ten minutes of fitful shut-eye, then awake and furious, all night long. Why hadn't Iris *told* her? After all they'd been through! Her own sister! They could have cleared this up with one simple conversation, twenty years ago. Iris wasn't bright, but she was always perceptive.

Well, not always. Not about Sheldon.

This would hang between them for the rest of their lives. They would never trust each other again. Not really.

BJ had tossed and turned and fretted, dozing off only to come awake with a start, her heart beating so loudly she could hear it. After a couple of hours her anger was spent and she was filled instead with something worse: sympathy and shame and guilt. How had she let Iris sink so far under Sheldon's spell? Why hadn't she noticed what was happening? BJ had always thought Iris tolerated the man only to protect Diane. She'd thought her sister's behavior was calculated and deliberate. But if Iris believed Sheldon had slept with BJ, just because he said so, then Iris had been in deeper than BJ thought. She was like one of those women at the domestic violence shelter who left her husband after he punched her but didn't stay away long enough for the bruises to heal because he sweet-talked her for ten minutes and she was too insecure to resist. Sheldon was the classic abuser. Iris was the classic victim. BJ hadn't recognized it until now.

If she'd been more perceptive, twenty years ago or anytime since, things might have turned out differently, for all of them.

Yet even so, she was too hurt to blame herself in a serious way. All her life, she'd been closer to Iris than to almost anyone. And all these years, Iris had believed she'd slept with the loathsome Sheldon.

Out of breath again, BJ did a slow backstroke across the pool and blinked to get rid of the little streaks of light flaring on and off in her right eye. She tried to think back to the months following the party. Had Iris behaved differently toward her then? BJ couldn't remember. One of the best things about Iris was her even temperament. Unlike most women, she wasn't moody. She made an effort to be pleasant even when people slighted her. If Iris had been angry with BJ, or resented her, or even hated her, why hadn't BJ known?

Iris was ten times more clever than BJ, when it came to matters of the heart.

Ten times sneakier, too.

Back on her stomach, BJ clawed at the water, doing a messy breast stroke with renewed energy. The new goggles were keeping her eyes dry, so the sudden mist in front of her vision must be tears.

She'd be damned if she was going to cry about this. She'd be damned if she would. *Iris* was the crybaby.

Afterward, under the dressing-room shower, BJ stood until the hot water began to feel like it was making dents in her shoulders. She toweled off quickly, too antsy to bother drying her hair. She wasn't calm. She was just tired. Outside, in the sunlight, BJ noticed that her right eye was full of floaters, those little strings and dots that were the bane of the nearsighted. Iris had them, too. But this seemed more than usual, practically a meteor shower. As she drove, a bigger shape kept crossing her line of vision, too, a sort of brownish, translucent circle. Creepy. The new goggles must have been too tight. How they'd produced this odd effect she wasn't sure. She meant to stop somewhere for breakfast and not go home before Iris went out (as Iris surely would, if only to the mall), but now BJ didn't feel like eating. She wanted to lie down, close her eyes, and wait for this junk in her eye to go away.

To Iris's credit, she was gone by the time BJ pulled into the driveway. At least they wouldn't have to make small talk. Randolph acted as if BJ had been gone for a week. Donning the dark sunglasses she usually reserved for summer and the beach, BJ walked him around the block. The smoky lenses distracted her from the floaters but didn't get rid of them. Later she'd call Fred Shulman and tell him his goggles were far too efficient, drying her eyes out like this. Back in the house, she closed the blinds and fell into her bed.

She couldn't sleep, of course not. It was ten in the morning. In the TV room she surfed channels until she found an old movie. She lay down on the couch. Too early in the day to be so unproductive. What the hell, it was Saturday. The room was dim, and as she stared at the TV, the floaters very nearly disappeared. She finally dozed off. When she got up, she assumed she was cured.

Downstairs, she made a sandwich. She picked up the newspaper to read while she sat at the table. Big mistake. The strings and dots were back, floating across the newsprint along with the pesky large round thing—

the Big Blob, she found herself calling it—that made her feel that she was looking through glue.

If Iris, that fool, would just come back (BJ knew she wouldn't), at least she'd have someone to confide in.

No! She wouldn't tell Iris a damned thing. The last thing she needed was Iris getting panicky over some irritation probably caused by a pair of *swim goggles*, for God's sake. Yes, it was weird. Yes, it was bothersome. But it was probably just some freak phenomenon that would play itself out in the next ten minutes.

Wasn't it?

A little thread of panic pulsed at the back of her throat.

Okay. More TV. She lay down and closed her eyes through an entire rerun of *Guys and Dolls*, a movie she'd always loved. Today, she didn't even perk up during the scenes with Marlon Brando. She didn't sleep, either. Two hours passed. Finally she got up and took another shower.

One of the most bothersome things about being widowed six years ago, BJ had discovered, was not having a Saturday-night date. Of all the lifestyle changes she'd had to endure, that was the one that nearly got the best of her. She sat home Saturday after Saturday, missing David and imagining that all her married friends were out having fun and *not including her*. After a while her home-alone status no longer made her despondent or sad; it just galled her. Finally she took matters into her own hands. Each week she lined up some social function to attend or asked some friend to go out for dinner and a movie. Lately, Iris had often been that companion, though luckily, not tonight.

Tonight's date was Resa Taub, who was picking her up at six so they could use a two-for-one coupon from Ruby Tuesday and then go to a show. Ready a few minutes early, BJ went outside to wait.

Oh, Lord.

With all the junk floating in her eye, the night looked like a blurred cloud of marshmallow haze.

The streetlight at the corner was surrounded by a big, diffuse halo. In the distance, the headlights from Resa's car bounced toward her like giant, fuzzy Nerf balls. BJ's night vision had never been good, but this was genuinely scary.

"Okay, there are a slew of new movies," Resa said as BJ got into the car. "Drama or comedy?"

"You decide."

Resa looked at her quizzically. "You never let anyone else decide. You always want to make the choice yourself. Are you all right?"

"Of course." They reached the end of the street and turned into a steady line of traffic. The haloed lights blended together, making her squint.

"Did I tell you I called your sister after she came to Singles Night Out?" Resa asked. "I offered to take her around to look at houses, but she said no. She said she was doing some looking on her own."

"Oh?" BJ wished the halos would go away. Blinking didn't help.

"You think Iris is working with another Realtor and didn't want to hurt my feelings?"

"I doubt it." In fact, BJ didn't know and—for once—didn't really care.

She would get through tonight. She would get through tomorrow, because it was Sunday and there was nothing she could do. Monday morning, first thing, she would find out what the hell was wrong with her eyes.

For anyone in the advertising business, November was always a busy month. With the holiday buying frenzy upon them, business owners who claimed they didn't believe in print ads could sometimes be convinced to change their minds. Clients who always advertised also tended to grow nervous. Should they add a large display ad even if it put them over budget? Or would customers come anyway, driven by their gift lists?

On Monday morning, the phone in BJ's home office rang three times while she was still in the kitchen having coffee. She never answered the business phone until office hours began. By the time she checked her answering machine, there were half a dozen messages. She meant to go upstairs and shower as soon as she got a break, but at ten o'clock she was still in the sweats she'd worn for walking Randolph three hours before. Even when she heard Iris sneak downstairs and leave stealthily by the side door, she looked up just long enough to calculate that she and her sister had not spoken for nearly sixty hours.

Iris, she noted with some satisfaction, would not have the wherewithal to make these same calculations.

She scribbled a few notes about the ad for Fountain Aesthetics: "The best holiday gift you can give. The fountain of youth." The Big Blob floated across her eye. She had meant to call the doctor first thing. She checked her appointment book. If she met with all the people she was supposed to see this afternoon, she wouldn't have time for the doctor until tomorrow. Would it make any difference? Her vision was no worse than it had been on Saturday.

No better, either.

On and off all afternoon as she drove from client to client, a pulse beat wildly at the top of her collarbone.

The Big Blob was not a normal floater.

Maybe she had a disease.

Daylight Savings Time had ended, so it was dark by the time she turned into her block on the way home. Driving at night was not impossible, but the halos around everything made it hard. Accommodating for the distortion exhausted her. She would walk Randolph and then go right to bed. In his yard, Harvey Sussman was still raking up pine straw by the illumination of his porch light, maybe because the evening was so warm and balmy. Without giving it a moment's thought, BJ pulled into his driveway and rolled down her window. She had not meant to do this. Sometimes you acted on instinct. "I think," she blurted as he walked over to her, "that I'm going blind."

Harvey rested his forearms on the frame of her open window and peered in. "You just drove up the street," he said amiably. "You just pulled into my driveway. How could you be going blind?"

In a rush, BJ told him. Harvey's expression changed as he realized she wasn't joking. He grew serious, then concerned. He opened her car door and said, "Come in for a minute," and helped her out with a solicitous hand on her arm. Harvey's attention alarmed her. This had not occurred to BJ before, but probably she had a brain tumor.

Inside his house, Harvey guided BJ to a couch in the living room. She noted distractedly that everything looked vaguely Oriental. *Second wife liked Asian touches*, she thought.

"And the flashes of light," Harvey was saying. "Are you still having them?"

"No. The only time I had them was the other day in the swimming pool. What's wrong with me, Harvey? It's serious, isn't it?"

"Probably not. You probably just had a PVD. But you still need to check it out."

"A PVD?"

"Posterior vitreous detachment. It's a normal aging process. The back of your eyeball is filled with a jelly-like goo called vitreous. When you're young, it's attached back there to the retina. But as you age, it can shrink and peel off. Happens to everyone, sooner or later. But especially if you're nearsighted, or if you've had cataract surgery, or a few other risk factors. Some people don't even have symptoms. I'm going to call Wayne Adams."

"Wayne Adams?"

"A former colleague. He's a retina specialist. Young, but very good. He can check you out."

"Check me out? Why? I mean, if it's a normal aging process?" BJ's heart did its alarming little dance.

"Because sometimes when the vitreous pulls off, it pulls off with enough force to tear the retina. And the symptoms of a normal PVD—those flashes and floaters—are exactly the same as the symptoms of a retinal tear, which needs to be fixed right away."

BJ didn't follow any of this. In Harvey's lamplit living room, her vision seemed normal. No distortion, no floaters. "I know," he said. "In muted electric light everything seems fine. You think it never happened." Abruptly, he rose and left her sitting there. She heard him talking on the phone.

"Wayne says come on over," he told BJ when he hung up.

"But it's night. It's not office hours."

"He doesn't mind." Unceremoniously, he strode over to the couch and more or less pulled BJ up.

Twenty minutes later, she was sitting in a darkened examining room, where Wayne Adams was holding her lid open while pressing on various sections of her eye. This didn't hurt, but it was uncomfortable and odd. He shone a bright light into her eye. He poked some more. He mumbled, "Hmm," and "okay, fine, very good." BJ said nothing.

Harvey, instead of remaining meekly in the waiting area like most people who accompany patients to an appointment, had come into the examining room and was standing to Dr. Adams's side, occasionally peering over his shoulder into BJ's eye. She couldn't see much, what with the bright lights and the pressing, but once she caught enough of a glimpse to realize that, while Harvey was definitely "older," Wayne Adams looked to be around twelve.

This sent her heart into its unwelcome flutter.

"Well," Wayne Adams finally said. "I'm going to tell you a story." He put away his light and sat down on the rolling stool across from his examination chair. Harvey, behind him, crossed his arms and remained standing. "As Dr. Sussman suspected, you've had a PVD," Wayne said. Then he proceeded to give her the information Harvey had given her earlier. "I don't see any tear. If there is a tear, usually it happens at the same time as the PVD. But it can happen later. So if the floaters get any worse, or the flashing comes back, you need to call immediately."

BJ could not imagine the floaters getting any worse.

"But for just a PVD, there's no treatment. Eventually the symptoms subside. In any case, call the office tomorrow morning and make an appointment for a recheck."

BJ nodded dumbly.

Outside the examining room, she had no idea what to do about paying. The office staff must have gone home an hour ago. Harvey solved the problem by shaking hands with Dr. Adams, saying, "Thanks, Wayne," and leading BJ outside. As soon as she sat down in the car, an unnamable emotion flooded her with the force of strong whiskey. Her hands began to tremble. She clenched them into fists to make them stop. Why didn't she feel relieved? She did not have a brain tumor. She was not going blind.

But the retina could still tear at any time. The floaters and the Big Blob were real. She hadn't been able to wish them away.

Relax, she told herself. She took what a yoga instructor had once called a deep cleansing breath.

She took another.

They drove through the balmy evening, with its swirling halos of light. BJ squinted. "It looks like somebody airbrushed the whole street," she muttered.

"That's because at night the light bounces off the debris in your eye and causes a lot of distortion. In the daytime when it's bright, you can see each individual floater—not that that's any fun, either. It won't last forever."

"It won't?"

"In a month, maybe six weeks, some of the floaters will start to drop below your line of vision. Even before that, you won't notice it as much. It's amazing how the human brain adjusts." Harvey's tone was perfectly matter-of-fact, as if he voiced these words every day.

"What about the Big Blob? I can't imagine not noticing it. What the hell is it, anyway?"

"A fragment of the tough connective tissue that holds the vitreous to the area around the optic nerve. When it pops off and floats right in front of the retina, it can look pretty scary. But basically, it's just a big floater."

"Oh." Only a floater.

"It'll go away, too," Harvey assured her. "Once it moves farther forward, the shadow will become more diffuse." BJ wasn't sure she understood everything he said, but there was something touching about the way he was explaining it all with such patience. She knew he was just acting in a professional capacity, doing what he had been trained to do, but it had been nice of him to treat her situation as a crisis, stopping only long enough to change out of his gardening clothes before rushing her to the doctor.

She said to Harvey, "Now I feel completely ridiculous."

"Ridiculous? Why?"

"Coming to your house in a panic. For a normal aging problem."

"You didn't sound like someone in a panic," Harvey said. "What you did was sensible. You should have done it a couple of days ago."

There was no judgment in that, just simple fact. Under the spell of Harvey's monotone, BJ's agitation gave way to a cautious unclenching of muscles she didn't even know she had. She yawned. The next thing she knew, they were in his driveway, beside the car she'd left there earlier. She had slept all the way home.

"You're exhausted," Harvey noted. "Come on, I'll drive your car home so you won't have to." He got out, walked around the car and opened her door.

"I can drive," BJ said. "I'm okay."

"Come on. I've driven you this far, I can take you the rest of the way." He led her to the passenger side of her car.

BJ was embarrassed, but she got in.

As soon as they pulled up to her house, they heard Randolph inside, barking and scratching at the back door. "I'll walk him for you," Harvey said.

BJ meant to refuse, but somehow she put her key in the lock without saying a word. Harvey leashed up the dog and was gone. BJ sank into a chair. She was so glad to be sitting there, so glad not to have to go out again, that she was filled with a sort of—well, treacly gratitude. She couldn't help it. She closed her eyes.

"Canine bowels and bladder good for at least another eight hours." Harvey was poking an index finger into her shoulder. It was embarrassing, not to be able to stay awake. He handed her Randolph's leash. He looked around. "Where's your sister?"

"She'll probably be in late," BJ said. It seemed far too complicated to explain that they'd had a fight and were avoiding each other.

"Too bad. I could explain this to her. She could help

you. Maybe she'd drive you around at night until you feel more comfortable with the distortion."

BJ's head began to clear. Now she understood. Here she was, getting all emotional about how kind Harvey had been—and Harvey was doing it in hopes of seeing Iris. He'd driven BJ's car home from his house rather than letting her do it herself just so he'd have a chance to come in. Not knowing Iris was out, he'd counted on this chance to run into her. Counted on having a little heart-to-heart with her about poor BJ and how they could help her.

Not in *this* life, BJ thought.

BJ had no problem with Harvey and Iris getting together. Quite the opposite. But she'd be damned if she'd be their mutual charity case.

"I know how terrifying it is, to think you're losing your vision," Harvey said. "It wears you out."

BJ meant to offer some clever retort, but the sound that came from her throat was more like a grunt.

"Get some sleep," Harvey said. He took her hand and helped her up, in the manner of someone aiding his frail and elderly sister-in-law.

He leaned over and kissed her forehead.

She felt like a damned fool.

CHAPTER 10

Iris stood in the middle of the Hebrew section of the cemetery, a fistful of stones in hand, flinging them one by one at Sheldon's headstone. It was eight in the morning. No one was there to see her. The sky was overcast. It was cold.

"You lying son of a bitch!" She threw yet another stone at the grave. "And to think I *believed* you!"

Or had she? On their way home from that long-ago party she had said to Sheldon, bluntly, "Where *were* you? You were gone, and so was BJ."

Sheldon had remained dramatically silent for a time. Then he had put on a frozen expression and said stonily, "Don't ask me this, Iris."

"Just tell me! Just get it over with and tell me." This had been so unlike her. Usually she never asked. Usually he behaved himself at parties. Usually he didn't disappear with her sister.

"We went over to the store." At that time, Sheldon had been working at The Sleep Shop. Iris had pictured him on a new Sealy mattress still wrapped in plastic, pants pulled down to his knees, humping BJ while the plastic crackled with every thrust.

"*And?*" Iris had pressed.

"I asked you not to ask me," Sheldon said. "But since you insist, I'm going to tell you the truth. You're not going to like it." Another loaded silence. "She came on to me."

Iris didn't believe it. She believed someone had come on to someone. But in her mind she cast Sheldon as the one coming on and BJ the one submitting.

It had been hard to imagine BJ submitting.

Then, a week and a half ago when BJ had denied the affair altogether, and so angrily, Iris had known at once that this was the only version of the story that made sense. BJ was telling the truth and Sheldon, two decades before, had been lying.

Iris had been exactly as stupid as BJ had said. For twenty years she'd believed the story invented for her by a man who'd been unfaithful on a regular basis. She hadn't even given BJ a chance to defend herself, then or later. She was a moron.

And to think how, for years, she'd worked so hard at forgiving BJ for her infidelity! To think of all the turmoil and distress! To think there had been nothing to forgive in the first place.

She threw another stone, which hit the headstone with a sharp, satisfying *chink*. "Asshole!" she said to Sheldon.

For the moment, she blamed her late husband for everything. For the fight with BJ. For making her feel so stupid that she had to sneak out of BJ's house every morning just to avoid talking to her. For making her hang at the mall so much that she knew where every piece of clothing was on every rack in every store. For making her go to the nine-thirty movie almost every night of the week, just so BJ would be in bed by the time she got home.

Another stone. *Chink*.

Iris knew she was pathetic, yes, and if it weren't for Sheldon, she'd be blissfully ignorant. She wouldn't know how truly pathetic her life really was. She had always loved shopping, and if not for this past week and a half, she still might. But no. Wandering endlessly through retail shops had made her realize that her unfaithful, lying bastard of a husband—*chink*—had left her enough life-insurance money to buy anything she wanted and pay for it without having to hock her soul. What fun was *that*? When Jonah had needed a new car seat, well, yes, then her old enthusiasm had come back. But to buy for herself? Who cared?

Chink.

When she couldn't stand being in stores anymore, Iris had had her hair colored even though it didn't need it. She'd made her quarterly appointment for Botox. She'd even spent a couple of afternoons doing what she'd told BJ she was going to do months ago: look at houses. Well, not houses, exactly. Condos. Everyone had said that now that she was alone, all she really needed was a one-bedroom condo. Maybe two

bedrooms. Maybe at that new place practically around
the corner from Diane.

Heaven protect her from condos.

Even in the cleverly decorated model with its mirrors
and compact furniture to reinforce the sense of space,
Iris had felt the walls closing in. And she was not even
claustrophobic! Crummy as her old house had been, it
had been spacious by comparison. She didn't want to
live in some ten-by-ten room where she'd have to open
the windows and stick her head out to feel she could
breathe.

She didn't want to live with BJ, either.

Clink.

"Son of a bitch," she said again. Then it occurred to
her: he wasn't. A son of a bitch would have a dog for a
mother. Sheldon was not the son of a bitch. His
mother, Anne Meyerhoff, had been good-natured and
funny and kind. Iris had learned a great deal from her.
At a time when it was fashionable to dislike one's
mother-in-law and make fun of her, Iris had loved and
respected hers very much. Dropping the stones into a
pile beside her, Iris sat down on the cold ground,
lowered her head into her hands and wept.

Anne had been living with her second husband,
Marty, in a small house outside Philadelphia when she
was diagnosed with breast cancer. Learning that her
chemotherapy wasn't working, she'd checked out of the
hospital and gone home to die. Sheldon and his brother
had rushed to Philadelphia to help their stepfather nurse

Anne through the difficult last week of her life, while Iris and her sister-in-law, by some communal, unspoken agreement, stayed home with their children. When it was over, Diane and Iris took an early-morning flight to Philadelphia for the funeral. Sheldon met them at the airport, already wearing the dark blue suit and somber tie he would wear to the service. He had never looked so handsome. But no: *handsome* sounded shallow and inadequate. In the morning sunlight, Sheldon looked transformed, and surely not just by the pain of watching his mother die. There was a kind of deep gloriousness about him, an evanescent, luminous quality of beauty she never would have expected, that spilled out onto Iris and Diane like a sheltering halo of love.

Sheldon kissed them and held his arm protectively around their shoulders as he guided them toward the parking lot. All the way to the suburbs, he steered the car with one hand and clutched Iris's hand with his other, in a gesture of neediness she had not known him capable of.

That night, Sheldon and Iris had slept in Marty and Anne's small spare bedroom. Although exhausted from the long day, they had reached for each other greedily—despite, or maybe because of, the whirlwind of emotions that had swirled around them. What they did that night was truly, in the best sense of the word, *making love*. Having sex wouldn't begin to describe it. The love they made was a marriage vow more binding than the one they had taken twelve years before. The love they made renewed them.

All that night Iris had felt—Iris had *known*—that Anne was with them, that she was showering them with love, her own love for them, and their love for each other. It was her parting gift. It lasted for years.

In the months before Anne's death, Sheldon had been involved with one of his women. For almost two years after, Iris was sure he was faithful to her.

Sheldon was not a son of a bitch.

And even after that magic time when Anne seemed to be sheltering them, even after Sheldon returned to his wandering ways, when he was at home with his family he was more *with* them than many men ever were. It was true that he cheated on Iris and lied to her even about his nonexistent affair with BJ. It was also true that sometimes he would come home and announce, "Spaghetti!" and usher Diane and Iris into the kitchen where he would don a ridiculous chef's hat, and with a phony French accent and great drama, demonstrate for them his technique for making "ze world's best pasta sauce," laced with oregano and wine. Brandishing his wooden spoon, he would give Diane and Iris detailed instructions for the simple task of slathering butter on the loaf of French bread he'd brought home, and show them how to sprinkle garlic powder on top of the butter, as if this were a magnificent feat. They laughed and cooked and finally ate, and they were as happy a family as any they knew.

Iris was wrenched from her reverie by the damp chill that was seeping through her slacks. Why was she sitting on the *ground*? It was November. It was cold and beginning to drizzle. Iris's bottom was as wet as if she'd peed in her pants. What was wrong with her? BJ was probably still at home, warm and dry, conducting business on the phone in her pajamas instead of at the newspaper office downtown. BJ might not get dressed until lunchtime, when she'd head out to make her sales calls. No way could Iris go back there and change her clothes. She got up, feeling as creaky as an old woman. Maybe she *was* an old woman. She brushed herself off.

The truth was, she *wanted* to hate Sheldon.

And she did hate him. But she loved him, too. Holding a grudge was beyond her.

That was why, even now, even after what BJ had told her, Sheldon was still on her list of people she loved.

She walked through the gate that separated the Hebrew cemetery from the main one, and headed down the path toward her car. There were no flowers in the Jewish section, just the stones people put on (or in Iris's case, threw at) the graves for remembrance. The rest of the cemetery was much more entertaining, in Iris's view—although she was careful never to describe it that way in public. People put silk flowers in the metal vases attached to the gravestones, or stuck small shepherd's hooks into the ground and hung them with different flags for each new season—appliquéd azalea blossoms and Easter bunnies in spring, beach chairs or stars-and-stripes in summer, and right now, displays of colorful autumn leaves and cornucopias and turkeys to replace the jack-o'-lantern flags that had hung all through October. At Bill Wilson's grave someone had placed a packet of the honey-roasted peanuts he'd always liked to eat. Nestled at the base of Ned Sutton's tombstone was a blue teddy bear his wife had brought after his grandson was born. It was as if the relatives wanted to keep their departed ones apprised of what was going on.

Iris knew you weren't supposed to feel cheerful in a cemetery, but by the time she reached her car, she always felt a little better, even now, walking through the drizzle with a wet bottom. She was grateful that today, for once, she didn't have to think about how to fill her time. This morning she was helping out at the temple, then lunching with a friend, and later watching Noah and Jonah so Patti Ann could leave early to go to the doctor. Best of all, she could stay through the evening because Wes was out of town and Diane had a meeting after work. She had a full schedule! What a relief!

At the temple, Iris headed for the social hall to meet Mitzi Rosen, who had recently taken over the Judaica shop and claimed she had no idea how or what to order, especially now with Chanukah coming up. There was actually no "shop," just a row of shelves lining the walls of the room, and a few glass cases for jewelry and other small items. Except before important holidays and on certain Sunday mornings during religious school, there were no shop "hours," either. People took what they wanted and sent Mitzi a check. Most of the buyers were honest, but sometimes they forgot. Dozens of boxes of Chanukah candles disappeared every year, and at least one copy of *The Jewish Book of Why*, a popular Bar Mitzvah gift. The Judaica shop had never been a well-run operation.

"Oh, Iris, you're a lifesaver," said Mitzi, rising from a table covered with a jumble of Judaica catalogs. "Look at all this."

"Catalogs," Iris said. "There's nothing I like better."

"Thank goodness one of us does."

Iris took off her heavy cardigan and tied it around her waist in case there was an actual damp *spot* on the seat of her pants instead of just the damp feeling. She walked over to the table and sat down quickly. Someone had turned on the heat, which floated in the air like a weightless blanket. The warmth was like a blessing.

Iris liked Mitzi, a pretty fortyish woman whose youngest child had just started school, and who, in desperation, had volunteered for everything she could think of, just to avoid the emptiness of her home. Although Mitzi had a master's degree (in what, no one knew), she couldn't take a paying job, Sarah Kline maintained, "because Eric is a gastroenterologist who needs more taxable income the way the rest of us need a clump of colon polyps."

Until Sheldon's death, Iris had never had the luxury

of too much free time, but since her falling-out with BJ, she'd begun to understand what a curse it could be. She'd offered to come here this morning because Mitzi seemed at such loose ends that Iris felt sorry for her.

After the gray morning outside, the fluorescent-lit social hall seemed exceptionally bright, and Mitzi even brighter. A redhead with creamy skin and only the tiniest sprinkling of freckles, Mitzi dressed in vivid primary colors that were supposed to flatter her complexion but somehow never did. Her hair, a true, brilliant red, was wavy-going-on-curly, falling to her shoulders in a fluffy style meant to be sleek. Today, frizzed from the dampness outside, set against her aggressively orange pullover and pale skin, it made her look a little like Bozo the Clown. Iris suppressed an urgent desire to put her arm around the younger woman and say, "Come on, Mitzi. Let's go back to your house and find something more flattering for you to wear. Let's get you dressed all over again."

They pored over the catalogs for most of the morning. Iris warmed to the task because she wasn't buying for herself, after all; she was performing a service. Everything Mitzi wanted to order was too expensive—embroidered wall hangings retailing for hundreds of dollars; breakable latke platters of high-quality porcelain; heavy, sterling silver menorahs and kiddush cups. Doctors' wives, Iris believed, often had no sense of the term, "affordable," a folly of which they were unaware after so many years of inflated income.

Gently, Iris guided Mitzi toward tasteful but less costly selections. Even then, except for the children's toys, Mitzi's taste ran to the funky or the bizarre—a lopsided cookie jar shaped like a spinning dreidel, a wooden Star of David with bright, cloth braids hanging from each of its points—items that would sit on the shelves for years. When finally they had completed their order, Mitzi noted with dismay that Iris was the one who had chosen almost every item on the final list: moderately-priced mezuzahs, Jewish-themed potholders, the chocolate Chanukah *gelt* everyone bought to give to their children.

"I'm hopeless at this," Mitzi groaned as they completed their order, and quickly excused herself to go to the ladies' room.

"It's an acquired skill," Iris called after, though she wasn't so sure. She'd always believed her own talent for shopping was inborn, like BJ's bent for selling. As a girl, BJ had set up lemonade stands and convinced the neighborhood children to buy shiny white pebbles collected from someone's landscaping bed. She'd won prizes for selling the most Girl Scout cookies and gone door-to-door with flower bulbs for a school fund-raiser. Iris, on the other hand, had hated all these projects and been terrible at them, even with the example of her older sister to guide her. What she excelled at was helping her mother buy clothes and household goods for the family. Frivolous as this seemed to her now, her talent, from the time she could read a price tag, was in being able to spot a sale. And even as a child, Iris had been fascinated by catalogs. The colorful photos and feel of silky paper beneath her fingers served as a kind of surrogate for the actual fabrics and styles. She *knew* what to buy. She was rarely wrong.

It was only years later that Iris had her first come-uppance, after BJ badgered her into learning how to use a computer and Iris realized with a shock that she had no talent at all for ordering online. Looking at a computer screen didn't give a feel for a product the way seeing it in a catalog did. It seemed like it ought to, but there was a world of difference. Iris had placed web orders only twice, and both times everything turned out to be the wrong color, the wrong texture, wrong in a thousand ways. In her heart of hearts, Iris feared that Mitzi had about as much aptitude for running the Judaica shop as Iris did for finding bargains on eBay.

"This is going to be a chore, isn't it?" Mitzi said when she emerged from the ladies' room. *More than you imagine*, Iris thought. "Only at first," she said aloud. "You'll see what people buy, and the next time you order, it will be easier. In the meantime, I'm always glad to help you."

Mitzi sighed. "Let's face it—I took on the worst possible project I could have volunteered for. I've never been a shopper. Look." She pulled at the fabric of her orange shirt. "When I saw myself in the mirror in the ladies' room, I scared myself half to death. I can't buy my own clothes, much less Judaica."

Sometimes Iris didn't understand why people couldn't see what was right before their eyes. "All you need," she said, "are two words of advice. Wear black."

"Black?" Mitzi looked down at herself. "Not a color?"

"Mitzi, you don't *need* a color. You *are* a color."

Mitzi opened her eyes wide as this critical and obvious truth dawned on her. A slow, easy smile spread across her face. Iris smiled, too, partly because as she rose from her chair to go, she knew that she had done a *mitzvah*, and partly because she sensed that the seat of her pants was finally dry.

CHAPTER 11

At three o' clock, Iris arrived at Diane's, ready to babysit so Patti Ann could leave early for her doctor appointment.

"Oh, no, I'll fold the laundry first. I wouldn't stick you with housework *and* watching both boys," Patti Ann said, as if these tasks were a snap for her but much too burdensome for poor Iris. "Jonah will be up from his nap any minute. He fell asleep before lunch, so he'll be grumpy and starving," she added ominously. "You know how *that* can be."

"Not a problem," Iris said. "Famished two-year-olds are my specialty."

Patti Ann handed Noah to Iris. Against her shoulder, he grew heavy as he settled into sleep. Iris knew better than to put him into his crib. Even in the throes of slumber, he would sense the change immediately and startle awake. He would nap only in his vibrating seat (but not for very long) or against the warmth of human flesh—including at night, when he snuggled between Diane and Wes.

Patti Ann pulled a handful of towels from the dryer.

"My appointment's not till four-fifteen, so I won't come back this afternoon," she said, looking worried. "I hope you can manage."

"I'll be fine," Iris said. Rocking back and forth on her heels to keep Noah asleep, she noted that Patti Ann, for all her recent medical appointments, looked perfectly healthy. Just fat. And causing no end of worry. "Patti Ann has to leave early—her third trip to the doctor in two weeks," Diane had informed Iris with a note of alarm. "I know she has her faults, but until now she's been completely reliable. She's never late and she never takes off. So it must be something serious. Can you come, Mom? I can't ask her to reschedule. Wes is out of town and I have a meeting after work." Iris had said of course she'd come. She hoped Diane hadn't heard the relief in her voice at having something useful to do for once. She was glad to be here, even if Patti Ann was terminal.

But Iris saw no signs of Patti Ann's imminent demise. Watching the nanny put on her Mary Poppins act, folding laundry with a long-suffering but beatific expression on her face, Iris doubted she was really on her way to the doctor. Yet where else would she go? Out to happy hour with a friend? Possibly a *male* friend? Unlikely. Patti Ann seemed dedicated to her husband. An early movie? From what Iris could tell, Patti Ann preferred TV. Shopping? She could shop after work, or even *during* work, when Jonah was in school and there was only Noah to lug around. Iris couldn't figure it out.

"Are you sick?" she finally asked.

"No. Just another checkup." Patti Ann piled the folded towels into a wicker basket and patted the top of the stack as if it were alive.

"Oh? Checkup for what?" Iris persisted.

"Sugar, I think."

"Sugar?"

"Yes. I take a pill for it. Then I can eat as much sugar as I want."

"You mean you have diabetes?"

Patti Ann looked up. "I don't think so."

"You mean you don't know for sure?"

"Like I said, I take a pill, and then I can eat as much sugar as I want." As if to reinforce this, she pulled a caramel candy from her pocket, unwrapped it and popped it into her mouth. "Want one?"

"I don't think it's healthy to eat between meals," Iris said.

Patti Ann frowned and looked at her watch. "Uh-oh, I better go."

Jonah woke up seconds after Patti Ann departed, and so did Noah. Neither was in a good mood. Noah didn't want to be put down, even in his vibrating seat. Jonah pouted as he shrugged off the fog of midday sleep, and then demanded to go outside.

"It's raining, sweetie. Besides, you need something to eat."

"I want to watch TV."

Iris fixed a plate for him, anyway, of leftover chicken and steamed carrots and broccoli, heated for forty seconds in the microwave. Although she thought it was healthier to warm food on the stove or in the regular oven, at the moment she believed time was of the essence. Or maybe she was just being optimistic. Jonah pushed the plate as far away from him as his short arms would allow. "I want to watch TV."

"Later." While Iris warmed a bottle of refrigerated breast milk and began feeding Noah, Jonah retrieved his plate and restlessly pushed its contents from one side to the other with his spoon. Tears of frustration shimmered in his eyes, too proud to spill over. Iris wanted to say to him, this is one of the few times in your life when people who love you will urge you to eat food they have prepared to help you grow up healthy and strong. What she actually said was "Okay, you can get down. But no TV. You can play with your toys."

Strangely submissive, Jonah did. He pushed a tractor across the carpet and brought it to a halt just before it hit a strangely shaped structure he had built with his blocks. He lost interest. He picked up a muscular blue action figure he had named La-La. He walked it across the carpet, sat it down, picked it up again and walked it some more.

"La-La has to go to the dokker," he told Iris.

"Oh?" Iris decided Noah was finished eating and took the bottle away. "Is La-La sick?"

"He got ooo-eys," Jonah said.

Iris was puzzled. "You mean cooties?"

"No. Ooo-eys." Setting La-La on the floor, Jonah rushed to the table and snatched a piece of carrot from his plate. He shoved it into La-La's face. "Ooo-eys all better!" Jonah told Iris.

"You should eat some supper," she replied. She believed all children were a little crazy, and that it was the job of adults to help make them sane. It was bad enough that the children themselves had to go to the doctor and be subjected to immunization shots, but now Patti Ann was seeking medical attention, too, and making no secret of it. This could not be good for a two-year-old. No wonder Jonah was obsessed with doctors and ooo-eys, whatever ooo-eys were. She put on his bib and kissed him on the head. "Eat some of your supper, and then I'll give you a Fudgsicle," she said. He did, and she did, and then, even though philosophically she was opposed to this, she turned on the TV.

By the time Iris heard Diane's car pull up just after ten, she and Jonah had watched two full-length DVDs, read half a dozen books, and played a game called *Find La-La*. She had swept the kitchen floor and loaded the dishwasher. She had given Jonah a bath. She had done all this between (and sometimes during) sessions of carrying Noah in her arms, which soon ached more than arms should if they belonged to a woman who regularly lifted free weights in the privacy of her room. After his long nap, Jonah resisted going to bed for an hour before finally falling asleep. The minute he quieted, Noah grew fussy but refused to take his bottle. He wanted his mama. Iris wanted her, too.

The only reason Diane had asked her to stay through the evening, she reminded herself, was because Wes was away, as he was so often lately and would be until the first of the year when his promotion took effect. This was an emergency of sorts. Diane hated evening meetings after her hour's commute to work and back. She preferred spending time with her family. When Iris heard Diane's key in the lock, she was certain her daughter would look even more tired than Iris felt.

But no: Diane came bursting in, briefcase and laptop and a shiny red gift bag in her hands, looking amazingly chipper for someone who'd been gone from the house for fourteen hours. Seeing her, Noah smiled and lurched in her direction. Putting down her bundles, Diane caught him in her arms and began to unbutton her jacket.

"Well, I'm glad to see you, too," she told the baby. "I'm about to pop." Already her milk had begun to let down and stain the front of the blouse Iris had bought her at T.J. Maxx, pure silk which would cost a small fortune to clean.

Iris let Diane settle onto the couch to nurse the baby. Then she asked, "How was your meeting? Okay?"

Diane repositioned herself for a long moment, as if she couldn't get comfortable, during which time Noah sucked greedily and seemed unfazed. "It wasn't really a meeting, Mom. It was more a—social event. I should have told you before." She lowered her eyes and studied Noah's head.

"A social event?"

"I knew you'd be mad."

Diane had kept her here more than seven hours for a *social event?* "I'm not mad. Of course not. I'm just surprised. What kind of social event?"

"I'm embarrassed to tell you."

A social event more important than her children— and now Diane *wasn't going to tell her?* "Tell me anyway," Iris said.

Diane readjusted her position a little more. "Well, sort of like a Tupperware party. But not a Tupperware party."

"So what kind of party *was* it?"

Noah closed his eyes. Diane detached him from her nipple. "They call it a passion party," she whispered.

"A passion party?" This took a moment to sink in. "You mean where men and women get *together?*" She didn't believe it. Diane wouldn't! The one time Diane had seen evidence of Sheldon's infidelity—some woman's lacy black *bra* left in the car—Iris had whispered, "Just don't ever let anyone do this to you. And don't do it to anyone else." With tears in her eyes, Diane had nodded. Iris had always considered it a pact.

And now, *this.*

"No, Mom. Of course not where men and women get together. Just women."

Oh, God, that was worse. Iris could feel the blood drain from her face. "Lesbians," she breathed.

"No, of course not lesbians. Where women get together to *buy* things." She laughed.

Iris was not in the mood to be laughed at. "To buy things, but not Tupperware," she snipped.

"Well, yes." Diane lifted Noah to her shoulder and patted his back. She did not meet Iris's eyes. "To buy…sex things."

"Sex things?"

Noah burped loud and long, and opened his eyes in surprise.

"Sex things?" Iris repeated. "You mean it's like a Tupperware party where they hold up *sex* products and demonstrate how they work?"

"Sort of." Diane wouldn't look Iris in the eye.

"And where they have a glossy full-color catalog so you can make further purchases in the privacy of your home?" Iris hoped this sounded sarcastic rather than desperate.

"Oh, Mom. It's more like—" Diane hesitated. "Okay, look. Bring me that bag."

Iris didn't move. One of the best things about having a daughter was the close relationship you had with someone you would choose as a friend anyway, but there were limits. No matter how chummy you were, there were some things a mother and a daughter shouldn't discuss.

"Go on, Mom. Hand it to me."

Reluctantly, Iris retrieved the glossy gift bag and set it on the couch. She braced herself as Diane's hand rummaged through the tissue paper. She tensed when Diane clutched an item at the bottom of the bag. Oh,

God, don't let it be a dildo. She didn't actually know what a dildo looked like. She didn't *want* to know.

It was not a dildo. It was a little bottle of something. A little round bottle with a gold top.

Iris allowed herself to breathe.

"Perfume," Diane said, holding up the bottle with the hand that wasn't cradled under Noah's head. "Pheromone perfume. It's supposed to attract the opposite sex." She giggled. "It's probably stupid."

"Perfume," Iris repeated, trying to sound normal and reassuring. She wanted to be modern about this. "Perfume isn't stupid. I've always liked perfume."

"*Pheromone* perfume." She handed the bottle to Iris, who had no choice but to take it.

"Oh. To use with your husband."

"With your husband, yes."

If Diane and Wes needed pheromone perfume, she hoped Diane wasn't going to tell her why. Idly, she twisted open the top, raised the bottle to her nose, and sniffed. The colorless liquid gave off a generic floral pleasantness that reminded Iris of the cheap colognes sold in the dime stores of her youth. It didn't smell sexy. She twisted the globe-shaped top back into place and set the bottle on the coffee table. "I just hope you didn't pay too much for this," she said.

"Why?"

"Just in case it's a hoax."

Diane responded with a sardonic smile. "No. They've done studies. On insects and animals and maybe even on humans. There's a bunch of information about their products on the Web site."

"Oh, Lord, a Web site." Iris imagined photos of garter belts and whips and chains. She lifted her arms in a gesture of surrender. "You know what? I can't do this. This discussion has to be over."

"Agreed." Diane nodded and moved the now-sleeping Noah off her shoulder and onto the couch beside her. She began to button her shirt.

"I ought to get going." Iris judged that by the time she drove to BJ's, it would be safe to go into the house. Thank goodness for small favors. She began to stand up, but Diane motioned her back into her chair.

"He had another checkup," she said, touching the baby's cheek.

"Another checkup? Is something wrong?"

"No. Just the regular checkup. He's fine. But, Mom—" Diane's pretty face began to crumple.

"*What?*" A little shiver of alarm skittered up the back of Iris's neck. "Is he sick? *What?*"

"He still hasn't turned over," Diane said weakly. "He should have turned over by now."

"He hasn't *turned over?*" Not, he has leukemia, he has cystic fibrosis, he has—Iris didn't want to think about it. She made herself inhale. "And the doctor is alarmed?"

"No. He says some babies are late. *I'm* the one who's alarmed."

"Why?"

"Because what if there's something wrong with him?

What if he's slow, and has special needs? How am I going to handle a normal child and a backward one, and have a career?" Her voice began to waver. "And lately with Patti Ann and all the doctor appointments— I mean, I really don't *know* what this meltdown is with her. If only she'd just *tell* me." Fat tears dripped silently from her eyes. "What if she's *sick?* I've actually been interviewing other nannies just in case. But it's hard. It's *hard*," she whimpered. "And what about when I have to travel, with Wes traveling so much right now, too? How am I going to do all that? Oh, *Mom*." She broke down into open sobbing.

So! This was what it was all about. When you were this desperate, *of course* you'd be tempted to go to a passion party, even on a weeknight when you'd normally want to be home. You might even tell your mother about it. Of course! Iris was no longer exhausted. She was full of energy and good sense. She was a mother. She was here to comfort her child!

Her first instinct was to rush over to Diane and embrace her, but she stifled the impulse.

"So. He hasn't turned over yet," she said sharply. "You know what I think?"

"What?"

"I think Noah doesn't turn over because he has no need to. His back never hits a mattress long enough to make it necessary. At night he's in bed with you and Wes, cuddled up and nursing—don't tell me he isn't. During the day Patti Ann carries him around all the time unless he falls asleep, in which case she puts him in that vibrating seat, where he couldn't turn over if he wanted to. Tell me the truth—would *you* want to turn over if your back was getting a massage like that all the time?"

"Well—"

"Noah's happy, isn't he? He clutches things. He smiles. He's fine." Iris certainly hoped this was true. "Besides, a four-month-old baby—"

"Five months, Mom."

"Five months, heaven preserve us. You think it's some critical skill he can't master a little later? Another month and they'll send him to the funny farm?"

"*Mom*," Diane wailed.

"Listen. Four months, five months, any age. They do things when they get ready. A baby doesn't need a big chart listing *skills*. You didn't walk until you were fourteen months old, and look at you now. Still walking. A miracle. Amazing."

Sensing she was overreacting, Diane took the tissue Iris held out to her. She sniffed. She blew her nose.

"And Patti Ann is probably fine, too." Just a malingerer, Iris thought. "And if she isn't, you'll find someone else. Someone better. It probably won't come to that, but if it does, I'll come every day if you need me until you've got someone you trust." Inwardly, Iris cringed. Although this would give her a place to be instead of at BJ's, and although it had always been her goal to shower her grandchildren with caring and kindness so they would grow up confident and secure, until now she had not necessarily seen this as a full-time job. She set her chin, got out of her chair and hugged her daughter. "Don't worry, honey. Everything's going to be fine."

"You think so, Mom?"

"I just know it."

Diane sighed.

"You know what? You're tired. You need go to bed. I'll watch Noah while you get undressed."

When Diane had trudged down the hall to her bedroom, Iris bent toward the sleeping baby, still on the couch. "You're driving your mother crazy," she told him. She kissed the fine cap of dark hair on top of his head and whispered, partly out of love and partly from pure self-interest, "Turn over, Noah. This is a direct order from your grandma. Do it in the next couple of days."

There. She felt much better. She felt in control.

The baby gave no indication that he heard.

CHAPTER 12

"Are you alone?" Harvey stood at the front door, hands outstretched toward the fast-approaching dog.

"Just me and Randolph and the Big Blob," BJ said as a pair of canine paws landed on Harvey's chest. He was wearing a dress shirt instead of his usual pullover, a spiffy sky-blue button-down that looked frighteningly vulnerable to grime and claws. "Get down," BJ said. Randolph ignored her. Harvey scratched the dog's ears.

"Hey, buddy. Hey, buddy." Harvey peered furtively into the entryway as he spoke, no doubt fearful that Iris might catch him calling the dog "buddy" instead of his given name.

"She's out," BJ said. She felt mildly sorry for Harvey, making his daily visit on the pretext of asking about BJ's eyes but actually hoping to catch a glimpse of the elusive Iris. *We had a fight*, BJ sometimes thought of telling him. *She's never here because she's avoiding me.* But then she'd have to explain that she'd been working at home so much these past two weeks not only because adjusting to the Big Blob made her want a nap every afternoon, but also because she was punishing Iris—or

rather, allowing Iris to punish *herself* for spending a
third of her life believing BJ was a slut.

Ever since the fight, Iris had left the house early and
returned late, even if she had one of her headaches.
Twice on what BJ assumed were headache days, Iris had
driven up the street at around noon, only to pass the
house without stopping once she saw BJ's car in the
driveway. Apparently she was more willing to endure
the pain in her temples than BJ's cold appraisal. BJ
imagined Iris gulping three or four Excedrin the minute
she got out of the neighborhood, and rushing off to her
massage therapist, who specialized in migraines.

To fill the rest of her day, Iris probably hung out
at the mall, visited Jonah and Noah despite the
presence of the evil Patti Ann and finally took in a late
movie—perhaps *dozed* through the movie, if the
headache hadn't gone away—to avoid coming home
until BJ was in bed. BJ knew her sister very well. And
though BJ allowed this because she was still stung by
Iris's failure to trust her, the whole situation made her
feel terrible. Iris had believed Sheldon because she'd
been mesmerized. Her judgment had been clouded. It
wasn't really Iris's fault. BJ figured she could endure
only a few more days of their standoff before she'd have
to insist on a reconciliation.

Randolph, having had his fill of jumping and slathering, sat down with his tongue lolling out. "Still
bothered by the Big Blob, then," Harvey said. "A few
more weeks and I'm sure it'll be less distinct."

"I hope so."

"So what else is the matter?" Harvey asked.

"What do you mean?"

"You're even snappier than your usual snappy self."

"By snappy, I take it you mean a person who snaps at you in an irritated way, as opposed to someone dressed in a snappy, attractive outfit?"

"Correct."

"There's not a thing the matter," BJ snapped.

"Such as?"

"My grandson." Other than Iris, this was her troublesome issue of the day. She had not meant to talk about it with Harvey or anyone else, but in the past two weeks Harvey had been around so much that they'd discussed virtually everything—except, of course, Iris—and BJ figured oh, hell, why not? "Eli is four years old and lives with his father on the West Coast. I almost never see him, but we usually have a little phone visit a couple of times a month. Now his stepmother is having a tough pregnancy and it's hard to get hold of him. Why am I upset? I have no idea. He and my daughter are coming at Christmas, and I'll have him for a whole week. Enough said. I have an ironclad rule that no one should ever have to listen to anything about anyone else's grandchildren."

Harvey nodded as if acknowledging the sense in this. He adjusted his glasses.

"You would think," BJ said, "that a retired optometrist would get glasses that don't slide down his nose."

"That's what I mean, snappy." Harvey pointed at her as if to say, "gotcha." BJ meant to respond sharply, but to her annoyance she found herself smiling, which would have ruined the effect.

"Your eye recheck is this afternoon," Harvey told her.

"Did you think I'd forgotten?"

"I'm here to drive you."

"No need. I've been driving my car every day in my effort to talk unsuspecting clients into buying ads. The Big Blob notwithstanding, I haven't driven into a single wall."

"Professional curiosity," Harvey said. "I want to be the first to know how you're doing. Indulge me."

Noting that Harvey's car was in her driveway, blocking hers, BJ didn't see that she had a choice.

In the doctor's office, BJ was handed a stack of insurance forms she hadn't filled out during her first, emergency, visit. Unlike the last time, she and Harvey sat in the waiting room for forty minutes, leafing through magazines of no interest to either of them. *Working Mother* was for women half her age. *Modern Equestrian* had limited appeal. BJ reminded herself that Dr. Wayne Adams was a much younger person than she herself or, from the looks of it, most of his patients.

When BJ was finally called back, Harvey made no move to accompany her. She raised her eyebrows toward him questioningly. Hadn't he gone to the trouble of driving her here so he could horn in on the exam? He only waved her off with a slight pushing motion, as if to propel her through the door.

Inside the dim examining room, BJ waited as long as she had in the reception area, except that now she had no forms to fill out and nothing to read. Dr. Adams finally swept in, lab coat flapping (did he really need a lab coat?), and began pressing on BJ's eyeball while blinding her with lights. He made small, contented humming noises as he worked.

"Well, good," he said after many long minutes. "No complications, at least so far." He then recited the same litany of information Harvey had been going over every day. The floaters should be less troublesome as time went on. BJ should call at once if she suddenly saw more of them or noticed more flashes of light at the edge of her vision. She should make an appointment for another recheck in a month.

It was dark when they finally left the office. This time BJ's hands did not tremble. Instead, she felt at once relieved, exhausted and euphoric as she told Harvey what the doctor had said. It took some moments for the gnawing sensation in her stomach to announce itself through these warring emotions. She remembered she had skipped lunch.

"I'm starving. How about you?" Harvey asked. Again a virtual stranger was reading her thoughts, a phenomenon that always left her defensive and belligerent. Somehow, her hostility seemed not to have reached her mouth. "I could eat something," she heard herself say.

They went to Genki, the only Japanese restaurant in town without a sushi bar. "Trend or no trend," Harvey told her, "I won't eat raw fish." As the hostess escorted them to their table he added, "'Genki' means 'good health.' In your situation, it seemed appropriate."

BJ was touched and embarrassed. "Probably means 'House of Roasted Lizard,'" she grumbled.

"You're thinking of 'gecko,'" Harvey said as if she'd been perfectly serious. "Genki for health. Gecko for lizard."

When she turned to glare at him, he winked. She was still searching for the proper clever retort when she remembered Harvey had chauffeured her here. She vowed to be kind. "My treat," she told him.

"Absolutely not."

He ordered plum wine, which they both agreed was too sweet but ought to be part of a Japanese meal. "To your health," he said. They clinked glasses, took one sip and ordered a bottle of Pinot Noir. Hungry as BJ was, the wine made her head feel clearer, as if it were sweeping away the accumulated fuzz and dust of the day. In the restaurant's muted light, even the Big Blob disappeared until she studied the menu, when it floated across her vision with its usual regularity, annoying but somehow not so maddening, now that she'd been assured once again that it would go away. Harvey ordered steamed dumplings, which arrived almost at once, and their pungent, warm taste didn't hurt her mood, either.

Over miso soup, Harvey talked about the Yoshino cherry tree he had planted in his yard and why fall was the best season for this. BJ was more interested than she'd expected to be, maybe because of the wine and maybe because she was trying to sell an advertising contract to a landscaping firm. *Yoshino cherry trees*, she added to her mental list of botanical names to drop at her next meeting. She let Harvey refill her glass.

The crunchy Japanese salad arrived in its little black bowl. BJ sometimes felt awkward with chopsticks, but under the spell of the wine, she found she could pick up even the smallest slivers of cabbage and get them to her mouth without giving the spicy ginger dressing time to drip. She hadn't felt this calm for weeks, since before her quarrel with Iris. She could actually feel the blood meandering through her arms and her neck like a slow, warm river.

The conversation drifted. Harvey talked about eyeglasses. BJ told him about her early days with the newspaper. "*Ads Unlimited*, it was called when I bought it. Can you imagine? I changed it to *The Scene* because I thought it sounded classy. I put on my best dress and went after ads from travel agents and nail salons instead of used-car lots and trailer parks. Sometimes it took me months just to get in the door."

BJ omitted the fact that it was Iris who'd finally turned the paper from a break-even operation into a profitable one, after she talked her plastic surgeon into buying a series of display ads. No self-respecting physician ever advertised in those days. BJ wasn't even sure medical ads were legal. Maybe Iris's boldness had changed some laws and started a nationwide trend. Ads for cosmetic procedures had flourished ever since.

"It's nice of you to keep checking up on me and my eyes," she said to Harvey over her third glass of wine, "but after this you don't really have to. It appears—" she paused for effect "—that I am going to be able to see for the foreseeable future." This struck her as clever and funny: *see for the foreseeable future*. Harvey smiled.

"So if you want to come over to see Iris," she said, twirling the glass in her hand, admiring the richness of its burgundy liquid, "then come on over. Or call."

"To see Iris?"

The waiter arrived with their salmon teriyaki. It was very beautiful, BJ thought, on its shiny black tray, garnished with parsley and radishes.

"I'll give you her cell number," BJ said.

Harvey looked confused.

The waiter set down their dishes and moved off. "We had a fight," BJ blurted. "I should have told you before. We had a fight and Iris is avoiding me. That's why she's never home." She was glad the words were out of her mouth. Yes. It was time. She felt much better.

"A fight," Harvey repeated blandly. "I see."

"Don't think I'm not grateful for everything you've done, but I know you've been expecting to see her."

Harvey frowned. He held a chunk of orangey-pink fish aloft, gripped tenuously between his two chopsticks on its way to his mouth. "You think I'm coming over to see Iris?"

"Well, aren't you?"

"No. Of course not. Iris and I don't…" He lowered the fish to his plate. "Don't you remember why I had your lawn mower serviced? To apologize for not getting along with her at Singles Night. I told you that."

"Yes, but I thought…actually, I thought you were testing each other."

Harvey looked puzzled.

"People will sometimes do that," BJ said lamely. "Do a little verbal sparring. See who can be more clever."

"You thought we were doing that?"

Now that she considered it, BJ wasn't sure.

"I'm not interested in Iris," Harvey said decisively.

"You aren't?"

"No. She's not my type. Michael Jackson never appealed to me, either."

"Well," BJ said.

"Yes. Well." Harvey set his chopsticks down as if he were finished eating, though he had barely started. His fingers were strong and square looking. He motioned the waiter to bring them some tea.

"I think you ought to tell me what's going on," he said, when the teapot had arrived and the brew been poured. "I mean, why you insisted I go to Singles Night. Why you invented the whole Singles project—which if I'm not mistaken was for your sister's sake. I think you should tell me the whole story." There was the hint of a smile under his words, not amusement, just kindness. "But first—" he tapped an index finger on the table "—tell me about your fight."

BJ ignored her tea and took another swallow of wine. Then she talked in a rush, at first just to get it over with and then because she was so glad to be *telling someone* that each word seemed like a weight being subtracted from her load. It occurred to her that until now she'd had no one at all to confide in, not even Resa Taub, who was usually reliable but at the moment so focused on earning a living that she probably would have used the information to try to sell Iris a house.

Now she told Harvey everything. About Iris believing for more than twenty years that BJ had slept with Sheldon. About BJ's stunned reaction when Iris confessed this to her. About their blowup. After a while she felt as if she was floating on the sea of her own words, sitting in her chair but also not, her body a fraction of an inch above the surface, her limbs suspended as if in water. Harvey listened with quiet attentiveness, his gaze alert but so mild that she told him more than she meant to.

She finished her tale about the fight, took another drink of wine and launched into the story of Singles Night. About Iris moving in with her. About her concerns. Harvey nodded and kept listening, not interrupting even once to make a sarcastic remark. BJ began to think that below the surface Harvey wasn't cynical at all, that his sharp edge was just a brave act he put on, and maybe BJ knew something about brave acts herself—a thought that struck her as odd, unrelated to her story, and proof that she was drunker than she thought, or why else would she feel she was about to burst into tears?

When she finally stopped talking, she noticed that her wineglass was empty and so was the bottle, and suddenly she wasn't sure what to do with her hands. Harvey pointed to her tea. She picked it up, one of those handleless cups that burn your fingers if the liquid inside is hot. The tea was lukewarm now, and tasted like an elixir.

"I still don't understand a grown woman—a grown man, for that matter—wanting to move in with a relative if she has enough money not to," Harvey said. "What was she thinking?"

"That's just the thing. She *wasn't* thinking. She *doesn't* think. I mean, well of course she thinks, but she isn't logical. She doesn't respond to things that way. Not that she's stupid. She's not. She's smart in other ways—in ways that don't show up on IQ tests."

Usually, trying to explain Iris to people made BJ defensive. She'd even been defensive with her own mother, who couldn't understand why, as a child, Iris did so poorly on her exams, unless she didn't study. "Ma, she did study," BJ would say. "She always studies. It runs through her brain like diarrhea. She can't help it!" Today, Iris would be diagnosed with a mild learning disability. In those days, it was called stupidity. Although everyone liked Iris and felt she understood them, and although everyone knew that, in her sweet, unassuming way, Iris got from them whatever small things she wanted, the *stupidity* label stuck. In return, BJ had always felt the need to defend her sister with a leonine ferocity far out of proportion to the slights Iris had endured.

But Harvey Sussman didn't call up BJ's need to do that. Not at all. Harvey, or maybe Harvey combined with the wine she'd been drinking, made BJ feel she could explain her sister to him the same way she explained Iris to herself.

"She's like a blind person who responds to the world by touch. Whose other senses get keener," she told him. "Iris's instincts are very good. Better than mine. Better than most people's. We even have a family joke about her 'people-meter' that only goes off if someone is no good. Well, except when she was around Sheldon. She could never see what was going on with Sheldon. But when it came to handling everyone else, she was wily—I know people don't think of her that way—and at the same time she was so *nice* that people would give her jobs and accept her in their social group and treat her daughter like all the other kids, no matter what they thought in private. It got her through all those years. And now, with Sheldon dead, thank goodness— I know she's relieved, but she's sort of in limbo."

BJ put her cup down. Harvey slid his hand across the table and put it on top of hers. "And so you feel you need to take care of her," he said.

"Yes."

Wrapping his fingers around hers, he squeezed as if to express approval. But then he said, "It's not good for either of you for you to take care of her. She probably wouldn't even want that. I think you know that. She has to develop some kind of life."

"I know," BJ said hopelessly, because the truth was, she *did* know—but what else was there to do except to marry her off?

"What is your sister good at?" Harvey persisted. "What does she like to do?"

BJ hesitated. She sighed. Then she said, "She likes to shop."

CHAPTER 13

It was close to nine when they got home, a clear moonlit night. They had sat in the restaurant more than two hours. BJ was a little dizzy from so much wine and so much confession and so little food, because once she'd started talking, she'd never seriously returned to her meal.

Harvey slowed as he turned onto their street, then pulled into his own driveway. "I'll leave the car here so Iris won't block me in when she comes dragging in at midnight or so," he said.

At the thought of this—Iris's absences that BJ could end with a simple word—she felt her accustomed pang of guilt. But also, as she pictured Iris "dragging in" at midnight as Harvey had described, she couldn't help smiling.

Harvey motioned BJ to remain where she was as he got out of the car and went around to open her door. It was like being nineteen and having a date. "I'll help you walk the dog," he said. Randolph had been alone in the house for hours.

They walked much farther than she normally did

after dark. When you had someone to go with you on a chilly night, she reflected as they strolled down the block, it was more of a pleasure than a chore. Even Randolph seemed cheerier than usual, sniffing and pawing at everything. "One of the reasons I kept my house after David died," BJ told Harvey, "was because I felt like I was a part of this neighborhood. Even though the neighbors come and go, still you feel they know each other, more or less. As much as neighbors need to. It makes you feel safe." BJ never told anyone about her need to feel safe. She didn't want to be perceived as weak. But the wine had unleashed her tongue, and it was running free. Since there didn't seem to be anything she could do to stop it, she no longer even cared. Pointing to the house they were passing on the left, she said, "Did you know Molly Gerber used to live there?"

"Molly from the retirement home? Lou Green's woman?"

"Yes. When David and I moved here, Molly and her late husband were still living in that house. They were the first owners. They'd raised their daughters there, and they stayed a couple more years before they downsized. Molly was a bigwig in the Sisterhood then. Before that, she was principal of the religious school. I always liked her."

She didn't add that lately, every time she saw Molly at temple or Over-Fifty Singles, the old woman seemed a little smaller. Molly had once been a pretty, plushly padded woman of medium height. Over the years, she had shrunk several inches and grown scrawny. Recently, her complexion had gone gray and dull, too, so much so that at the last Singles Night BJ had thought, *Why, her skin is exactly the color of dirty snow*. It had made her sad.

Yet even now as they walked down the block, twenty years after Molly had moved away, BJ was aware of the other woman as a kind of melody of feeling—the sense of Molly's sweet, effervescent presence from all those years ago—now and every time she passed her house.

BJ sighed. She couldn't remember the last time she'd felt this sappy and nostalgic.

"What are you thinking about?" Harvey asked.

"Nothing."

But Harvey patted her arm, as if to say, *I know it isn't nothing*.

She knew then how glad she was that he wasn't interested in Iris.

Back at her house they stood in the entryway as she took off Randolph's leash. "Thanks for dinner," BJ said. "Thanks for everything." Harvey made no move to go. BJ took off her blazer, and though she didn't exactly mean to, it was easy to turn toward him, very slightly, and lift her face for his kiss.

It was sweet and deep, and lasted quite a while. She had almost forgotten the twin sensations of a man's soft lips combined with the sandpapery scratch of his whiskers against her face. She luxuriated in that now. Even nicer was the way Harvey held her to him, the way she hadn't been held for years, breast to chest and belly to belly.

Well, he didn't have much belly. But there was certainly something else.

"Oh, my," she said when he released her.

"Not all men of sixty-something have erectile dysfunction," he whispered hoarsely.

"So I noticed," BJ said.

It wasn't until morning, with the sweet late-autumn sun pouring in and Harvey creating a substantial presence on the other side of her bed, that BJ's mind began to function again in something approximating its normal way.

I have not had sex for more than six years, she thought. *Closer to seven.*

She smiled.

She hadn't thought she'd ever have sex again. She hadn't thought she cared.

Wrong.

She'd thought she was too old. Or at least that she'd feel guilty.

Well, so much for *that*. She felt marvelous. She'd slept like a log.

Beside her, Harvey shifted position and ran his hand up her back. "I thought you were asleep," she said.

"Not exactly." He made a sound somewhere between a sigh and a moan.

"Disgusting," she mumbled.

"Mmm," he agreed, and repeated the sound so forcefully that Randolph raised his head and regarded him from the corner he had managed to claim at the foot of the bed.

It was then, with Harvey looking far more comfortable than he ought to in a strange woman's bed, that BJ grasped the logistics of what must have happened.

"You *planned this,*" she whispered with feigned horror.

"Planned what?" All innocence, Harvey kept rubbing her back.

With an effort of will, BJ shifted away and narrowed her eyes at him in what she hoped was an expression of accusation. "You parked your car in your own driveway so if Iris came in and we weren't downstairs, she'd never know you were here."

"You give me too much credit. I parked there so she wouldn't block my car when she came in. Just like I told you." Harvey grinned.

"Liar," BJ said. Neither of them could stop grinning.

Actually, it had been a relatively quiet moment when Iris had come "dragging in," as Harvey had predicted she would, a few minutes before midnight. By then, BJ and Harvey had been sharing BJ's bed for several hours and had spent the better part of their passion—or at least enough to make them vigilant. Speaking in stilled voices after Iris passed BJ's door on her way down the hall, they decided it would be wise, in order to escape discovery, for Harvey to remain in

BJ's room until after Iris's departure in the morning. By necessity—it was only a double bed, not a queen— they had spent most of the night curled in each other's arms, which BJ had found remarkably pleasant. They had slept through the dawn and into the bright morning.

"Actually, I wasn't smart enough to plan this," Harvey said softly, "but if I had been, I would have." With what felt like genuine reluctance, he pulled back the hand that had been caressing BJ's spine and reached toward the night table for his glasses. Without them, the pouches beneath his eyes looked not so much like signs of age as pockets of caring and concern, and his dark eyes were surprisingly cowlike and warm.

Randolph, glancing expectantly from BJ to Harvey and back again, wagged his tail and pawed gently at their intertwined feet, as if to ask when someone was finally going to take him out to pee.

BJ checked the clock. It was after nine. The mall would open in an hour. Iris would leave in a few minutes. The best BJ could figure, her sister usually went somewhere for breakfast before she began shopping. Despite her myriad diets, she had always believed in breakfast.

"Get dressed," BJ said. "The minute Iris gets out of here, the coast is clear."

"Or we could stay right here a little longer."

"No!" It was odd enough, having a man in her bed at all, much less having slept with him *all night*, and now talking in whispers as if they were teenagers hiding from a parent in the next room. Not that it really mattered if Iris discovered them. It was BJ's house; she could do what she liked. But since this was likely to be a one-night stand, and considering what Iris had already thought about BJ's moral character for the past twenty years, it was best to be discreet.

"We both need to get dressed right now," BJ asserted in her most dramatic whisper. "You need to get out of here as soon as you can. I have to work."

Harvey lifted an arm into a languid stretch. He lifted the other arm. He was in no hurry. He reached over and crunched a wad of BJ's hair in his hand. "Springy," he said. "Nice consistency." He traced the line of her jaw with the back of his hand and ran a fingertip over her little hoop earring. "Pretty," he said. "You never take them off, do you?"

"It's not intentional. I just forget."

"It's unusual when someone wears the same earrings all the time."

"Is it?" BJ didn't mention that these were the only earrings she wore because they were the only ones she'd ever found that didn't make her feel she was carrying weights in her ears. Someday she might tell Harvey about her aversion to jewelry in general, but she'd have to know him a lot better and be able to judge how he'd probably react. For the moment, she'd just as soon not have him think she was weird.

Harvey turned his whole body toward her and reached

in her direction. BJ was tempted. But before either one of them could do more, Randolph scooched between them and whimpered his bladder-full-to-bursting plea.

"Sounds serious," Harvey said.

"All right. I'm getting up." BJ suppressed an outrageous urge to giggle. Now that she'd declared herself, what was she supposed to do? Her clothes were on the other side of the room, in the untidy heap where they'd fallen hours before. Her robe was in the closet. Was she supposed to get up in front of him *naked*? No! She was sixty-two years old! She sagged! She bulged! Unlike the old-lady calendar nudies who'd gone public for charity, she wasn't ready to go public at all. Seizing a corner of the top sheet, she wrapped it around her and rose from the bed.

"Cheated," Harvey groaned as she retreated into the bathroom, "of the best show of all."

Five minutes later, dressed and presentable, BJ walked out of the room with Randolph at her heels. She closed the door behind her. The guest room where Iris slept was at the far end of the hall. Without venturing closer, BJ paused and strained to listen. She was sure she heard Iris moving around.

Outside, the weather had turned warm again overnight, as it often did in the months before Christmas. Stretches of real cold—if there *was* any real cold this year—wouldn't set in until January. Maybe it was the mild sunshine that made BJ feel so light. Even the hangover headache behind her eyes when she'd first opened them was gone. It was as if for years every muscle in her body had been in a state of tension and now had relaxed, not in a staggering, losing-balance way but in a free, loose-limbed one, that allowed all her limbs to work as smoothly as they had when she was thirty. She walked Randolph an extra two blocks, partly for the joy of it and partly to give Iris time to clear out.

They rounded the last corner and started back toward her house. Uh-oh. Iris's car was still in the driveway. Of all the days to be getting a late start. Well, no matter. She'd be out of the house in a few minutes.

But no, they came in the back door and *voila*. Iris stood at the counter in the kitchen, clad in the turquoise leggings and baggy black shirt she wore only around the house. She had fixed her hair but not put on any makeup. She was dunking a tea bag into a cup of steaming water. Milk and a carton of eggs sat on the counter. For the first time in two weeks, Iris was *making breakfast at home*.

Alarmed, completely at a loss, BJ blurted, "Aren't you going out?"

And poor Iris—who obviously *wasn't* going out, who was probably ready to make amends and start over—looked up, startled, before regaining herself and saying with guilt-inducing mildness, "Well, sure, BJ. I was just getting ready right now." She poured milk into her tea, although she never used milk in her tea, only sweetener. She put the eggs back into the refrigerator. "Going to the grocery," she said crisply. "Checking the supplies." Then she picked up her cup as if she'd meant to take it with her all the time, seized the purse lying beside the newspaper she'd obviously meant to read at her leisure, and left the house in a rush.

BJ's cruelty echoed in her ears: *Aren't you going out?* She couldn't believe she'd said that to her own sister.

CHAPTER 14

*A*ren't *you going out?*

Iris couldn't believe BJ had said that to her own sister! Not after telling Iris two weeks ago that she didn't want her to leave, only to go to bed. Not after Iris had stayed away so much since then, as a way of providing a cooling-off period. After all that, Iris thought BJ would have calmed down.

Well! Apparently not! Apparently BJ was still steaming! And just when Iris had said to herself, okay, this is crazy, it's time to make up. Just when she'd decided to stay home and present a peace offering of French toast just the way BJ liked it. She would mix the milk and eggs with cinnamon (she could do without the cinnamon, herself), slice the bread thick so it would have to cook for a while, and let the aroma drift through the house until it drew BJ downstairs. She would say to her sister, "Come on in. Have some." BJ would not be able to resist. They would eat, and they would talk, and bygones would be bygones.

But no. There she came, Miss Priss herself, marching in through the back door with Randolph, looking as if she'd discovered an intruder.

Well. Now the die was cast. The writing was on the wall. If BJ wanted her out, so be it. Iris would stop procrastinating. She would find a suitable house. No more haphazard driving around or looking at condos she didn't want. She would call Resa Taub, or some other real-estate agent. She would complete her search.

But first she would eat. It was a known fact that dieters who ate breakfast lost more and kept it off longer than those who skipped the meal. Iris had started out the morning with notions of French toast, and there was no reason she shouldn't carry through. She drove to Angie's Diner.

The trouble was, once she'd settled into her booth and ordered, she wasn't the least bit hungry. Her coffee came and she drank it, but what she had really wanted was tea and BJ's company. The French toast turned out to be thin and undercooked. The minute she poured syrup over it, it sank in the middle. She put money on the table and left. The day was so warm and beautiful that it mocked her. She didn't think she could stand to go to the mall. Aside from the weather, there was her outfit to think of. Never before had she worn this particular shabby shirt and leggings outside of the house. She bought a newspaper from the stand in front of the diner and drove to the park.

By noon she'd circled every real estate ad that interested her even a little. She'd check these out herself before calling Resa Taub, who might spread the details of her house-hunt through the entire congregation.

Hiking the strap of her purse to her shoulder, she rose stiffly from the wooden bench she'd been sitting on all morning, and started back to her car.

She'd gone only a few steps when a small muffled noise began to rise from the depths of her purse. A feeble *meep, meep*, and then silence, then *meep, meep* again. Had some little bird or chipmunk crawled into her purse and now was crying to get out? For a second she toyed with the notion of emptying everything onto the grass so the trapped creature could escape without her having to touch it. Then she realized what she was hearing. Her cell phone. Much as Diane badgered her to keep it charged and ready, no one ever called. Iris plunged her hand into the purse to retrieve the thing before it went to voice mail. She had no idea how to retrieve a voice-mail message.

"Oh, Mom, I'm so glad you're there!" Diane said in a panicky voice that sent Iris's heart into overdrive.

"Honey! What's the matter?"

"I'm not sure. They just called from Jonah's preschool. The class let out half an hour ago and Patti Ann hasn't come to pick him up. She doesn't answer the phone at home, either. I don't know where she is. Somewhere with Noah. I just hope nothing's happened. I'm leaving the office right now, but I'm forty minutes away. Can you get Jonah for me and meet me at home?"

"Of course." Iris took a breath and aimed for a tone of unconcerned calm. "I'm sure by the time I get him home Patti Ann will be there, too, and there will be some logical explanation."

"I hope so," Diane sputtered.

"Drive carefully. It's going to be fine." Iris marveled at how the steadiness of her voice gave no hint of the intemperate beating of her heart.

Ten minutes later, Iris was at the preschool. "Gamma!" Jonah shouted. He didn't seem upset; quite the contrary. One of the teachers, Lacey, was showing him how to play hopscotch.

Gushing her gratitude, Iris lifted Jonah into the larger of the two car seats she'd bought for her car.

Diane's house was empty. No sign of Patti Ann. No sign of Noah's stroller. No note. With shaking hands, Iris retrieved a can of tuna fish from the pantry and said to Jonah as she mixed it with celery and mayonnaise, "I bet you're *starving*, after all that hopping around."

"*Star*-ving," Jonah repeated with perfect intonation. He retrieved his favorite action figure from the floor and set it on the table. "La-La starving, too."

Most children Jonah's age didn't like tuna fish, but Jonah considered it a treat. He downed a respectable amount and fed the rest to La-La while Iris repeatedly checked her watch. She looked out the window and scanned the street for Patti Ann's car. She gave Jonah a box of the sweetened juice she normally didn't approve of. She checked the driveway again.

"All done!" Jonah said. Iris wiped his face and took off his bib. *Think*, she told herself. Where could Patti

Ann be? Her mind was blank. She cleared Jonah's dish from the table.

At his construction site, Jonah marched La-La into a stack of blocks. Iris's heart fluttered. Palpitations? Fibrillation? "Do you know where Patti Ann is?" she asked, aware how desperate she must be, to ask a two-year-old.

"She go dokker," Jonah said without looking up, creating another stack of blocks. Iris understood that *dokker* might have been yesterday's answer, last week's answer, any answer, just to get back to his game.

"Did she take Noah somewhere?"

Jonah picked up La-La and swooped him down into the newly stacked plastic blocks. "Kazam!" He had disappeared with La-La into la-la land.

The front door opened. Diane flew in, hair disheveled, eyes wild. "Anything?"

"Not yet." Iris shook her head.

"Mommy!" Jonah dropped his toys and rushed to hug Diane around the legs. Absently, she ruffled his hair. "Hi, sweetie." And to Iris, "Something must have happened. Or else she kidnapped him."

"*Kidnapped* him?"

"It's all I can think of. I'm going to call the police."

"Mommy!" Jonah squeezed Diane's legs harder, demanding attention.

"She wouldn't kidnap him," Iris said. "She *loves* him. She carries him around as much as you do."

"All the more reason she might want him to herself."

"No. That's crazy. She has a husband to go home to.

She's not going to go running off. She probably forgot what time it was. Maybe her watch stopped."

"At the very least the police could track down her car," Diane said.

"I don't think—" Iris began, trying to sound reasonable. She stopped because she didn't know what she thought, except that calling the police seemed extreme. "Do you have her husband's number at work? If something happened, he'd be the first one she'd call."

Diane shook her head. Jonah let go of his mother's legs. Agitated at being ignored, he ran back to the construction site. He picked up La-La and set him down violently down on the carpet. "Uh-oh. La-La got ooo-eys!" he shouted. He rushed to the table, found a scrap of tuna salad that hadn't been wiped up, rushed back, fed it to the doll. "Ooo-eys all better!" he shouted.

"Hush," Diane said.

"Oooh-eys!" Jonah yelled, lifting La-La triumphantly into the air.

Iris sometimes wondered what went on in a two-year-old's brain. It was a mistake to treat a child that age like a logical creature. Cognitive reasoning wouldn't come for years.

"What about her doctor's number?" Iris asked Diane.

Again, Diane shook her head. "On TV they always say to call the police right away," she told Iris. "They say not to wait because in cases like these, the sooner they get on the trail, the better." She picked up the phone.

Jonah seized La-La again. "Ooo-eys!" he said insistently. For a moment Diane gave him her full attention. "Jonah, *stop*."

Jonah burst into tears.

"He needs his nap." Diane put down the phone and picked him up. Jonah did not stop crying.

Iris looked at her grandson. She looked at La-La still clutched in Jonah's fist. "Eating made the ooo-eys better?" she asked.

Jonah wailed.

Iris tried another tack. "What does La-La do when he has ooo-eys? What's the *first* thing he does?" She was pretty sure she knew.

Jonah rested his head on Diane's shoulder. He sniffed as she turned to carry him to his room. Just before burying his head in his mother's sweater, he said, "La-La *sit*."

At that moment, Iris understood everything she needed to about ooo-eys.

"Give me fifteen minutes," she called as Diane walked down the hallway. "If I don't get back to you by then, go ahead and call the police. But I don't think you'll have to. Just give me fifteen minutes."

"*Mother*—"

Iris grabbed a juice box from the refrigerator, snatched her purse from the chair and was on her way to the mall.

She found Patti Ann exactly where she expected to, not inside the pet shop but on one of the benches next to it, in the wide center hallway. Noah, in his stroller, was sound asleep. Patti Ann sat motionless, face pale, skin visibly clammy even from a distance.

"Patti Ann?" Iris asked.

The nanny looked vaguely in her direction.

"Are you okay? You're having a woozy, aren't you?"

A flicker of recognition registered in Patti Ann's eyes. "I ran out of candy," she said.

"So I see." Easing herself onto the bench beside the other woman, Iris pulled the juice carton from her purse and unwrapped its cellophane-clad straw. "Here."

Patti Ann looked at it blankly.

Iris stuck the straw into its prepunched hole. "Drink."

Patti Ann obeyed. Iris stood up, nodding encouragement, and moved a few steps away while she called Diane. "I found them at the mall. Noah's asleep in his stroller. Everything's okay. We'll be there in a few minutes." She hung up before Diane could ask questions.

Patti Ann sucked on the straw. After a few sips of the sweet juice, her ashy complexion began to pink up.

"Better?"

Patti Ann grunted. "I ran out of candy," she said again.

Iris already knew what must have happened. Made restless by the warm weather, most people would have taken the baby outside, but Patti Ann's aversion to the sun sent her to the mall instead. No doubt she'd wheeled the stroller to the food court for a snack. Maybe two snacks. Fearing she'd overdone it, she'd taken an extra dose of her medication. Then she'd headed for the pet store to show Noah the parakeets. And pretty soon, this.

"What did you have to eat this morning?" Iris asked her. "Did you get something here in the mall?"

"A smoothie."

"Anything else?"

"A doughnut," Patti Ann whispered.

"And that was too much sugar. So you took a pill?"

Patti Ann lowered her head. Fat tears ran down her cheeks and fell into her lap. She didn't try to wipe them away.

"Here." Iris handed her a tissue. "You told me no when I asked if you had diabetes. Why did you lie to me?"

Patti Ann sniffed and blew her nose. Iris didn't feel sorry for her. "*Answer*," she said.

"I was afraid I'd get in trouble," Patti Ann mumbled.

"You wouldn't have gotten into trouble for being sick. You're in trouble for playing games with the children's safety. When you're spaced out like this, you can't take care of them."

"I didn't drop Noah. I put him in the stroller. I didn't hurt him. I didn't fall."

"Did you know you forgot to pick up Jonah from school?"

Patti Ann looked at her watch. She seemed confused. "It's hard not to eat sugar," she said.

Wes had arrived by the time Iris and Patti Ann returned to the house in Iris's car, his tie undone and flapping against his shirt. Diane snatched Noah from his car seat and held him to her, kissing his head, squeezing him so hard that a less mild tempered child might have raised a fuss. Wes put his arm around Diane's shoulders as if protecting her from a chill on this warm, sunny day, and led her back inside.

Patti Ann hadn't budged from Iris's passenger seat. Her normal color had returned, but her expression was grim.

"Come inside," Iris told her. "You owe them an explanation. Diane almost called the police." She wanted to add, *It would have served you right*, but didn't because then she would have to pull Patti Ann bodily from the car.

"Tell them," Iris demanded when they were all seated in the den.

"I had a woozy," Patti Ann said in a flat tone. "I had to sit down. I forgot what time it was. I didn't mean to upset anyone. I'm sorry."

"I think," Wes said in a voice that didn't allow for refusal, "that you'd better start at the beginning." Wes was such an ordinary-looking man, of medium height and build, with such a familiar-looking narrow face and high forehead and slightly receding hairline, that Iris never failed to be surprised at the authority in his voice. Patti Ann froze at the sound of it. She didn't say a word.

"She has diabetes," Iris prompted. "Patti Ann, tell them."

"I have diabetes," Patti Ann repeated woodenly.

"Tell them about the pills."

Patti Ann clenched and unclenched her fists in her lap.

"Patti Ann, look at me," Wes told her.

Defiantly, the nanny looked up. "I take a pill, and then I can eat all the sugar I want."

"You know that's not true," Iris said.

"If I eat a certain amount of sugar, then I just take another pill." Patti Ann looked boldly from Wes to Iris and finally to Diane, who had begun to nurse the baby.

"Does the doctor say you can eat all the sugar you want?" Wes asked.

"No, but I can. The pill lowers the sugar in my blood. If it lowers it too much, I know right away because I start to feel dizzy. So I suck on a hard candy, and then I'm all right."

"You weren't all right today," Wes said.

"I ran out of candy."

"Oh, for God's sake! She *never* knows if she's all right!" Iris might not be good in math, but she grasped medical details as well as anyone. "The medication lowers her blood sugar, so she thinks she's safe and eats however damn much sugar she wants. Then her sugar skyrockets and she takes another pill. This drives her blood sugar too low, so her head feels foggy and she's so woozy she has to sit down. Then she eats a piece of candy. Her head clears, and it starts all over again. It's like playing Russian roulette."

Diane stared at her mother, transfixed.

"It's more complicated than she thinks," Iris said. "The pills are time-released, so she can take one now and the full effect doesn't kick in for hours. If she takes too many, her sugar can plummet half a day later, when she least expects it. She could end up in a coma right here on this floor with no one else home. She could end up dead."

Gape jawed, Diane turned toward Patti Ann as Iris's explanation gradually sank in. Patti Ann returned to studying the clenched fists in her lap.

"And now she's got Jonah thinking woozies are a fact of life," Iris continued. "He says La-La has to go to the doctor. Or he pretends La-La has the woozies, only he calls them ooo-eys, and he makes the doll sit down while he feeds him something to make him feel better. What kind of example is that to set for a child?" She sounded loud and sharp, even to herself. She sounded like BJ. "It's just luck Jonah wasn't there today after Patti Ann ran out of candy and got so disoriented. And it was luck that she didn't pass out before I came along with some juice!" She turned to the nanny. "I'm sure the doctor told you messing with your medicine doesn't always work. Didn't he? I'm sure he told you to keep away from sugar altogether."

Patti Ann looked up and spoke directly to Diane. "When I started to feel dizzy, I put Noah in his stroller," she said boldly. "I didn't fall on him. I kept him safe."

Iris drove Patti Ann to get her car at the mall. They

made the trip in silence. When Patti Ann got out, she kept her hand on the door handle for a long moment. "Am I going to lose my job?" she asked.

You already have, Iris thought. Aloud, she made herself say evenly, "There's no point talking about this now. First, you have to get help."

Patti Ann walked away, toward her car. Iris shifted into drive and headed out of the mall parking lot, shaking all over as if she had the chills.

Back at the house, Diane seemed not to have moved an inch. Still on the couch with Noah dozing in her arms, she sat with her legs stretched out to rest on the coffee table. Wes was slumped in a chair. Both of them were glassy-eyed with shock.

"We don't know how to thank you," Wes said in a gravelly voice.

"And to think that a week ago all I worried about was when Noah was going to turn over," Diane added. "Now I don't care if he ever does." She ran a finger up and down the sleeping baby's arm.

Both Diane and Wes looked as if they were about sixteen, raw with emotion, trying so hard to hide it that their faces were contorted with the effort.

"You figured all this out, Mom," Diane said. "Nobody else had a clue. The ooo-eys and the woozies. And where Patti Ann was. What made you think she was at the mall?"

"The pet shop. I saw her once with Noah in the pet shop."

"A regular Sherlock Holmes," Wes said.

"Well, I was worried that you'd call the police and make it even more complicated. I'm not crazy about Patti Ann, but she never set off my people-meter. I knew she wouldn't hurt Noah if she could help it. I didn't think she'd kidnap him, either, and I didn't think it would help to have her arrested. It's bad enough for her that she'll be out of a job."

Diane regarded her mother with an expression Iris identified as awe, as if the extent of her feat was too much to take in. "It's amazing. You were so *in charge*."

Well, she *had* been, hadn't she? She'd been too angry to be tentative or unsure, at least until it was over and she started shaking. She wouldn't mention the shaking.

"What was I supposed to do?" she asked gruffly. "Leave my grandson in the mall with a spaced-out nanny?"

Diane laughed, but the merriment didn't reach her eyes, which were ringed with worry and exhaustion. Wes looked beat-up, too, not just from the hard afternoon, but deep-down weary from lack of sleep. Maybe it wasn't right to think what popped into her head right now, but Iris couldn't help it. No wonder Diane had been buying things at a passion party, hoping they'd revive her sex life. She and Wes were both numb from fatigue.

CHAPTER 15

Three nights with less than six hours of sleep! Three nights because she'd been too busy cavorting under the covers with Harvey! Imagine! A woman her age. BJ should have been dragging herself around in the morning with her eyes half-closed. Instead, she was wide-awake and focused. "I only wish I could bottle this," she told him.

He winked. "We'll work on it," he said.

Best of all, Iris had left a message on the answering machine that she was staying at Diane's for a few days—nothing serious, just nanny problems—and would be back on Saturday. Listening to the tape made BJ feel exactly as she had nearly fifty years ago when her parents had left her alone for the weekend while they took Iris to summer camp—that unforgettable deliciousness of knowing that no one would come home and discover her, no matter what she was up to. Back then, she'd invited seven girls to a sleepover. They'd tried out her mother's makeup and given each other pedicures with her mother's manicure kit. They'd eaten chocolate ice cream for breakfast, and every cookie in the house. In some respects, BJ supposed she was having the adult version of a sleepover now.

As in the days of her teen slumber parties, she and Harvey hadn't slept. They'd dallied the night away (never mind how), eaten questionable foods (leftover Cloggeroo straight out of the freezer) and exchanged tidbits of intimate personal information.

Lying on his back staring at the ceiling, hands clasped behind his head, Harvey had confessed that he'd refused to wear shorts the hot summer of his ninth year, because he thought people would laugh at his legs. "They were skinny. I didn't think I could show them in public unless the calf muscle rippled every time I took a step."

"Does it ripple now? I must have missed something."

Harvey leaped out of bed and rose repeatedly on his toes to demonstrate.

"Surprisingly muscular for an old coot in his sixties," BJ conceded.

"Old coot!" Harvey flung himself back onto the mattress in imitation of a boy of seventeen. BJ hoped to hell he didn't break something. He grinned maniacally.

Harvey Sussman, BJ jotted in her mental notebook, *is a bit of a wacko.*

She didn't care.

In their lists of personal favorites, there was no overlap whatsoever. Harvey, BJ learned, read nonfiction history books, went to war movies, listened to classical music and turned on the TV only to watch sports. BJ preferred novels, dramas, show tunes and sitcoms. Their interest in each other wouldn't last a month. BJ didn't care. She revealed her weakness for shrimp, crab and oysters. Except for salmon, Harvey claimed an aversion to anything that lived in water.

"Now, fried chicken, that's another story. When I was a kid my friend's mother made terrific Southern-fried chicken. My own mother always baked it until it was dry. When I came down here, I discovered she wasn't alone. Southern Jews aren't really Southern, when it comes to cooking, are they?"

It was on the tip of BJ's tongue to say, *Oh, you should taste Iris's fried chicken*, but after Harvey placed his right ankle over her left one as if it belonged there, she didn't. "Most of my friends are too health conscious to fry anything. Too stingy to provide the added cholesterol you crave."

"Added cholesterol. I *do* crave it. Yes." He shifted in her direction on the bed and reached a hand toward her waist. "Although I crave other things more."

Randolph, unwilling to relinquish the space he'd reclaimed beside BJ and retreat to the bottom of the bed, held his position. When Harvey nudged him away, he wriggled back. Harvey gave up but regarded the dog sourly. "Randolph. Such an important name, he thinks he has to be a person instead of a Fido or a Rex. It's a lot of pressure for him. Why Randolph?"

"It's short for William Randolph Hearst. The news-paper magnate." BJ did not add that both the dog and his name were gifts from Iris after David's death. BJ hadn't wanted a pet but had no choice. She hadn't wanted to call him Randolph, either, but Iris had been unaware of the irony of naming the beast after an empire builder known for journalistic excellence, when BJ owned only a third-rate shopper. Some things, BJ judged, were too personal to reveal.

On their second night together, it had occurred to BJ that since her time with Harvey would be an interesting but probably short-lived interlude, and perhaps an unwise one, as well, it was best if the whole neighborhood didn't know. "It's one in the morning," she'd said to him. "Time for you to go home."

"Better to leave under cover of darkness than go sneaking off at dawn when everyone is waking up and peering out their windows?"

"Exactly," BJ said.

"Agreed." But Harvey made no move to get up, and a few minutes later, both of them were so sound asleep that they didn't stir until Randolph barked at something at three in the morning. Each opened a bleary eye just long enough to rule out the possibility of intruders. Neither awakened again until sunlight streamed through the window. They didn't revisit the issue of Harvey's staying over. He simply did.

For three days, BJ rode on a tide of joy she thought had ebbed along with her youth. She threw out a whole raft of long-held tenets. It was rather liberating. A week ago, she wouldn't have considered even the mildest flir-

tation with a neighbor or a colleague. At best it was bad
for business, and at worst it could make you feel you had
to move to a different neighborhood or take a different job when you liked the current one perfectly well.
Now she didn't care.

Until now she had also believed that men not only
died younger than women (statistical fact) but also
aged so much less gracefully that she'd never want to
touch some old man in an intimate way for the rest of
her life. She didn't think any old man would want to
touch *her*, either. Well, so much for that. BJ's sense of
touch was quite intact. Harvey's, too. Despite his state-
ment when she'd first invited him to Singles Night
that he was interested only in females under forty, he
had proved he could find a sixty-something woman
quite stimulating.

Couples, BJ had read somewhere, had lower blood
pressure and fewer heart attacks and strokes than their
single counterparts. They were happier. They lived
longer. Whatever her previous beliefs had been, now
she converted to this one. She was having a fling. She
was enjoying it. For as long as it lasted, she wasn't
asking any questions.

On Friday morning after Harvey left, BJ determined
to finish her piled-up end-of-the-week newspaper tasks
so she could enjoy the weekend guilt-free. Not that she
would have felt guilty in any case, but she might as well
be practical. She made out her invoice, ticked her way
through her to-do list, planned her schedule for the fol-

lowing Monday and Tuesday. She didn't even answer the phone until noon, when Janelle's number appeared on the caller ID. Her heart leaped in her chest at the sight of it. Noon in Fern Hollow was nine in the morning on the West Coast. Janelle usually called at night.

"What's up, honey? Are you okay? Is Eli?"

"Nothing serious. Just a change in plans."

"Oh?" BJ felt herself sitting taller, tensing her muscles to hold everything in place.

"About coming east for the holidays."

"Oh?"

"Marianne—" this was the ex-husband's new wife "—is due December nineteenth, and with all the problems she's had, Luke feels Eli should stay with them and be part of the new-baby experience. Not feel excluded when his little sister comes along."

BJ took one of her yoga-class deep cleansing breaths. Okay. There were worse things. Eli could be sick, the way he'd been last spring when he and Janelle were supposed to visit but couldn't because, despite his immunization shots, Eli had gotten the mumps.

"I thought the idea was to let Eli have a special holiday celebration with you and me while they got the baby settled in," BJ said.

"It was, originally. But with Marianne in and out of the hospital for tests, and then on bed rest for so long, it's been a confusing time for all of them. I know I'm supposed to get Eli for Christmas this year, but Luke thinks it will be better if he stays with them. I'm inclined to agree. He's promised me an extra week in the spring."

For the past month, in anticipation of the visit, BJ had been buying small gifts for Eli. At night, sitting in front of the TV, wrapping toys in glossy Chanukah paper from the Judaica shop, she'd imagined the "pretend Chanukah" they'd have together. The actual holiday would be over before Eli and Janelle arrived just before Christmas, but they would recreate it. They'd light the candles in the menorah BJ hadn't taken out of her china closet since David died. They'd make potato latkes and fry them in oil while discussing the miracle of lights that had allowed one day's supply of oil to last for eight days in the newly purified Temple. It would be a perfect project for a woman and her four-year-old grandson, educational but just difficult enough (grating the potatoes) and dangerous enough (hot oil!) to be interesting.

The expanding circle of plans BJ had carried in her head now slowly collapsed, leaving behind only a mother-of-pearl sheen of memory, like the skin of soap bubbles Eli liked to blow in the bath.

Then she realized Janelle must be hiding her own disappointment at having to spend the holidays without her son.

"You could still come," she told her daughter. "I'd love to have you. We can do some mother-daughter things. See a dozen movies. Shop. Eat fattening foods."

Janelle laughed. "I don't want to use your frequent flyer tickets for just me. We'll wait until I can bring Eli."

"I hate to think of you being all alone."

"Don't worry, Mom. Daniel will be off." This was the new boyfriend, perhaps the next husband. "Christmas is the only vacation he has for months. If I can't have Eli, I'll probably go with Daniel down to Monterey."

Then BJ understood this was not about Eli, it was about Janelle. "Oh. Good," she said. "At least you won't be alone."

Staring at the phone after they hung up, BJ felt the hollowness of knowing she wouldn't see her grandson mingle with her guilty relief that Janelle had declined her invitation to visit solo. Although she missed her daughter in the dreamy way that parents do, on the rare occasions when Janelle took pains to fly across the country to be with her, BJ was always aware of a little pocket of sadness in her chest, not for the grown woman who was in so many ways a stranger, but for the child Janelle had once been, who had needed her and brought laughter and a sense of fullness to her life. Sensibly, BJ and David had raised their daughter to be strong enough to leave them. "What if something happens to us?" they'd asked each other. "She needs to be able to make it on her own." Later, BJ wondered if they hadn't done too good a job.

Janelle was a graphic designer. She'd learned her craft first as a young teenager at BJ's paper, under the patient tutelage of BJ's designer. Before the end of her first summer, she'd created a new logo for *The Scene* that BJ still used. She had been so proud of her daughter's

talent and quickness that she sometimes imagined
Janelle taking over the business and molding the paper
into something bigger. Then Janelle went off to college
and the West Coast. She loved Seattle. And when she
found Luke, a marine biologist with a specialty in some
unpronounceable Pacific rim creature, BJ hid her disappointment at realizing his work would always keep
him in Washington State. Later, when Eli was born, BJ
held back her emotions again because she sensed that
her daughter's marriage was in trouble. It was only
when Janelle brought the baby east to visit, filling her
house with more noise and purpose than it had contained for years, that BJ realized how much she was
missing. In better circumstances, *this* was what you
could have when your children were grown. This bois-
terous new generation.

Well, not really. Not in BJ's case. During the divorce,
Janelle gave Luke custody of Eli as blithely as if she'd
been giving him a bottle of cologne, claiming her son
would need a male role model as he grew up. BJ had
refused to criticize her daughter for this. She had simply
said to herself then, in the most nonjudgmental way she
could, *Eli will never live on the East Coast.* He will always
be three thousand miles away. This will be hard.

She had accepted this, or she thought she had. But
it hadn't gotten easier. Eli was a real person now, not a
baby. Talking on the phone wasn't the same as visiting.
After not seeing him for a year, except in the photos
Janelle dutifully e-mailed, BJ wondered if she'd even

recognize her grandson in person—or if he would recognize her. She accepted the fact their lives had unfolded in ways that kept them apart most of the time. But until now she had not expected Janelle herself to participate in the conspiracy.

Staring at the phone after she had hung it up, BJ thought, for a long angry moment, that she could let her daughter go. She already had. But not her grandson. Not entirely. No!

She was so swamped by this emotion that when the back doorbell rang, BJ looked up in total confusion. Even the cacophony of Randolph's barking didn't clear her head right away. She walked mechanically through the kitchen and caught a blurry glimpse of Harvey through the small side-window, standing on the back stoop. She opened the door. Flashes of light suddenly spangled the edges of her vision. Panic threaded through her. Oh, no! A retinal tear, just as the doctor had warned!

Harvey grinned and held up a bucket of fried chicken. BJ glared at him through the haze of her impaired vision. Couldn't he see she was having an ophthalmic emergency?

He stepped inside and closed the door. BJ blinked. As suddenly as they had come, the flashes were gone. She closed her eyes and opened them again. Her vision had cleared. Everything was normal.

What the hell—?

Well, of course.

Thinking about Eli had brought tears to her eyes. Tears! And when she'd opened the door to the bright sunlight, the sun had flashed off the wetness and made her see the flashes.

Retinal tear, indeed. Her thinking was as flaky as Iris's. Whatever happened to being *strong*?

At least the tears hadn't overflowed and run down her face. And at least Harvey didn't seem to notice them. There was something to be said for the block-headedness of men.

Harvey set the bucket of chicken on the table with a flourish. "Cholesterol!" he exclaimed. "I thought we needed something that would satisfy my craving for cholesterol."

BJ was inclined to agree with him. The scent of chicken that wafted up from the bucket was familiar and comforting. Her stomach began to growl a little. She hoped Harvey didn't hear it. "Cholesterol. Absolutely," she said.

Harvey had showered and put on some kind of aftershave. Mingled with the aroma of the chicken, it reminded her of the combined satisfactions of food and sex.

It occurred to her then that the chilly, unsettled weather at Christmastime wasn't really ideal for Eli's visit. Spring, on the other hand, would be a warm, sunny splash of azaleas and dogwoods, in contrast to Seattle's gray drizzle. They could go to the park and play ball.

If Janelle wasn't coming for Christmas, then BJ

might as well spend her time with Harvey. Iris would be mostly at Diane's. If they wanted to, she and Harvey could spend all day in bed.

What kind of person *was* she, to be thinking about this not ten minutes after her daughter had bailed out on her? Was it really possible, at age sixty-two, to value a few hours with a man more than a visit from her own family?

Well, no. She missed Eli. She always would. But she was glad—and why the hell shouldn't she be?—to be sitting here with a man who cared enough to bring her something warm and greasy for lunch.

CHAPTER 16

After three days and four nights with the grandchildren she loved, Iris felt as if she'd just been released from a sentence of Chinese water torture. She intended to reclaim her place in BJ's guest room, at least for the weekend, regardless of what BJ thought. She'd left a message on her sister's answering machine that she was coming. She'd warned her. That was the best she could do.

It hadn't been Iris's plan to stay at Diane's so long, but once Patti Ann had left, there was really no choice. "I'll take a few days off work to reorganize," Diane had said when things calmed down. "I'll interview the rest of the nannies on my list and make a decision." Diane sounded almost like her calm, take-charge self. Then she closed her eyes and raised her hands to her temples as if jolted by pain. "*Shit.*"

"What?" Iris asked.

"I just sent out a memo to all my staff saying no personal time off until after the holidays, unless it's already been scheduled." She gazed wistfully down at Noah, still sleeping in her arms. "Well, too bad."

Wes regarded the baby, too. "I'll cancel my trip." To Iris he explained, "The last big sales conference before the holidays."

"When?"

"The rest of this week." After the New Year, he was scheduled for a promotion that would mean less travel and more money. In the meantime, the sales meeting sounded important. He and Diane exchanged glances.

"Oh, stop it," Iris said with a false brightness that made her think of a chirping bird. "Of course you both want to put the children first. But you both have work responsibilities, too. You don't need to feel guilty for that. I'll stay until you hire someone new."

Diane eyes widened, the way Jonah's did when being offered ice cream. "Oh, Mom. Would you?"

It was then that an image of Diane's passion-party perfume in its gold-topped bottle popped into Iris's mind. "I'll stay on one condition," she said. "As long as I'm here, Noah sleeps in his crib. He doesn't sleep in bed with you, even for a minute. If he gets up in the night, I'll give him a bottle. But he stays in his crib."

"He'll scream."

"Trust me on this, Diane. And right now while Jonah's sleeping, you should take a nap yourself. You can leave Noah in the trusty hands of his grandmother."

"And I can get back to the office," Wes said, standing up.

"No!" Iris exclaimed with such intensity that everyone jumped. "How much do you think you'll get done in the next hour and a half? I need you to run over to BJ's and get me some clothes." No way was she running the risk of facing her sister again that day. "I'll give you a list of what I need. When you come back, you can take a little nap, too."

"Well…okay." Wes spoke with the robotlike inflection of someone not awake enough to question why Iris didn't want to do her own packing.

Diane rose wearily from the couch and handed Noah to Iris. "Thanks for everything, Mom." She touched her husband's hand and leaned over to stroke the baby's cheek. "I'm so glad to have him back."

Iris wasn't sure which "he" she was talking about but figured it didn't matter. "So am I, honey," she said. "So am I."

That night, Iris got up with Noah four different times. Once, she gave him a bottle, but otherwise, convinced that he craved comfort rather than nutrition, she only patted him on the back until he quieted. On the next few nights she offered no milk at all, only the patting. Last night, he'd finally taken the hint and slept straight through. Pleased as Iris was at this accomplishment, she had been so alert to Noah's every move and sound that she felt like she herself hadn't closed her eyes all week.

Each day Diane had taken an extralong lunch hour so the prospective nannies on her list could come to the house for an interview. She and Iris agreed there was really only one good choice: Gina Buono. Gina was sixty-five, a retiree who'd run a day-care center and now was bored. Her references were excellent. Although her age sounded alarming, when they actually met her it was clear that she looked younger than Patti Ann, sounded smarter and moved faster. In Gina's presence, Iris's people-meter remained comfortingly silent—but then, it had remained silent around Patti Ann, too. Just to be sure she wasn't making another mistake, Iris offered to help Gina for a few hours each day next week, until the nanny knew her way around. But first Iris meant to go back to BJ's and sleep the whole weekend. Maybe watch a few old movies on TV. Nothing else. If BJ didn't like it, too bad.

On Saturday morning Iris rose at dawn and packed her things with a giddy sense of impending freedom. She was nearly finished when Jonah padded into her room, so innocent in his little footed pajamas, so un-suspecting of the grandmother who was plotting her escape, that she decided she'd better cook breakfast before making her getaway. After all, Jonah had had a tough week. They had just reached the kitchen when Wes wandered blearily out of the bedroom and said with forced heartiness, "How about I make us some eggs, Jonah? Just you and me and Grandma can have bacon and eggs."

Iris begged off, saying she wasn't hungry. Happily, she started carrying her belongings to her car. Wes rushed to help, probably as relieved to see her go as she was.

Now she pulled into BJ's driveway, glad she'd arrived

while the street was still quiet and empty. She wouldn't have to talk to a soul.

Locking the car without even popping open the trunk—she'd unpack her things later—she got only halfway to the house before she spotted Harvey Sussman loping down the street toward her. He had on his usual tattered yard clothes, indicating he'd probably been slogging around in his flower beds for hours. Stuffing his dirt-encrusted gloves into his pocket with one hand and waving to her with the other, he shouted, "Iris, wait!" The grubby gardener strikes again.

He gestured more frantically, then caught up with her just as she reached the door. "Iris," he panted. "I'm glad I caught you before you went in. I need to talk to you. Do you have a minute?"

Well, of course she had a minute. She'd just hoped it would be a minute to herself, after three days without one. "Sure, Harvey," she said. "What's wrong?"

Before she knew it, she was sitting in Harvey Sussman's kitchen, a place she'd never been or expected to be. He had poured her a cup of coffee from an ancient coffeemaker with a warming coil that obviously didn't work, considering that the brew was tepid rather than hot, and tasted sour as well. It ended up not mattering, because after Harvey told her about BJ's eye problem—a normal aging phenomenon, my foot—and suggested that BJ could have used Iris's help driving at night, Iris wouldn't have been able to taste the coffee anyway.

"Why didn't she tell me?" Iris was mortified that she hadn't known.

"I take it the two of you had a fight."

"Yes. I insulted her. It was my fault."

"I think the PVD happened the next day. I don't think she wanted to ask you for any favors."

Iris put her cup down with a clunk. That was just like BJ. Not to want to ask favors, when Iris would have been perfectly willing to help. She felt tears welling up, but had no intention of crying. She didn't know Harvey Sussman well enough to cry in front of him. She remembered her vow to practice being meaner.

"Well, let me tell you, I know I insulted her, but that was twenty years ago!" she forced herself to say. "And BJ wasn't nice about it." She sniffed back the tears, hoping she sounded as if she had a cold. "I'll be moving out of her house as soon as I settle on a place," she continued. "I wanted to do that, anyway."

"And once you move out, what will you do with yourself?" Harvey asked.

Why was he asking her this? Why was it his business?

Then she realized she'd been waiting for someone to pose this question for a year. She just hadn't thought it would be this annoying stranger.

"I wish I knew!" What *would* she do? "Years ago when I was raising Diane and had to work full-time, I thought there'd be nothing better than having a little free time. Now I have too much. I could sit and eat bonbons all day—don't think I'm not tempted—and for a while I thought I'd give my eye teeth for a fuller schedule. But after three days of nonstop grandchildren, I'm not so sure. Not that I don't love my grandchildren."

"Well, of course you love your grandchildren. There's a difference between being a grandmother and being a babysitter."

Iris nodded in agreement. She'd been truly distressed to find that when her time with the children was no longer a visit but a *task*, it hadn't been nearly as much fun. While Diane and Wes were at work, she was *entirely responsible*. If anything bad happened to the children on Iris's watch, Diane and Wes would never forgive her. She'd never forgive *herself*. She was holding the survival of the whole family in the palm of her trembling hand. It was quite daunting. A childless man like Harvey could never understand.

Drinking his coffee, looking thoughtful, Harvey lowered his cup and leaned slightly in her direction. "What do you like to do, Iris?" he asked. "I mean, in the interest of keeping away from bonbons. BJ says you like to shop."

Iris put aside her worries about grandparenting in order to consider this. Very interesting. BJ and Harvey had been discussing her. Iris could picture it. Harvey standing on the front porch, having come over to check on BJ's eyes, and before they knew it, the two of them chatting it up about poor Iris with nothing to do with her time.

Iris wasn't sure if she was insulted. Considering all that had happened, probably not. If BJ was gossiping about her, she must have begun her descent from her towering mountaintop of fury.

"Yes. I like to shop. I'm good at it, too. But I only shop in stores or through catalogs. Not online. You can't tell anything about the look of a product on a computer."

"Fine. Then that's what you should concentrate on. Shopping. You can start a shopping service. Set it up as a regular company, maybe an S-corporation. You can be president."

Iris laughed, but it came out more of a snort. She had no idea what an S-corporation was. "You know the last time I was president of anything? In seventh grade. The candidates went out of the room while the class voted, and when we came back in, everyone was clapping. But I didn't know who they were clapping for because I was too nearsighted to see my name written on the blackboard at the front of the room. As an optometrist, you can appreciate that. I had my first pair of glasses a week later."

"It's not unusual to become nearsighted in adolescence," Harvey said.

"Anyway, that was my one experience with high office."

"All the more reason to be president of something now." He sounded a little like her cousin Gerald, who'd always thought Iris could do a lot more than she actually could.

On the other hand, maybe Harvey had a point. If a woman could save her grandson from a two-hundred-pound nanny so spaced out from the sugar blues that she was likely to collapse on him at any moment, and if she could train a five-month-old to sleep through the night so his parents could have some privacy, who was to say she couldn't also run a business?

"A personal shopping service," she said with a kind of bravado she hadn't expected from herself. "Fine. Done. Perfect."

Harvey seemed surprised. "Well, good," he said uncertainly. He rose to carry his coffee cup to the sink.

"Wait. Sit." Iris motioned him back to his chair. "So. What do you need?" she asked.

"Pardon?"

"From the personal shopping service. What do you need?"

Harvey frowned. "Wait a minute. I didn't say I would—"

"Be my guinea pig? Why not? How else will I get my feet wet?"

"You can—"

"Never mind, I know what you need. A man your age, even when he's working in the garden, he needs presentable clothes." She waved in the direction of his outfit. "Shorts, not frayed cutoffs. A comfortable shirt."

Harvey opened his mouth, then closed it without speaking.

"I'll go to the store for you. I'll bring you a few things

to try on. You decide what you want, and I'll take the rest back. You pay me a ten percent commission of what you buy."

Harvey nodded, dumbstruck. Iris felt as if she'd been taking lessons in assertiveness from BJ all her life, but it had taken this week's avalanche of dramas to finally loosen her tongue.

Energized by her sudden entry into the world of business, Iris walked back to BJ's and got her bag out of the trunk, no longer too tired to lift it. She greeted Randolph on her way in. She lugged her clothes up the stairs. At the top, an odd sound drifted into the hallway from the master bedroom suite. BJ was singing in the shower. "Put your head on my shoulder…" Iris could make out only those few words, and no tune to speak of, because BJ couldn't carry a tune. To avoid embarrassing herself, BJ never sang, not even the national anthem at sports events or old show tunes like this one in the privacy of her bathroom. Puzzled, Iris continued down the hall to unpack her clothes.

The shower had stopped by the time Iris ventured into the hallway again, but BJ was still singing. "You're not sick, you're just in LUH-UV." The song was so ancient that at first Iris couldn't even recall the show it came from, though BJ had started her collection of musical soundtracks when she was still in her teens and had played them constantly until the old, long-playing records wore out. Then Iris remembered: *Call Me Madam*. One of BJ's favorites. The show was probably older than Iris herself.

It occurred to Iris then that BJ's unprecedented singing must be the outward expression of something really special to her—perhaps her pleasure at having Iris back in the house. No, that was too much to hope for. More likely BJ was singing to distract herself from her eye problem, to cheer herself up. Iris knocked on BJ's bedroom door. "BJ? Are you all right?"

The singing stopped. BJ, clad in terry-cloth bath-robe, with a towel around her wet hair, opened the door. "So," she said. "You're back."

"I left a message on your tape."

"Got it." BJ motioned Iris in. She pulled the towel from her head and began drying her hair with it, rubbing so vigorously that she might have been trying to coax blood to flow faster through her scalp.

"Are you okay?" Iris asked again.

"Yes, of course. Why do you keep asking?"

"You were singing."

"I was?" Sounding surprised, BJ lowered the towel to expose a mop of wet curlicues. "So. Are you back to stay for a while? Or just passing through?"

"Back to stay. Here to help you turn Randolph into a seeing-eye dog. To take you to your Braille classes."

"I take it Harvey Sussman caught up with you outside and told you about my eye."

"You should have told me yourself."

BJ crumpled the wet towel between her hands. "How could I tell you? You were in hiding."

"I was at Diane's!"

"Before that."

"Before that I was here every night. I got out of the house early because you were mad at me. I was trying not to get on your nerves."

"I wasn't mad."

"Good. All the more reason to have called me. I have a cell phone."

"You never turn it on."

"That's not true."

BJ dropped the towel on top of her expensive satin bedspread. Iris sat down on BJ's bed and casually lifted it off the dry-clean-only fabric so the water wouldn't make a stain.

"I see what you're doing." BJ crossed her terry-cloth-clad arms across her chest. "Trying to preserve my bedspread. You're not my mother."

"You should have told me about your eye," Iris persisted. "I could have driven you around, at least at night."

"I was all right." BJ, too, sat on the bed. "The lights all have haloes, but you get used to them. The human brain adjusts."

"What if it had been worse? What if you had really needed me?"

"I was okay," BJ repeated.

"Even so."

Taking one of the washable cotton toss pillows from the head of the bed, BJ put it behind her head and lay down, staring at the fan hanging from the ceiling directly above them. On the other side of the bed, Iris did the same.

"Well, there was one good thing that came of this," Iris said.

"What?"

"I stopped feeling guilty about Noah." Iris stared upward and wondered if ceiling fans ever fell off their fittings, decapitating the sleepers below.

"You felt guilty about Noah?" BJ asked.

Iris settled deeper into her pillow. "By Jewish tradition, you name your child after a dead relative, right? So here was Sheldon, the grandfather, dead only a year when Noah was born. Naturally I thought they'd name the baby Sheldon. Diane even apologized to me when they didn't. She said something about wanting to stay Biblical, I can't remember exactly. All I remember is, I was glad. Really *glad*. But I felt guilty for it. I mean, what wife is glad her daughter doesn't want to name a child for her husband? Then I found out you didn't sleep with Sheldon, that he'd lied to me about it all those years. And boom, I stopped feeling guilty."

"Well, I'm glad I could be of assistance," BJ said.

"It's a relief, believe me." Both sisters regarded the ceiling fan. Iris wondered if BJ, too, was thinking about decapitation. In a minute she'd divert her attention by telling BJ about Patti Ann and the shopping service.

Sometimes it was easier to talk if you were studying a ceiling fan instead of each other.

Then BJ said softly, "He lied to you about a lot of things." She paused as if to think about this. "He was a lying bastard."

"I wish you wouldn't call him that," Iris said, aware that she herself had called him that and worse back at the cemetery.

"Call him what?"

"Bastard. It's not respectful." Iris sat up. She threw the toss pillow back toward the head of the bed.

"Respectful!" BJ also sat up, running her fingers through her hair, making it stand up a little more. "You know what?" she snapped. "I don't get this at all. The minute Sheldon died, you started getting rid of everything you ever owned with him. You couldn't wait to get rid of the house where you lived while he was cheating on you. You were glad Diane didn't name her baby after him. But if I call him a bastard, all of the sudden I'm out of line. How does that make sense?"

"It makes sense because there was more *to* him than that. He was Diane's father. He was my husband for thirty years!"

"Which probably qualifies you for sainthood!" BJ sprang from the bed and started pacing the floor. "I just don't understand you!"

"No! You don't! I knew it was a mistake to come back. I'll clear out as soon as I can." Iris stood up, but a wave of exhaustion more powerful than her anger made her sit right back down.

BJ stopped pacing. "Oh, Christ. Now we're fighting again. We're having the exact same fight." She hugged herself into her bathrobe as if she were cold. She rubbed her forehead and frowned. "This is crazy. You finally came back. We were going to make up. I thought we were finished with this."

"So did I," Iris mumbled.

"I don't want you to go. I don't want to start all over."

"Me, neither," Iris agreed. She was too tired to fight. "Maybe there are some subjects we should just avoid."

"Exactly. No more discussion of the S-word," BJ said.

"The S-word?"

"Sheldon."

"Oh." Iris made herself stand up. "No more mention of the S-word."

"Friends?" BJ said the words but stood her ground like she always did, so Iris was the one who had to walk over and give her a hug. "Maybe we should have a peace offering," Iris said.

"What?"

"We should all have Thanksgiving dinner at Diane's."

BJ stiffened. "You know I always go to the soup kitchen."

"You don't have to."

"I don't do it because I have to. I do it because I like it."

Iris knew this wasn't true, but she was too tired to pursue it. "Suit yourself." If her sister wanted to spend her whole holiday being lonely, well, BJ had made her bed.

For that matter, Iris was about to make her own bed. All she had to do was stay awake long enough to get all the way down the hall.

CHAPTER 17

"We should cook a turkey," Harvey said.

"What?" BJ turned to frown at him in the darkened car. The idea was ridiculous. They were on their way home from Over-Fifty Singles Night and had just eaten.

"For Thanksgiving," he explained. "You don't really want to go to the soup kitchen. I don't really want to eat with the Gordons. Your sister will be at Diane's. Turkey is easy. Did I ever tell you my mother taught me to make gravy? An unparalleled treat for the palate. You'll love it."

"Well—" BJ knew it was bad policy to agree to a project too quickly, even when the proposal sounded reasonable. Raising a few objections allowed for compromise later. But it had been a difficult evening, and she didn't want to fight. "Well, sure," she said. "The soup kitchen always has too many volunteers anyway."

After all, Harvey had taken her to this Singles Night under protest, after she insisted that, as the originator of the project, she had to be there. "I'm sure everyone would understand if we didn't show up once in a while," he'd said. "I mean, now that we're a pair." Although, as BJ reminded him, they were a clandestine one. She'd let him drive only because, as neighbors, they might logically arrive in one car.

"I'm doing this to show you what a *mensch* I am," he'd said as they pulled into the parking lot. "But put it on the record that I don't get it. What would be wrong with having dinner out, just the two of us, once in a while?"

"Oh, Harvey, we can't. Not until I get around to talking to Iris. If she hears from someone else that you and I are 'a pair,' as you call it, she'll sulk for a month. Anyway, I'll still have to go to Singles Night. The retirement-home women count on it. I can't just abandon them."

"The retirement home," Harvey groaned.

It was true that Singles Night had undergone a metamorphosis. The younger group, relatively speaking, had shrunk. Iris boycotted the dinners in order to avoid Arnold Lieberman, who had come regularly until Iris's absences finally cued him to drop out. Maybe he'd also been hoping to see Sarah Kline, who had expressed interest back at the *oneg*. But Sarah hadn't appeared at Singles Night or anywhere else lately, and it was rumored she'd reconciled with her husband. Resa Taub and Fred Shulman still came, but they talked only to each other, as if the outing were a private business meeting where they could discuss the latest rental properties Resa wanted to show him. Despite repeated invitations in the temple e-mail and by phone, BJ's efforts to attract other singles under seventy had failed.

Yet the group's numbers had swelled. Sometimes they took up two whole tables, or a single long table that stretched the length of the back room, because of the influx of retirement-home ladies who were now enthusiastic regulars. They no longer arrived in cabs. Enough of them had joined their ranks that they were able to commandeer the retirement facility's "coach," a van which brought them to the restaurant and took them home. The women, and occasionally a man or two, claimed the dinners were the highlight of their week. When else did they get to eat where there was actually *salt* on the table? It was a relief, they all gushed, to dine at a real restaurant for a change, instead of in their dismal dining hall.

BJ now spent much of her evening reading menus to frail old women whose sight was failing, or helping them unfold their walkers before escorting them to the ladies' room. She and Harvey both cut meat for those whose hands were too arthritic to do it themselves. They performed miscellaneous small tasks that somehow did not get done anywhere else: changing a hearing-aid battery for Lottie Solomon, placing masking-tape over the zero and the seven on Anna Moskowitz's TV remote, so she could feel the numbers for her favorite local news station when the light in her room was too dim for her to see. BJ always felt, as Iris would have put it, as if she were doing a *mitzvah*.

BJ was sure Harvey felt that way, too. He always seemed happy to help, and he was by far the most patient of the able-bodied diners at the table. The truth was, he was not irritable because he'd had to spend his evening at a singles outing but because, since Iris had returned to BJ's house, BJ hadn't allowed him to spend the night. She was a little cranky about this, herself. During those first long nights together she had enjoyed a reawakened life of the body that had lain dormant for years, an intimacy not just of sex, but also of holding, talking, joking, dozing—an unhurried, lazy togetherness. In the morning, she'd gone to work well rested and alert, and sometimes during a difficult business meeting, her unflappable cheerfulness had actually startled her. For someone who was only an interesting diversion, Harvey had a powerful effect on her. Now that they had to plan their bedroom time carefully, the sight of him tended to speed her pulse even more alarmingly than before. She had made a mental note to check with her doctor in case the phenomenon was related to heart health rather than sex.

"I would have told Iris by now that we're seeing each other if she wasn't so busy starting up her business. Really, the shopping-service idea was a stroke of genius on your part." Actually, BJ thought Harvey had been humoring Iris by suggesting it. She thought Iris's enthusiasm would be short-lived and the project would soon fizzle out. In a tone so bright she was sure Harvey could hear its falseness, she added, "And she's been helping with Diane's new nanny, too."

BJ didn't say that the real reason she hadn't talked

to Iris was that she felt a little odd about spending time with the man she'd chosen for Iris back when she first started Singles Night—not that there was anything wrong with this. But she was afraid Iris would think that, secretly, BJ had actually recruited Harvey for *herself*. Well, she hadn't! Not at all. It didn't matter much, since Iris had disliked Harvey on sight. Even so, she felt funny about it. Aloud she said, "I'll talk to her any day now."

"Well, I hope it's any day because I want to ask you a favor." By now they had turned into their neighborhood. Harvey had slowed down far more than he needed to and was inching the car up the street.

"What favor?" BJ prodded.

"Come to a party with me." Harvey didn't turn to look at her. "It's the Eyes to the Future holiday party. I'm being recognized because my company donates some of the eyeglasses. Believe me, I would rather not be 'recognized.' All it means is that you have to make an acceptance speech, and the next day every organization in town calls you thinking maybe they, too, can benefit from your generosity. But there's nothing I can do about it. You've probably been recognized a few times, too."

"Oh, yes," BJ admitted.

"Anyway, I can handle social events as well as the next guy, but this one would go down a lot smoother if I didn't have to go alone. So please. Talk to Iris or don't talk to Iris, but come to the party with me."

"Well, sure." Again, BJ sensed she was agreeing far too easily. She couldn't seem to help herself.

"It's dressy. Very—" Harvey lifted his arm from the steering wheel and gave a helpless wave. "Very froufrou."

"You mean you aren't wearing your cutoffs?"

"According to Iris, I shouldn't wear them even in the garden."

"Maybe she has a point," BJ said. "Those flexible calf muscles and all."

Harvey smiled and pulled into his driveway. He would walk BJ home and kiss her chastely at the door. The idea was depressing.

He had invited her, several times, to come to *his* house, now that hers wasn't so accessible. BJ had refused. She'd been afraid she'd fall asleep in his bed and Iris would find her gone in the morning. She'd been afraid of— Actually, she wasn't sure what she was afraid of, or if she was afraid of anything at all. Somehow, in her mind, her place was "their" place, for however long they lasted. Not to mention that she recalled the Oriental touches in his decor that screamed "former wife," even though they'd been divorced for years.

"Come in for a minute," he said now, motioning her toward the door.

"Harvey, we've discussed this."

"Just for a minute. I want to give you something. A gesture of gratitude for bailing me out of the Eyes to the Future thing."

"As long as the something isn't inside your pants."

"You're such a cynic." He fiddled with his key chain until he had the proper key in hand and unlocked the door.

"Wait here." Leaving her standing in the entryway, staring at a wall covered with rice paper and a long Japanese print of a waterfall, he headed in the direction of what she supposed was his bedroom. A moment later he returned with a little white box. "Here."

Oh, God, jewelry. At least he hadn't had it wrapped. She lifted the cardboard top. Inside, two big, round, sparkly earrings sat on a bed of cotton. If she had to choose absolutely the last gift she'd want anyone to give her, this might be it.

"Oh, Harvey," she said.

"I thought you'd like to wear them to the party. You always wear these same little hoops." He brushed his finger against her earlobe. "I thought you might like something else for a change. Something dressy."

BJ didn't lift her eyes from the contents of the box. Compared to her tiny hoops, the earrings were enormous. They probably weighed a ton. She wouldn't be able to make it through the cocktail hour with those weights hanging on her ears, much less the dinner. She hoped her dismay wasn't visible.

"You don't like them," Harvey said.

BJ inhaled and put on what she hoped was an expression of gratitude. She looked up. "*Like* them? I love them. I'm just...they're so extravagant."

"Don't get too excited, they're not diamonds, just Austrian crystal. But pretty, huh?"

"Beautiful." At least he wasn't aware that her distress was not about cost—which might have made some sense to him—but about cumbersome materials that often made earrings impossible for her to wear. "Really lovely," she added. If it meant so much to him for her to have them, what else was she going to say? Later—tomorrow—she'd explain. She'd tell him she wore the same hoop earrings all the time because they were so light. She'd tried others, but none of them worked. The weight was just too much for her. And not just on her ears. She didn't wear necklaces or bracelets, either, only a watch that for some reason didn't bother her wrist, which she'd replaced with the identical model every time it gave out. She'd lift her arm to show Harvey what she meant. She'd say she was sorry.

She'd give the earrings back.

He moved closer, pulled her toward him, kissed her. She had to kiss back because, after all, he'd just given her this lavish gift, even if she didn't want it.

Once they were kissing, a pleasant little thread of fire sliced through BJ's belly, producing a sensation she thought she'd been finished with decades ago. It took her some moments to pull away. "I thought this wasn't a seduction," she said in a voice even hoarser than her usual low growl, so husky it sounded like something out of a porn film. Good Lord. She backed away and cleared her throat.

"Okay." Harvey let his hand rest in midair for a few seconds, as if he were debating whether to embrace her again. Then, true to his word, he walked her home.

Iris was in the den, feet propped on the coffee table, sleeping in front of the TV. Her mouth was open, and a dab of red lipstick clung to an upper front tooth. BJ stuffed the earrings into the pocket of her coat and hung it in the closet. When she returned to the den, Iris was snoring.

"Iris?"

"What!" In one panicky movement, Iris startled awake and leaped to her feet.

"I didn't mean to scare you."

"Oh! It's you. BJ." Iris took in her sister's identity and suddenly seemed fully alert. A sheepish expression crossed her face. "I guess if I'm going to sleep in front of sitcoms, at least I should do it in my room." She sounded like someone who'd been caught raiding the liquor cabinet. "I should go upstairs."

"No need. Stay here all night if you want to." BJ kept her tone light. She didn't want Iris thinking she had to hide in her room. "Just don't complain about the crick in your neck in the morning."

Iris sat down again, as if she'd been commanded. Her eyes darted from place to place. Given her apparent insecurity, BJ thought this might be a good time to tell her about Harvey. She'd ease into it slowly. She'd be gentle. She'd work up to it. "I bet you're exhausted," she said. "I bet you helped the nanny again today."

"Gina?" Iris paused as her tongue found the tooth with the lipstick on it. She raised a finger to wipe it off. "Oh, no. Gina hasn't needed help since the first day. She's a whiz, no kidding. Compared to Patti Ann, anyway."

"Probably younger and spryer than Patti Ann, too."

"Well, spryer, yes. But not younger. She's sixty-five."

"Sixty-five!" What was Iris's family thinking? "You were worried Patti Ann would collapse on you, and now you've hired woman of *sixty-five*? She could have a heart attack while the kids are in the bathtub. A stroke."

"Sixty-five, oh my," Iris said, all at once sounding much stronger. "Need I remind you that you yourself are sixty-two, three years younger than the ancient Gina?"

"Oh, God." BJ pondered this for a moment. "Actually, I forgot. I forget. I do. I forget I'm old."

"That's because you're not old. Neither is Gina. She'll probably work till she's ninety and then get hit by a truck."

This was not going exactly the way BJ had predicted. "So you like her."

A cloud of doubt shadowed Iris's face. "The first morning when she got there, Jonah wasn't too happy about having a new sitter. I guess he made a fuss. So what did Gina do? By the time I arrived, she had him in the kitchen baking cookies—these wonderful anise cookies with little sprinkles on top. If you want to win over a two-year-old, let him help make cookies with sprinkles. They're delicious, too. An old Italian recipe. She wrote it down for me."

"Ah, the way to a woman's heart…"

"Well, *of course* I'll make the cookies," Iris said sharply. "Why shouldn't I?"

"I didn't *say* you shouldn't. Iris, what's wrong?"

"Nothing, really." Iris sank lower in her seat, morphing from irritation into mildness. "You know what else Gina did? She taught Noah to turn over."

"No. She couldn't possibly," BJ assured her. "It's not something you can teach."

"I didn't think so, either, but she really did it." Iris sounded despondent. "Noah was flailing around on his back—you could see he *wanted* to turn over. So she set a shiny red ball just out of his reach. Sounds sort of mean, doesn't it? But in less than a minute he was so frustrated, not being able to get that ball, that finally he turned over like he'd been doing it all his life, and reached out to grab it." Iris sighed heavily. "Why didn't *I* think of that?"

"So you *don't* like her."

"I *do*."

"You're jealous," BJ said. She knew she ought to keep her mouth shut, but the words seemed to flow of their own accord before she could censor them. "You're afraid Gina's going to steal the children's hearts."

"Dream on," Iris huffed. "I'll let you know the children's hearts have been stolen after Jonah starts calling her Gamma and me Mrs. Meyerhoff." Then she stopped short. It seemed to have occurred to her that this was a real possibility.

"Hey, I'm sorry," BJ said. "I was just teasing."

"I know you were." Iris stood up. "I'm just tired. I better go to bed."

BJ almost motioned her to stay but didn't. Maybe it wasn't such a good idea to tell her about Harvey right now. If Iris had a man in her life, she wouldn't feel so insecure about being loved by her grandsons. After all, wasn't Iris's sense of security the main reason BJ had started Singles Night in the first place? And what had she accomplished? BJ, who had no need of a man, had gotten involved with the very man she'd picked out for her sister, while Iris, the needy one, had ended up with no one. This was not the time to rub it in.

CHAPTER 18

Iris could smell it as soon as she walked in. A turkey. It permeated the air, too strong to be leftovers from the soup kitchen. BJ had waited until Iris went to Diane's this morning and then, instead of devoting her day to charity as Iris had been led to believe, *cooked a turkey*.

"BJ!"

"In here."

BJ sat in the den, glass of wine in hand, clad in a silky pink bathrobe Iris had given her when she turned sixty. Iris remembered the occasion well, because BJ had lifted the shimmery garment from its box, dangled it from her hand as if it were a particularly repulsive kind of worm, and said, "If you're trying to convince me I'm a Victoria's Secret model and not a widowed, older-than-middle-aged businesswoman, good try."

Then, in an effort to be kind in those days of financial uncertainty before Sheldon's demise, BJ had said, "I know you're trying to be nice, honey, but you can't afford to buy me expensive gifts that are going to sit in a lingerie drawer until I'm carted off to the old-age home and everything goes to Goodwill."

The best Iris could tell, the lingerie drawer was exactly where the robe *had* sat, until now.

"Holy moly," Iris muttered as she stared at her sister. "Are you all right?"

BJ took a sip of what looked like Merlot or Pinot Noir—not that repulsive Drambuie, for a change—and turned away from what appeared to be a football game on TV. She gave Iris a loopy grin. "More than all right," she said, staring dreamily out beyond the open drapes to what would have been the backyard if she could have seen it in the dark.

BJ was drunk. BJ, who did not wear silk and did not watch football, and who drank only in moderation.

"What's going on?" Iris demanded.

Randolph appeared then, padding down the stairs from the bedroom. He had not barked when Iris came in. He had not greeted her in any way.

Behind Randolph, fastening his watch as he descended to the first floor, was Harvey.

Iris might have passed out from surprise, if this hadn't been too interesting to miss.

"Oh," Harvey said. "Iris. Nice to see you. I was just going home." His tone was matter-of-fact, not at all "uh-oh, I've been caught." After retrieving a jacket from the hall closet, he kissed BJ on the forehead and let himself out.

Still too stunned to speak, Iris went into the kitchen, spotted two empty bottles of merlot and a nearly full one sitting on the counter, and poured herself a glass.

The kitchen was a mess. Bones from the turkey languished in congealing grease in the roasting pan. Dishes had been stacked by the sink but not rinsed or put into the dishwasher. A roll of aluminum foil sat partially unraveled, as if something were just about to be wrapped when the person in charge was urgently called away. Aware of the nature of that urgency, Iris took a hefty swallow of wine and carried her glass into the den. "I see you didn't make it to the soup kitchen."

"No." She had the grace to look sheepish. "I meant for us to talk about this. I just didn't think you'd be home until later."

"I guess not." Iris tried not to smile. "So. Did he just happen to be on the second floor of your house using the facilities? Or is this what I think it is?"

BJ twirled the burgundy liquid in her glass and looked remarkably pleased with herself. "Let's just say he could do the Viagra commercial, only he wouldn't need the Viagra."

Taking another swallow of wine, Iris raised her eyebrows as high as she could, considering the Botox. "Good for him. Good for *you*."

"It is. Good, I mean."

As a virtual teetotaler, Iris could feel the alcohol immediately. It coursed through her arms and down to her fingers, making them tingle, making BJ's affair perfectly all right. She relaxed. She settled into the armchair. "I thought when you get to a certain age—" She had no idea she was going to say what came next. "At a certain age, for a woman, it doesn't always...things don't always hit on all cylinders."

BJ pulled the slinky robe closer around her, almost in a caress. "All my cylinders seem to be working."

"I could never do it," Iris said.

"Have sex?"

"Let some other man sleep in my husband's bed."

"Is that what you think?" BJ shook her head. "I moved that bed out of my room a month after David died. It made me sad even to look at it. I bought the double bed I sleep in now and put the queen-size one in the guest room. Harvey's not sleeping in David's bed. *You* are."

"Holy Toledo! I would never—"

"Well, you are."

"You could have told me." Iris could feel the wine begin to curdle in her stomach, which was already too full from Diane's turkey and stuffing and pie. She strove to regain her composure. "I don't mean you could have told me about the bed. I mean you could have told me about Harvey."

"I meant to. I almost did, a hundred times. But what was I supposed to say? That I was innocent in the case of the S-word, but in the case of the neighbor I tried to set you up with, I decided to sleep with him myself? You already thought I was a slut."

"That was different. I was never interested in Harvey. He has all those...opinions." Now that Iris considered this, maybe that was just what BJ liked about him. "The man can't even dress himself." Not that BJ would notice.

BJ set her glass on an end table and tried to look sober. "Listen, Iris, I'm glad you know about this. I'm glad you don't mind. But it doesn't—"

Iris raised a hand to stop her. "Don't say another word. I'll clear out as soon as I can."

"No! That's exactly what I *don't* want. This is exciting and fun, but it's not necessarily a big deal for me. It's more like—sort of a vacation."

"Having an affair with a man is a vacation?" Iris pondered this. "Well, maybe it is."

"The point is, it doesn't change anything. It makes absolutely no difference to *us*, to you and me. I still want you to live here. To consider this your home."

Iris felt a little clump of tears lodge at the back of her throat. One reason she didn't drink very much was that alcohol made her cry even more easily than she already did. She swallowed hard. "Oh, sweetie, that's so nice of you." She reached in BJ's direction and made patting motions, though her sister's hand was at least six inches beyond her reach. "But you don't want some relative infringing on your love nest. And besides, I can't stay here anyway."

Iris wasn't sure if BJ looked more relieved or more puzzled. "Why not?"

"Because I've found a house," Iris said.

At ten the next morning, Iris and BJ were in Iris's car, pulling into Iris's future subdivision. Iris had made BJ get out of bed despite her hangover, herded her sister into the shower, and then fed her eggs and aspirin and several cups of coffee to minimize her headache.

"You must be dedicated," BJ grumbled. "Taking me to see a house on the day after Thanksgiving, the biggest shopping day of the year."

"I can shop later." Iris *was* dedicated. The last thing she'd expected, after all her dutiful real-estate shopping, was to actually find a place that she loved. A place that was perfect in every way. The house was what the sales people called a "patio home," but instead of looking sleek and modern on the outside as most of them did, it was designed like a tiny Victorian house, with a steep-pitched roof and lots of ornamental trim, and a miniature front porch surrounded by elaborately carved railings. Iris loved both the homey old-fashioned exterior and the modern, practical touches inside, like the cozy eat-in kitchen and the three cute bedrooms, the master at one end and the guest rooms at the other. There was a "great room" instead of separate living and dining areas, and a set of French doors that led into a little backyard surrounded by a wooden privacy fence. Small boys would be perfectly safe out there, playing in a sandbox or on a swing, should she choose to buy one. Not only was the house a quantum leap better than the claustrophobic condos Iris had looked at, it was also the ideal midlife residence for a grandmother who was starting a home-based business.

She pulled up in front of the model house and stopped.

BJ made a show of retrieving her sunglasses from her purse and putting them on, though the sky was overcast. She got out of the car with the dramatic slowness of a woman of eighty and stood in the grassy front yard—which would be maintained by the management, Iris was happy to report—and squinted in the direction of the front door. "Why, if it isn't the gingerbread cottage where the witch was going to eat Hansel and Gretel," she said.

"Say that in front of my grandchildren and I'll disown you."

"You were going to leave me your fortune?"

"No, of course not. But you get the gist of my meaning." Iris opened the door and ushered her sister in.

The model was decorated beyond any normal degree of ornamentation, down to the floral wallpaper with the color-coordinated plaid window treatments, and the fake cookies in the fat-bellied teddy-bear cookie jar. But if the decor was excessive, the ambience was just right. Iris could tell BJ was impressed.

"When did you find this?" she asked as they inspected the master bathroom, complete with garden tub and optional Jacuzzi jets.

"The week Patti Ann left. I had dropped Jonah at school and Noah had fallen asleep in his car seat. I knew he'd wake right up if I took him home, so I drove around." She waved a hand blithely in the direction of the French-horn-patterned towels on the towel bar. "And here's where we ended up."

"Have you bought it? Have you actually signed a contract?"

"Yes, of course." This was a lie, but BJ never had to know. Iris didn't want to admit that she'd come back only two days after her first visit to put down earnest money and reserve one of the units under construction, but that since then, she'd done nothing. Well, not exactly *nothing*. She'd driven up to the sales office twice, intending to sign her contract, make her down payment, and choose cabinets, countertops, and flooring—and both times, instead of going in, she'd driven away.

BJ opened the bifold door off the kitchen that led to the laundry room. She made a little cluck of approval. "What does Diane think of this?"

"I haven't told her yet. They've been through so much with nannies and jobs and all that I figured it could wait until after the holidays." The truth was, even though Gina was working out so far and Diane seemed somewhat less tired, Iris wasn't at all sure Diane and Wes were on solid ground. Wes was about to switch jobs. His promotion would mean less travel, but it might also mean late hours and more evenings alone for Diane. The chilly winter was also about to arrive, which always brought its share of colds and flu. What if it all proved overwhelming? What right did Iris have not just to start a shopping service, but to burden herself with moving into a new house and buying furniture to replace the things she'd sold—tasks that would consume all her energy for months—when Diane and the grandchildren might still need her?

"So. What upgrades are you getting?" BJ asked. "What's the total price tag going to be?"

"I'm debating about the fireplace," Iris said. "In this climate, you don't really use a fireplace." BJ nodded, apparently satisfied with this non-answer. They completed their tour of the rooms in agreeable silence, and as Iris opened the front door to leave, BJ reached into her coat pocket, maybe for her gloves. Instead, she came up with a white jewelry box. "Oh, *this*!" She held it gingerly, as if it were toxic. "I completely forgot. I meant to give these back."

"These what? Back to who?"

Stepping out onto the sidewalk, BJ opened the box and showed Iris the contents. Very nice. "Earrings," Iris observed. "A gift from Harvey?"

BJ put the top back onto the box and stuffed it into her pocket. "He asked me to go to the Eyes to the Future party with him. He's being honored for giving them free eyeglasses. He gave me the earrings for the occasion. I was going to give them back yesterday and completely forgot."

"Well, no surprise. Cooking a turkey took all your concentration." Iris opened her eyes wide and clowned.

BJ scowled at her.

"Anyway, you ought to wear them. They won't kill you."

"They might." They had reached the car. BJ snatched her door open and plopped down into her seat.

"Well, I see your point," Iris persisted when they were both inside. "The earrings probably weigh more than a hundredth of an ounce. Maybe half an ounce. Holy cow. The weight will probably pull your earlobes clear to the floor. You'll probably be deformed forever."

"Lay off, Iris."

Well, maybe for the moment she would. "But you're going to the party with Harvey, right? What are you going to wear?"

BJ lowered her head and, with thumb and index finger, took hold of the skin between her brows and squeezed. It wasn't clear whether her hangover was getting the better of her or she was still distressed about the earrings. Either way, Iris hated to see anyone pinching facial skin that had lost its youthful collagen and was unlikely to lie smoothly back in place.

"Oh, Lord, it's black tie," BJ groaned. "That means I have to buy a dress. I hate formal dresses almost as much as I hate jewelry."

"No, you don't. You never hated formals. You always looked good in them. You're tall. You're swanky. What you hated was the *last* formal dress, the one you wore at Janelle's wedding. David was dead less than a year, you were alone three thousand miles away, and you didn't know a single person at the ceremony. I would have come, believe me, if Sheldon hadn't just lost another job."

"Iris, for heaven's—"

"You also didn't have a good feeling about the marriage, as I recall. You thought Luke seemed ready and Janelle didn't. Yes? So it's no wonder you opened your suitcase in the ladies' room in the airport before you checked it to go home, and stuffed the dress in the trash. It's what any rational person would do."

"I should never have told you," BJ said.

"The point is, you don't really hate formal dresses. You just don't have good memories about the last one, so you don't want to shop for this one. When is this party, anyway?"

"After Chanukah's over. Right before Christmas."

"Good. Plenty of time. I know just the person who can help you."

BJ looked over at her, momentarily bewildered. Iris pointed dramatically to her chest. "President and owner of Iris's Personal Shopper."

"That's what you're calling it? Iris's Personal Shopper?" BJ frowned.

"You don't like it?"

"It sounds like you're buying people underwear and sex toys."

"Holy catfish." Iris called up an image of thirty-something passion-party types, clandestinely handing her lists of scented oils and leathers.

"How about something like—" BJ pinched the skin above her nose again. "I don't know, exactly. I think better when I've been sober for a while. It'll come to me."

"Iris and Company," Iris said. "If you don't like Iris's

Personal Shopper, then it'll be Iris and Company." This had been her alternate name all along.

"Iris and Company? Who's the 'and company'?"

"Never mind. It's a nice name, don't you think?" She didn't elaborate on the appeal the word "company" had for her—she who had worked for dozens of companies over the years but never owned even a single share of any of them. To Iris, "and company" didn't mean a living person. It meant a business. An entity outside of her. "And company" was a heady concept.

"Okay. So how much is Iris and Company going to charge me for its services? More to the point, how much of my time will it take?"

"The fee is just enough to cover my back rent. And it will take exactly one afternoon of your precious time. I'll scout the stores first. You're dealing with a professional here."

"Okay." BJ sighed like a much older woman. "But don't think I'm excited about this."

"The deal is, you have to try on anything I bring you. I'm not asking to you to go to the stores. I'll do that. I'll choose what I think you might like."

BJ looked skeptical.

"You get to try everything on in the privacy of your own bedroom. You don't have to like it. You can reject it the minute you look into the mirror. But you have to try it on." Iris knew how important it was to lay down the ground rules, especially with someone like BJ.

BJ paused for longer than Iris thought she should have. "Agreed," she finally said.

It took Iris nearly three full days to narrow her selections. She rejected a gorgeous beaded dress because BJ would say it was too heavy, and another because it was turquoise, which had always been "David's color." If it ever got to that, "Harvey's color" would have to be something entirely different.

Eventually Iris settled on four dresses: one a rich chocolate brown, one royal-blue, one peacock-blue, and one red. She thought BJ would tolerate four. Three would have been better, but Iris couldn't decide.

In BJ's bedroom, with the dresses laid out carefully on the spread and Randolph sitting on the floor, his ears cocked as if aware that something significant was going on, BJ regarded each of the dresses with equal distaste. "What happened to black? I thought people went to these formal occasions in black."

"That's why you've hired a personal shopper. Black is out this season," Iris lied. BJ wore too much black already. "Color is back. A personal shopper knows these things."

In the end, BJ hated the brown dress and the peacock, and Iris had to agree with her. About the royal-blue, a long, flared skirt and a matching jacket with glass buttons, BJ said, "I could live with this. But just."

Then she tried on the red gown, a satiny, floor-length sheath with spaghetti straps, and an elegantly embroidered matching jacket. It was clear to Iris that even BJ, regarding herself in the mirror, could see it was perfect.

"It's red." BJ said. "I don't wear red."

"Yes, you do. What about your red turtleneck?"

"I mean red all over. So *much* red." She indicated the length of the garment.

"It's not *hooker*-red. It's not red with those cheap orange undertones. It's red with a touch of brown. It complements your coloring. It's first-lady red."

"No," BJ said, though she continued to study her reflection.

Iris noticed then that the earring box had made its way from BJ's coat pocket to the top of her dresser. Interesting. Iris opened it, lifted one of the earrings off its cottony bed, and held it up to BJ's face. "You should wear these," she said. "A little pizzazz is just what the outfit needs. Even red can be too plain otherwise."

BJ's expression told Iris that BJ agreed. The earrings would be perfect.

"No. It's a matter of principle. They're pretty, but why should I pretend to like something I won't be able to wear for more than five minutes? That's not what I do. That's not who I am."

"Honey, you can tell him later. After the party. In a tactful way."

"Oh, be the sweet little woman. That's me, all right."

"It *is*, BJ. You're sweeter than you think." Iris threw her arms around her, hugging the silky fabric of the gown.

"Get off, Iris!" BJ swatted her away.

Iris laid the earring back in its box. She left the box open, for BJ to see.

They kept the dress.

CHAPTER 19

In the temple kitchen, BJ and Iris and three other women had spent most of the afternoon making potato latkes for that evening's Chanukah dinner. By five o'clock, BJ felt like a grease ball, although a grubbily satisfied one. The latke dinner was never just the usual kiddie-party it was at some synagogues, but a huge social event that drew most of the congregation, pre-schoolers to octogenarians.

Earlier, each of the women had arrived with her food processor, which she'd used for shredding dozens of potatoes. Then, under Sally Solomon's expert direction, they'd divided the potatoes into large bowls, added salt, onions and flour and shaped the mixture into enough pancakes to serve the entire crowd. They'd fired up a dozen electric frying pans recruited from Sisterhood members, and fried and fried and fried, arranging the finished products on pans in the oven to keep them warm.

The kitchen had been uncomfortably hot for over an hour, but no one had complained. They were all too filled with a sense of purpose. Even BJ felt that way, although she was a little surprised because, for many years, she had believed cooking projects were beneath her. She was a professional who owned a business! Let the housewives work in the kitchen! Even after Janelle and David were gone and BJ's emotion had segued from a sense of superiority into a fear of being seen as one of the old ladies not good for much except preparing and serving food, she'd walked a wide path around this kitchen.

Yet somehow, here she was. Over the past few years, as Iris had gently recruited her into the "womanly" Sisterhood activities, BJ had begun to enjoy them in spite of herself. She was beginning to believe that, in a practical, down-to-earth way, older women ran the world.

Now, although she jumped and cursed at the occasional drop of hot oil that landed on her arm as she added a new batch of potatoes to the pan, the pain made her feel vaguely heroic. A few blisters were the price you paid for feeding the masses.

At the same time, she hoped she'd get finished in time to spruce up a little before she saw Harvey.

For all its homey feel, the latke dinner was orchestrated like a Broadway production. Depending on the first letter of their last name, each family had to bring a main dish, a vegetable, or a dessert. BJ's famous Asian slaw—her *only* famous recipe, compared to Iris's half-dozen or so—was in the refrigerator. Iris's anise cookies—actually the new nanny's anise cookies, from the recipe Iris had wheedled out of her—sat on the dessert

table in the social hall. Half an hour before the main
event, a cadre of women began bringing in platters of
chicken for the entrée. Some of the chicken was home
cooked, but most was the same fast-food fare BJ had
relied on during her busy working-mother years when
Janelle was still at home.

"Where do you want this?" a sweet voice trilled.

BJ turned to face Mitzi Rosen, the flaming redhead
whose husband performed most of the congregation's
colonoscopies. She was holding a platter of chicken
breasts and drumsticks.

"Stick it on one of those baking sheets and put it in
the warming oven," BJ said. Usually, attractive as Mitzi
was, BJ found it painful to look at her. The young
woman's hair was bright and her clothes were always
bright, too: garish neon shades of primary colors. But
today she sported a whole different style, striking but
soothing. Except for a long silver-and-turquoise neck-
lace, she was dressed entirely in black.

"Mitzi. You look terrific," BJ said. "That outfit is
wonderful."

Mitzi beamed. "You like it? I never wore black in my
life until your sister told me I could. She said, 'Mitzi,
you don't need to *wear* a color. You *are* a color.' It was
like—a revelation."

"So you used her shopping service."

"Her shopping service?"

"Iris and Company. Didn't she tell you?"

Mitzi blushed scarlet. "Well, no. She just gave me

her advice. But if she has a service... If she charges a fee..."

"No. No. She's just getting started. Maybe next time." BJ concentrated on turning a row of latkes while they were still golden-brown instead of burned. Then she said to the departing Mitzi, "You look so good, you're probably the one who made her decide to go into business."

Mitzi laughed. "Then I'll be sure to spread the word."

Twenty minutes later, Iris and BJ were carrying platters of warm latkes into the social hall and placing them on long tables spread with white cloths and decorated with menorahs. Most of the food would be on the buffet, but the latkes, the committee had decided, needed to be right at hand, along with the dishes of applesauce and sour cream to complement them.

The room looked beautiful, cheerfully decorated for the holiday and not unpleasantly crowded, even with the steady stream of arriving families and the gaggle of small children running up and down the aisles between the tables. Years before, BJ had sat on the design committee for this room. The previous social hall had been too small, and its kitchen woefully out-of-date. She still remembered her months of lobbying for recessed incandescent lights rather than economical fluorescent ones, so the large new room would look cozy rather than institutional. Every time she came to an event here, she was glad she'd prevailed.

From across the room, Harvey waved to her and

pointed to the seats he'd saved for them at a table with some of the other Singles Night regulars who didn't have family in town. Although BJ had washed her hands and face and felt less oil-slick, the sight of Harvey made her wish she had another top to wear, instead of her greasy blouse.

Iris elbowed her. "Look." She nodded toward the entrance, where people were giving their tickets to the check-in committee. There, arms linked with her husband—apparently they had reconciled and then some—stood Sarah Kline. She was beaming. Well more than beaming. She was exultant. Her gray hair was now a soft honey-blond. Her outfit, instead of her usual too-short skirt, consisted of a slim-legged pantsuit like the one Iris had described months ago when they were making fun of Sarah's skinny legs. The suit was a becoming shade of coral Sarah herself would never have chosen. If Iris had helped her, as BJ suspected, and if Iris was also giving advice to Mitzi Rosen, then maybe she was more serious about her shopping service than BJ thought. BJ couldn't focus on this the way she meant to, because she couldn't take her eyes off Sarah. The woman's new look was more than just clothes, more than just hair, more than the glow of her newly kindled romance with her husband. Sarah didn't just look well dressed and well coiffed and happy, she looked…well, *transformed*.

Then it occurred to her why they hadn't seen Sarah for all these weeks. "She had a face-lift!" BJ exclaimed.

Iris grinned. "Nice, isn't it?"

"You knew!"

"Yes," Iris admitted, "but she made me promise not to tell."

"You could have told *me*." Inwardly, BJ fretted about this while outwardly she and Iris both beamed goodwill on the families at the table where they were setting down platters of latkes. When they turned to head back to the kitchen, Iris patted her jaw near her earline and said, "I think her doctor pulled the skin back a little too much. It should ease some with time, but still. My own surgeries came out better. Except maybe for the nose."

"I thought you always looked fine, even before all that surgery," BJ said. "You never needed it in the first place. And surgery or no surgery, it wouldn't have affected how Sheldon—excuse me, the S-word— behaved. It was always his problem, not yours."

"We were never going to mention the S-word," Iris said.

"Using the term 'the S-word' isn't the same as uttering the word itself."

"It's very close," Iris protested as they re-entered the kitchen.

"Anyway, my point still stands," BJ whispered. Sally Solomon, manning the warming oven, handed her the last platter of latkes.

"Well, don't worry. I was finished with all that when Jonah was born," Iris whispered back. Sally seemed miffed at being excluded from the conversation, but Iris ignored her. "Jonah was the ugliest baby ever born. Red, and his face all squooshed." Raising her hand, Iris squooshed her face. "But I loved him. I knew I'd love him if his face looked that bad his whole life. He probably wouldn't care how my face looked, either." She scanned the counter for another latke platter, saw that they'd all been taken out to the tables, and motioned BJ to exit the kitchen in front of her. "I figured if the S-person wasn't going to change—I guess I always knew that in my head but didn't admit it in my heart—then I certainly wasn't doing all that surgery for *me*. Not to mention that I'd just as soon not lose my mind because of too much anesthesia, like that article said I might. So I said to myself, okay, Iris, now you're a grandmother—so *be* a grandmother. And *voila*."

Iris flung her arms out in a dramatic *ta-da* gesture and then, realizing they were once again in public, moved her hands chastely to her side. "Also I had this brilliant revelation," she said. "Once you get old, you can't get young again, even if you have face-lifts and go to the gym."

"For heaven's sake, Iris, you're not *old*."

"I know, but I hope to be." Iris gazed wistfully at Sarah. "She does look good, doesn't she?"

"Not as good as you do. So don't get any ideas."

"Don't worry." Spotting Diane and Wes and the children at their table, Iris made a beeline in their direction, leaving BJ to set down her platter alone.

When everyone was seated, it was apparent that the

Singles Night table now contained mostly couples,
except for two ladies from the retirement home who sat
on either side of—unaccountably—Arnold Lieberman,
who wasn't even a temple member and who, at sixty-
plus, was young enough to be their nephew or son. Like
Mitzi and Sarah, Arnold looked amazingly good,
having acquired—perhaps with Iris's help?—a new
hairpiece that might have passed for the real thing.

Beyond that, it was all couples. Molly Gerber and
Lou Green had brought another eighty-something
couple as their guests. Resa Taub had brought a man she
introduced as Joel. Fred Shulman, always openly gay,
had arrived with Barry Pearlman, who until now had
remained steadfastly in the closet, appearing in public
with one woman after another but never settling down.
Tonight, sitting next to Fred, he looked like he was
finally in love.

"You should be ashamed," BJ whispered to Fred.
"Barry is at least ten years younger than you are."

"*Fifteen* years," Fred whispered back.

"I just don't want to see you get your heart broken."

"No chance," said Barry, who had overheard.
Fred's smile had a glow BJ hadn't seen since his days
with Tommy.

The way everyone treated them, it seemed clear that
BJ and Harvey were also, so to speak, out of the closet.

Sitting directly across from BJ, Molly Gerber looked,
as always, as if she had shrunk since their last time
together. She had to rise from her seat and lean over the

table to do this, but she seemed determined to pat BJ's arm with one hand and Harvey's with the other. "You make a handsome couple," she told them. "Congratulations."

"No congratulations are in order," BJ said quickly. "We're just seeing each other, that's all."

"Oh, you're an item," Molly assured her, and sat back down.

Obviously dumbstruck, Harvey stuffed his mouth with green bean casserole so as not to have to talk. BJ was embarrassed. *Harvey*, not BJ, was the one who'd wanted them to appear in public together, openly, even before Iris knew they were seeing each other. *He* was the one who ought to say something. *He* was the one who had invited her to the Eyes to the Future party next week, where they would be "a couple" to the entire world.

The thought of this served as an uncomfortable reminder that the earrings he'd given her were still sitting on the bureau in her room. She'd meant to return them a dozen different times, and a dozen times she hadn't—partly, she was ashamed to admit, because of Iris's warnings.

"You're crazy if you give them back," her sister had snorted every time BJ was about to make her move. "You think he gave you fancy earrings for you to spit on them and trample them under your feet? No! If you return them, he'll be insulted. He gave them to you to wear."

"An optometrist gives you eyeglasses to wear, too," BJ had maintained, pleased with the patience she managed to infuse into her voice, "but if the prescription turns out to be wrong, he doesn't get offended when you bring them back."

"This has nothing to do with that! This is personal! This could affect your whole relationship!"

"Oh. The whole relationship. Maybe also the Mideast situation and the prospects for world peace."

At that, Iris usually rolled her eyes and went sulkily silent.

But the more the two of them argued, the less sure of herself BJ felt. Now, watching Harvey cut his chicken and pop a piece into his mouth so that all he could do was chew, she was suddenly irritated by the very sight of him. Most people looked silly when they chewed. Harvey looked as if he were advertising some especially delicious food product a consumer would do well to rush out and buy. It seemed to BJ, as she watched Harvey's mouth work so energetically—the chicken was a little bit tough—that Iris might be right. Harvey might not be the *mensch* she had taken him for but the kind of typical, egotistical man who knew he looked decent even when he was grinding poultry between his teeth, and who thought, therefore, that a woman would fall all over him just because he gave her a pair of torture-chamber earrings it would practically kill her to wear.

Not that he *knew* they were torture-chamber earrings. She wiped that troubling detail from her mind. Harvey swallowed, dabbed his lips with a napkin and smiled at something Lou Green was saying. BJ had noted weeks ago that Harvey had excellent, straight teeth. She had tried not to dwell on this because she was afraid it would make her feel disloyal to David, who had not been just a general dentist, but a tooth-implant specialist. In the end, she had felt guilty for not feeling more disloyal than she actually did. But David was six years dead, and BJ was pretty sure Harvey's teeth were the originals, set in his strong and annoyingly attractive jaw.

Turning away from Harvey, BJ speared a latke from the serving tray, put it on her plate and slathered it with sour cream. She took a bite. She didn't even *like* sour cream. Pushing the mess to the edge of her plate, she took another latke from the platter and put a dollop of applesauce on top.

The Eyes to the Future party was a week away. If Iris was to be believed, once BJ gave the earrings back, it was possible—maybe probable?—that she and Harvey would not be an item. Or maybe that wasn't what Iris meant at all. BJ felt thoroughly confused—an emotion she wasn't used to and didn't like. The latke in her mouth was barely lukewarm. If she had been six years old, she would have spit it out, applesauce and all. She chewed and swallowed. She got up. She went to the dessert table.

As usual at temple functions like this one, there was an astounding array of choices. Cakes, brownies, two kinds of pie, a fancy bowl of English trifle, cookies of every description, even a platter of Rice Krispies Treats to please the children, although BJ noticed that it was mainly men who were putting them on their plates. As BJ spooned up a bowl of fruit salad, Iris came up beside her and did the same. Seconds later, Arnold Lieberman appeared, plate of goodies in hand. "Let me guess," he said to Iris, pointing to the various items on his plate and then lifting one of the anise cookies in a kind of salute. "These are yours, right? Delicious."

"Thank you," Iris said, deftly moving away from Arnold as she spoke, putting herself on the other side of the table. "They're from an old family recipe."

"You and your old family recipes," BJ said when Arnold was out of earshot.

"I didn't say it was *our* family. Gina says her family has made these cookies since they were back in Italy. I wasn't lying."

From out of nowhere, Iris's grandson, Jonah, appeared and latched onto BJ's knee. "Aunt BJ!" he exclaimed.

"Jonah!" BJ picked him up and cradled his small, compact body into a hug. He had grown, even in the few weeks since she'd seen him. If Jonah was this tall at two and a half, how big must Eli be, at four? It was impossible to tell just from pictures. "I bet you want some cookies," she said to the boy.

"Yes!"

"What? You're going to make Aunt BJ get you cookies before she even finishes getting her own dessert?" Iris laughed from beside them. "Here, let Grandma help you instead."

Jonah dove for her, and in a single, graceful motion, Iris caught him and set him on her hip. She pointed out the various cookies until Jonah chose the ones he wanted.

"And what else did we have to eat, sweetie?" Iris asked her grandson. She put his dessert plate down long enough to point to a platter on another table. "What are those?"

"Lakkas!" Jonah exclaimed.

"Yes! Excellent. You're so *smart*."

"I smart!" Jonah smiled winningly as Iris carried him off. There was no arrogance in a two-year-old's confession of brilliance, BJ decided. Eli, at that age, had loved running away from BJ, beating her in a race, declaring as he ran away from her, "I fast!" He had been, too.

It was then, standing in front of enough sweets to satisfy the most demanding sugar craving, that bitterness rose in BJ's mouth so intense that for a moment she couldn't swallow.

Harvey touched her gently on the arm. "You miss him, don't you?"

She hadn't heard him come up. When she opened her mouth to answer, the bitterness eased some, and in a moment evaporated so thoroughly that it might never been on her tongue but only in her mind. "Miss who?" she asked.

"Your grandson. Eli."

"I haven't seen him in a year. He probably doesn't even know who I am."

"Of course he does. You told me the two of you talked on the phone all the time until just recently." Harvey's expression was of warm concern. She wasn't going to cry.

"It doesn't take long for kids to forget," she said harshly.

"Then go see him. Maybe right after the holidays, when your business is slow. I bet he'd love it."

BJ shook her head. "Too awkward. Too many people involved. Janelle and the new boyfriend. Luke and the stepmother and the new baby by then."

"Maybe everyone would welcome a grandma on the scene. Maybe *especially* when there's a new baby. Don't you think Luke might be happy to have Eli off his hands for a long weekend? And if Janelle wants to go off with the boyfriend... You might be surprised."

"Maybe."

"You should be visiting on a regular basis, anyway," Harvey told her. "Two or three times a year. More if they don't come here. You're a rich woman. You can afford it."

"You're so bossy, Harvey."

"Yes, but in a good way."

BJ couldn't do this anymore. If she didn't want him instructing her, why did the whole back of her throat ache with emotion? If she tried to say another word, it would come out as a croak. As she touched his arm in a gesture of thanks, the tug of something powerful as a riptide pulled her toward him, as if she were the swimmer and he were the sea, and she would drown if she weren't careful. But the sensation wasn't scary like a riptide was, it was as sweet as summer—and it had nothing, or at least maybe only fifty percent, to do with sex.

CHAPTER 20

"Would you mind telling me where we're going? I feel like I'm being kidnapped," Iris said as they made their way through the traffic. It was the Saturday morning of the Eyes to the Future fete, and she was sure BJ had a million other things to do.

"We're going to the mall. You know how much I hate the mall. You're coming for moral support. I haven't been there since 1997."

"You were there two weeks ago to sell that jeweler an ad. What are we going there for?"

BJ jerked her head in the direction of an old Belk bag in the back seat. Iris leaned over and retrieved it. "Holy cow!" BJ had stuffed her beautiful red formal into the bag, where it was getting creased and rumpled.

"I'll have it pressed. But first I need a bra. I tried it on with my other bra and decided I need...more lift."

"So for more lift you're blindfolding me and rushing me off to the lingerie department? Holy Toledo."

"You're not blindfolded. Although it would have been a nice touch." BJ looked fiercely at the road. "And what's with this 'holy' stuff? Holy moly. Holy cow. Holy catfish. Holy Toledo. You never talked like that before. Where'd you get it?"

"From Gina, I guess." Until now, Iris hadn't given the matter much thought, but yes, Gina was the one who said holy everything. And BJ was right—now Iris was doing it, too. "Holy hamburger!" she exclaimed without thinking. She clapped her hand over her mouth. "Listen to me! I can't believe I'm such a puppet."

"Don't be so dramatic, Iris. You're not a puppet. This is actually a good sign."

"A good sign?"

"It means you think she's okay. You don't pick up speech patterns from people you don't like."

"Well, I hope so." It was true that Gina's "holy" expressions tickled Iris. It was also true that she seemed a decent nanny. She took the children outside every day. She fed them nutritious meals. She seemed fond of them without being possessive the way Patti Ann had been. If Iris did something for Jonah or Noah, Gina didn't try to one-up her. She had her own four-year-old granddaughter to dote on. She made excellent baked goods and was generous about sharing her recipes. So far, Iris's people-meter had remained soothingly silent. In the unlikely event that Gina was Dr. Jekyll and Mr. Hyde after all, Iris meant to keep dropping in at unexpected moments. Just as a precaution. Just for a while.

BJ gave a false cough and cleared her throat to change the subject. "At the Chanukah party I saw evidence of Iris and Company in the wardrobes of Mitzi Rosen and Sarah Kline. Yes?"

"Yes." This was interesting. BJ was dense as mud about fashion, so if she'd noticed, other people must have, too.

"But what amazes me is Arnold Lieberman. What I want to know is, how did you convince Arnold Lieberman to buy a new toupee?"

"It was easy." Iris suppressed a smile. "He has the hots for me, you know."

"I've noticed. I thought you were trying to avoid him."

"I figured if I brought up a business subject, he might leave me alone, personally."

"And?"

"Big mistake."

"Yes. But what about the hair?"

"I lied to him. I told him I used to work for a wig company and I bet he had on a hairpiece." Iris remembered this conversation with satisfaction. "He was a little embarrassed at first, but then he asked how did I like it. I said he looked fine, but did he know the finest hairpieces had gradations of color. I told him if he ever wanted to look into getting an upgrade, I could help."

"Ah. And did Arnold's new rug make a good profit for your company?"

"It was a *mitzvah*." Iris had been afraid BJ would ask this and had prepared her answer. "A *mitzvah* for the visual well-being of the congregation. To give them something nice to look at. For that matter, for the visual well-being of the whole town."

"So true." For the briefest second, Iris thought her sister might leave it at that. Then BJ said, "But Iris, did you ever actually charge these people money? The idea of going into business is to make money."

"I know, but while I'm getting started, I want to let people see a few samples of what I can do. It's good advertising. Nobody knows that better than you do. Besides, I don't actually *need* any money."

They had reached the bottleneck around the mall, even more crowded than usual today, with Christmas so close. BJ bore down hard on the brakes as the light changed and a domino line of cars stopped short. Maybe that would shut her up. But the moment they were on their way again, BJ said, "Needing money is not the point. Business is business. Otherwise people will be calling twenty-four hours a day asking you to help with this and that for free, and then where's your life? Pay your expenses with money from the shopping service and let the S-word's money pay for Jonah and Noah's college."

"Hmm," Iris said. This was an intriguing concept—that she could see to it that her grandsons' educations were paid for. If Sheldon had lived, they never would have been able to afford it.

"There are all kinds of funds you can set up, with tax breaks, too. You need a good financial advisor."

Iris groaned. "That's what Arnold said. He wants to help me set up my books. If I accept, next thing he'll be wanting to take me out to dinner. Or to services, which he didn't attend for twenty years until this fall.

He'll want me to drive two hours up the road with him to meet his grandchildren. I'd rather have a root canal."

"Root canals aren't so terrible anymore," BJ said, automatically defending David's profession. Why hadn't Iris known better than to make disparaging remarks about dentistry?

"Anyway, you don't need to let Arnold help you." BJ rushed on. "There are other possibilities. I know someone who spent many years establishing and running a business."

"Oh? Who's that?"

In the second before she realized Iris was putting her on, BJ looked crushed, an interlude that Iris enjoyed greatly.

Then BJ was all business. "Iris, I'm happy to set up your books for you. I'll show you how to manage them. I'll go over them every month with you if you need me to. I'll keep you out of the clutches of Hairy Arnold."

"No need," Iris said as they turned into the mall parking lot, which was already packed with holiday shoppers despite the early hour. They'd be lucky to find a space at the very perimeter. "You've already put me up for months without letting me pay. You've done enough." Iris didn't add she might be in residence a few months more, since she'd yet to sign her contract for her house. She bore in silence the knowledge that the saleswoman had called to say she'd lose her reservation if she didn't complete the paperwork this weekend. She'd driven to the office every day this week, checkbook and pen in her purse. Each time, she'd gotten halfway up the block and then turned away. Diane's family was still her first responsibility. True, Gina seemed satisfactory. True, Wes would be in town more after the holidays. But just in case things didn't work out, it wasn't fair to be preoccupied by real estate.

"Well, it's certainly a fact that I've done a lot for you," BJ said as she cruised the lot. "I've been the soul of generosity." She kept her tone so sober that only a blood relative would detect the overtones of tongue-in-cheek. "But in matters of bookkeeping and profit-and-loss, it's better to keep it in the family. You don't want Arnold to know your net worth. You don't want many people to know, period. I'll set up your books and find you an accountant."

"You make it sound like the Sopranos."

BJ slowed the car to a snail's pace. "This is not an offer you'd be wise to refuse," she growled ominously.

Not that there was any question of that, Iris mused. But she was annoyed with herself for feeling so grateful.

Miraculously, just as they crawled past Belks, a space opened right in front of them, not ten steps from the door. BJ swung into it, inching out another driver.

"Good job," Iris noted in the exact words and tone she usually saved for Jonah. In addition to being an ignoramus about business matters, she was now beginning to sound like someone running a day-care center. Holy shit.

BJ assigned Iris a seat just outside her stall in the lingerie dressing room. She would try on her selection of bras in private, slip the dress over them, and then come out to model for her sister.

"All I can say," Iris called in as BJ was changing, "is that you must like him a whole lot if you're fighting Christmas shoppers in the mall just to get a little 'lift.'"

"Sure, I like him, but don't get any ideas." BJ emerged from the dressing room in bra number two at store number three. Iris had told her in the beginning there was no use going into Victoria's Secret, but BJ had insisted. "They cater to women half our age!" Iris had whispered as BJ picked up one flimsy bra after another and hastily put it down. The next shop, which featured tiny camisoles and see-through nighties, was even worse. Now, judging from the way BJ tugged at her gown in the area of her rib cage, she had gone to the opposite extreme and chosen an undergarment meant for the matronliest of matrons—a long-lined bra with stays that poked. "Nix," Iris said, giving a thumbs-down sign, "unless you want to pull at yourself so much he'll think you have fleas." Rather than taking offense, BJ shot her a look of gratitude and went back into the dressing room.

"You obviously adore him," Iris said when BJ came out in bra number three. "You're obviously gaga over him."

BJ narrowed her eyes. "I don't *adore* him. What kind

of description is that? I'm certainly not *gaga*. I'm too old to be *gaga* over anybody."

"Then why are you looking for lift mere hours before a social event?"

"Because I don't want to look like a saggy old hag," BJ said—a comment so un-BJ-like that Iris almost laughed.

"This one is good," Iris said instead. "This is the bra of choice."

"You think so?" BJ sounded as if she wanted reassurance, also un-BJ-like.

"Yes. Lift, but not so much as to look phony. Lift without bounce."

BJ sighed. "I feel like a damned fool. You're the one who should be here looking for lift. You're the one who should be getting ready for a party. I'm not comfortable with this…this being *involved*. Not that I'm very involved."

"You're such a liar, BJ. Anyway, don't be planning me any men. I've got enough with my new house—" this was a lie "—and my family and business, without thinking about men."

BJ went back into the stall and changed into her street clothes. "I never knew you to be sour on men," she said en route to the cashier. "Even after living with you-know-who."

"I'm not sour," Iris said as BJ swiped her credit card. "I'm just realistic about relationships in midlife. Or beyond. I guess we're beyond, aren't we?"

"Speak for yourself."

Well, Iris would. BJ glared, but Iris couldn't stop talking. "I mean, people have raised their families by now. They're devoted to them. It causes trouble. A woman meets some man and thinks he's wonderful. It never occurs to her that she'll have to go to Chicago for his daughter's seder, where she'll freeze and catch pneumonia because spring there doesn't come till May. Or he thinks it's her job to send birthday cards to all his grandchildren when she can't even remember their names, or want to. Believe me, I've seen how these things turn out."

BJ looked insulted. She seized Iris's arm and directed her toward the exit. Iris wasn't sure she could make this good.

"I mean, sometimes things turn out fine," she gushed on. "Like you and Harvey. I think you'll be fine. You always liked medical professionals, for one thing."

"*Medical* professionals!"

"David was a dentist. Harvey is an eye doctor." Why was BJ so upset?

"Harvey is *retired*." BJ was walking fast, practically pulling Iris toward the door.

"What I mean is," Iris said, "you'll be good together because you don't want him because he's a man—I mean, not *just* because. You want him because you like *him*. His profession. His personality. And he doesn't have children to get in your way. If you go to see Eli, you won't be competing with some other kid." Iris knew she was babbling. "With me, I'm too involved already. That's all I'm trying to say."

They had reached the door to the parking lot. BJ stopped and turned around to face Iris. "So. You're ruling out a relationship with a man?"

"No. Of course not. Not as long as he's single, healthy, heterosexual, childless, and no older than forty-seven." She pulled her arm out of BJ's grip. "You go on ahead. Get that gown pressed before it's too late. I'll stay here for a while and then take the bus." Iris loved BJ, but she didn't think she could endure another second with a sister who'd turned into a lovesick wacko.

Also, even though Chanukah was over, Iris had no desire to leave the mall. She was never able to stay out of the stores in the weeks before Christmas. She loved the crowds. She loved the last-minute sales. She loved to stock up. Already she'd bought a tricycle for Jonah's third birthday, months away, and dozens of marked-down winter clothing items for the boys, some for this year and some for next. She'd even fallen in love with a couch in her favorite furniture store—a bright, cheerful couch almost the same red as BJ's gown for tonight's party and sturdy enough for her grandsons to jump on, ideal for the great room of the cottage she would probably never buy.

BJ would have a fit when she learned Iris was going to take her up on her offer to move in permanently. Iris tried not to think about this. She busied herself in a survey of all the shops along one arm of the mall, mentally noting which items had been marked down even further since the last time she'd checked. She was completely lost in this activity for over an hour, until she came to the pet store and stopped short.

She spotted Wes first. He stood close to the front, with Noah in his arms, peering through the glass into the puppy area, where each animal was held in its own pathetically small cage. Her first instinct was to march in and announce herself, but then she saw Diane, kneeling beside her husband at Jonah's level as mother and son, too, surveyed the lineup of puppies. Jonah looked very serious. He peered up at his mother and asked, exactly as he always did when they looked into the communal cage of parakeets farther back in the shop, "Which one is *you* favorite, Mommy?"

Iris melted back a few steps into the dimness of the mall, wanting to watch without being discovered.

Diane made a show of thinking Jonah's question through, putting an index finger to her mouth to indicate concentration. "Let's see. I think the little black one over there." She pointed at a puppy Iris couldn't see. "The one trying so hard to get out of his cage."

Jonah nodded approval. "And what's *you* favorite, Daddy?" he asked.

"I like all of them," Wes told his son. "We need to take home the one *you* want."

So. They were getting a dog. They were going to take it home. No one had told her.

Maybe it was supposed to be a surprise.

All the same, she wished they'd mentioned it, if

only so they could have discussed the role a pet might play in their overextended lives. New jobs, a baby and now a *puppy*....

On the other hand, Jonah was clearly thrilled.

And then again...

Maybe it had nothing to do with her. Standing there discussing a future with Fido or Queenie or Rex, it was pretty clear they were a family all by themselves. They didn't need her. Not now.

Later they'd call and tell her about the puppy, and invite her over to celebrate. *She* was the one they'd need then, to make a fuss over the new addition and share their joy.

They loved her but didn't need her. There was a big difference.

Huge.

Something else occurred to her then. Patti Ann had always insisted she wouldn't work in a house with a dog. She claimed every dog she'd been entrusted with tried to bite her. If Iris had been a canine, she would have bitten Patti Ann, too. Gina was a different story. Gina liked dogs. She liked living creatures in general. And if Diane and Wes trusted Gina to take care of their children and their pets, Iris supposed she had to trust her, too. Whatever life she was going to have from now on, Iris was on her own.

She expected to feel downcast. Rejected. Discarded. But the emotion that seized her was relief. She could build up her business: consult, shop, advertise. She could decorate her house.

Holy gardenia! Her house! She was going to lose it, if she didn't buy it *this minute*. For once, her cell phone was going to come in handy. She used it to call a cab and let herself be chauffeured at great expense to the sales office to sign her contract.

After that she was too excited to go home. The best alternative, she decided, was to go back to the mall. Another cab whisked her there. She wandered for more than an hour. Then, as she knew she would, she walked out of the mall and across the street to the strip of shops that housed her favorite furniture store. If she was going to spend all of Sheldon's money, she might as well enjoy it. Casting her eyes on the couch she'd chosen a week ago, she was gratified to find that it pleased her as much as ever. She was also pleased that it wasn't exactly the color she remembered, but far more festive. It looked like a holiday. It was valentine-red, the color of cut-out cards and candy hearts and love. It wasn't at all, as she had thought at first, the elegant, standoffish first-lady red of BJ's gown.

BJ's gown!

Did BJ still plan to give the earrings back? The woman was so stubborn, she probably did. Holy churchmouse! Iris had to get back to the house *right now*, before her prideful, idiot sister ruined her life.

CHAPTER 21

BJ was glad when Iris decided not to drive home with her from the mall. She'd wanted to be alone from the minute she finished buying her bra. One more "holy moly" or "holy catfish," and she would scream. One more word of analysis about male/female relationships, and she would strangle her sister with her bare hands. It wasn't even Iris's fault. BJ was just too keyed up for conversation. She was too keyed up, period, though she didn't know why. A formal dinner/dance...she'd been to a lot of them in her time. They were always more work than you thought they'd be. They were never any fun. Why should she be *keyed up*?

All the same, BJ was restive as she drove to the dry cleaners. Fidgety as she waited for the gown to be pressed. Nervous as she drove home. Randolph met her at the door, wagging his tail in anticipation of their walk.

Good, she thought. Exercise. It was just what both of them needed.

Harvey's car was not in his driveway when they

passed, and BJ was glad. If he was home and saw them, he'd come outside. Usually she loved that, but right now this was better. She'd be with him soon enough.

A couple of mornings ago, Harvey had rushed out to join her on her early-morning walk, wearing only the ragged cutoffs he'd obviously thrown on the second he'd seen her ("Don't tell Iris," he'd said) and a light shirt not warm enough for the weather. He hadn't seemed to care. It had been just after sunrise, one of those crystalline days when the trees were almost bare and all the lawns had been raked, and everything appeared astonishingly clean. Looking into the rising light, BJ had been reminded of how much better her eye was, lately. The week before—or so it had seemed—the Big Blob had begun to break up into smaller pieces that didn't distort her vision as much. She knew that wasn't the process that had been explained to her. The Big Blob was simply supposed to drop below her line of vision. Maybe that was what had happened. Maybe the sense of the tissue breaking apart was just an illusion. In any case, it didn't matter. With the maddening Big Blob out of the way, the remaining floaters in her eye seemed inconsequential. Her clear vision, on that clear day, had seemed a gift.

"Mornings are so beautiful here," she'd heard herself say, startled to hear such gushy sentiments issuing from her own mouth.

Harvey had smiled. "Mornings are beautiful everywhere, if you're where you want to be," he'd replied.

Maybe that was true. Maybe it also applied to other

times of the day. Right now, this was exactly where BJ wanted to be, walking with her dog through the honeyed light of a December afternoon that reminded BJ a little of herself: mellowed and mature. And maybe a little bit weary, but that was part of its charm. As if the light were saying: *I have been here before. I have seen it all, and look: it's still pretty good.*

She felt—how could she describe it?—well, joyful.

Randolph tugged on his leash, full of energy, willing her to go faster. They walked for over a mile. The sun began to drop low in the sky, filling it with a slant of many colors: pink, purple, gold. BJ turned back. She wanted plenty of time to get ready. To take a bubble bath. To dress.

And—oh—to practice what she'd say when she gave the earrings back.

Why the hell hadn't she done this weeks ago?

By the time she got home, the color had drained out of the day. She didn't feel joyful anymore, either.

An hour and a half later, she had forgotten all that. She was almost ready. She was going to be fine.

Unless, of course, she died from the heart attack she nearly had when Iris burst into the room behind her, still wearing her coat, her face in a contortion of full-blown panic. Ignoring BJ entirely, she rushed over to the dresser. "Oh! Good! They're still here!" She seized the earrings in their little box, where BJ had set them in advance of carrying them downstairs to return to Harvey.

"Don't bother to knock," BJ said.

Iris clutched the jewelry box tighter to her chest.

"Put it down, Iris. And don't get started. I'm giving them back."

"Well, you shouldn't." But Iris set the box back on the dresser. She put her hands on her hips and looked belligerent.

"Listen to me, Iris. I'm wearing the gold hoops I always wear, just like I told you. These other earrings will be back in Harvey's possession before the beginning of the party. This is not the catastrophe you think it is. It will be perfectly all right."

Iris abandoned her hands-on-hips posture in order to take off her coat, as if she meant to stay a while. "Oh, brilliant. Now you're not only going to insult him, you're going to do it just when you're sure to ruin his evening. You can't do this now. It's too late."

"What do you mean, too late?

"For someone who's supposed to be smart, you're so *stupid*, BJ." She threw her coat on the bed. "Jewelry is not about *itself*. It's about what it symbolizes."

"What? A willingness to have your ear fall off? A tendency to masochism?"

"It symbolizes," Iris said slowly, as if speaking to a severely challenged child, "how people feel about each other. As in friendship ring. Engagement ring. Wedding ring."

"Don't kid yourself. This is not an engagement situation. *Certainly* not a wedding situation. And just barely friendship."

"You're the one who's kidding yourself! Once you sleep with somebody, it's friendship and then some!" Iris stabbed a finger in the direction of BJ's décolletage.

"Okay. Agreed. Friendship. Nothing more."

"Pay attention to me, for once, BJ!" Iris yelled. "The earrings won't kill or maim you. Wearing them won't make people think you're a shrinking violet. You're sixty-two years old. You've already made your point. Nobody will think you've given up your principles and are caving in because you're wearing a pair of *damn earrings*."

BJ didn't move, but Iris must have thought she intended to argue, because she held up her hand like a traffic cop. "I won't say another word," she huffed, and then turned away from BJ with her too-short, too-pointed nose in the air, trying to look haughty. Plopping herself down on BJ's bed, she shoved the toss pillows out of the way, threw BJ's sleeping pillow on top of them, and arranged herself, tailor-fashion, against BJ's headboard, with her arms crossed in front of her. BJ wasn't sure if she looked more like a demonstrator daring police to drag her away, or a small, hostile Buddha with lacquered black hair. Randolph, who had been lying on the floor, jumped up and sat next to her.

Even Randolph was on Iris's side.

It strengthened BJ's resolve. She would ignore both of them.

Looking in the mirror, she noted that her gown fit perfectly, especially with the new bra. Lift was a good thing, in a woman of sixty-two. Lift was important.

Even her hair looked decent. She'd had it done. Her fingernails, too, although she'd been smart enough to ask just for polish, not tips. And her toenails: the first pedicure she'd ever had in her life. She peered down at her feet, wiggling red-tipped toes that exactly matched her dress. Harvey would be proud to be seen with her, even without the earrings.

"This is really none of your business," she said to Iris.

Keeping to her vow not to say another word, Iris didn't.

BJ opened the jewelry box one last time and peered down. The earrings were sizable, each one a dazzling cluster of Austrian crystals interspersed with pearls. After a couple of minutes, they'd feel like five-pound dumbbells. What fool would subject herself to *that*?

She couldn't accept another man's gift of jewelry, anyway. What would David think? She tried to call him up, but after all this time he was hard to capture, the image sweet but formless, as elusive as the memory of light.

Without exactly meaning to, BJ lifted one of the earrings to her face. She put it down. Iris was watching her like a hawk. All the same, she picked it up again and this time slipped it into place with practiced fingers. In the mirror she was bright and sparkly, her dress look-at-me! red and not at all the elegant first-lady color Iris had described. Well, too late.

She took the earring off.

The doorbell rang. Randolph leaped off the bed, barked, and raced out of the room. Iris, too, stood up.

Breaking her vow of silence, she said. "I'll let him in." With a fierce glare, first at BJ and then at the earrings, she said, "Don't be a fool, BJ. Make up your mind."

BJ made up her mind. A minute later she descended the steps toward Harvey in the entryway, a solid, living presence, dignified in his tux, deserving of being recognized as the good man he was, regarding her with warm, approving eyes. The baubles gleamed in her ears. She would give them back later, after they began to feel like bowling balls. She would slip them off in the middle of the party after everyone had had a few drinks. No one would notice. Well, except maybe Harvey. She'd explain to him then.

"Wow," he muttered. He puckered his lips and issued a perfect, piercing wolf whistle that made Randolph spring to attention.

Iris gasped.

BJ laughed.

Harvey winked.

And that's when she knew she'd wear the earrings all night, even though they were a little heavy, as love always is.

A few of Iris's and BJ's Famous Recipes

THE CLOGGEROO
(also known as Chocolate Delight)

This is Iris's most famous chocolate cake. Everyone loves it. It's so rich that some people think of it as brownies. Iris and BJ call it The Cloggeroo because they think it has enough fat in it to clog even the healthiest artery. But they call it Chocolate Delight in public.

1 18.25-oz. package devil's food cake mix
1 3.9-oz. package chocolate instant pudding mix (If you don't have pudding mix, use 1/4 cup cocoa and 2 tbsp. sugar instead)
2 cups sour cream
1 cup butter or margarine, softened
5 large eggs
1 tsp. vanilla extract
3 cups semisweet chocolate morsels, divided
Chopped nuts, if desired

Beat first six ingredients at low speed with an electric mixer 30 seconds or just until moistened. Beat at medium speed 2 minutes. Stir in 2 cups semisweet chocolate morsels. Pour batter evenly into 2 greased and floured 9-inch square pans.

Bake at 350° F for 25 to 30 minutes. Cool completely.

Microwave remaining 1 cup of chocolate morsels at High 30 to 60 seconds or until melted, stirring at 30-second intervals until smooth. Drizzle evenly over cakes. If you're going to take this cake to a public event, it looks very nice topped with the chopped nuts.

SOUR CREAM COFFEE CAKE

Iris's and BJ's grandmother was a wonderful cook, but she made very few desserts. This is the one the sisters remember best, and that Iris makes all the time.

For the cake:

2 cups sugar
1/2 pound oleo
3 eggs, beaten
3 cups flour
1 tsp. baking powder
1/2 pint sour cream
1 tsp. baking soda
1 tsp. vanilla

For the topping:

1/2 cup sugar, mixed with cinnamon (a tablespoon or more), raisins and nuts, to taste (Iris usually uses just the cinnamon).

Cream the sugar and oleo. Add the eggs. In another bowl, sift the flour with the baking powder. Mix the baking soda and vanilla with the sour cream. Alternately, add the flour mixture and the sour cream mixture to the sugar/oleo mixture and stir together until well blended.

Pour half the batter into a greased, floured 9 x 13" baking pan. Sprinkle half the topping mixture over this. Then add the rest of the batter, and put the remaining topping mixture on top.

Bake at 350º F for about 40 minutes.

CHICKEN ENCHILADAS

Iris likes this because it's an easy dish to put together one day and bake the next, or to reheat. Men like it a lot (well, women like it, too, although they will complain that it's too rich even while serving themselves a second helping). It's even a favorite with Iris's two-year-old grandson.

1 medium chopped onion
2 tablespoons butter or oleo
1 1/2 cups shredded cooked chicken
12 oz. picante
1 3-oz. pkg. cream cheese
1 tsp. cumin, if desired
2 cups shredded cheese
8 six-inch flour tortillas

Heat oven to 350° F. Cook onion in oleo. Add chicken, 1/4 cup picante, cream cheese and cumin, and stir until thoroughly heated. Add 1 cup cheese and mix. Put 1/3 cup of mixture in center of each tortilla and roll up. Put seam side down in 12 x 7" baking dish. Top with remaining cheese and picante. Bake 15 minutes.

BJ'S FAMOUS ASIAN SLAW

BJ doesn't like to spend a lot of time in the kitchen, so she likes this because you don't have to cook it. Someone (she can't remember who) brought this dish to a potluck meeting years ago and gave her the recipe. It's easy to throw together from ingredients you can pick up in the grocery on the way home, and people always make a fuss over it.

> 2 3-oz. packages of ramen noodle soup mix (beef flavored)
> 2 8.5-oz. packages of slaw mix
> 1 cup almonds, sliced and toasted (BJ doesn't always use these)
> 1 cup sunflower kernels
> 1 bunch green onions
> 1/2 cup sugar
> 3/4 cup vegetable oil
> 1/3 cup white vinegar

Remove the flavor packets from the soup mix and set them aside. Crush the noodles and place them in a bottom of a large bowl. Top with slaw mix. Sprinkle with almonds, sunflower kernels, and green onions.

Whisk together the contents from the flavor packets, sugar, oil and vinegar, and pour the mixture over the slaw. Cover and chill 24 hours. Toss before serving.

GINA'S ANISE COOKIES

Iris's grandson likes to help his nanny, Gina, make these cookies, because he is allowed to put the sprinkles on top of them. Gina claims this is an old recipe her family made back in Italy. Iris describes it to friends as "an old family recipe" but doesn't say whose family.

For the cookies (makes three dozen):

5 cups flour
6 eggs
5 tablespoons baking powder
1/2 cup vegetable oil
2 cups granulated sugar
2/3 bottle anise flavoring

Mix eggs in large bowl by hand. Add all other ingredients and mix together. Refrigerate for one hour. If dough is still sticky after refrigeration, add a little more flour (or powdered sugar, if you prefer). Roll small pieces of dough into a ball. Then, with your hand, flatten the ball and roll it into a stick about two inches long. If you're right-handed, hold the stick toward the top with your left hand and, with your right hand, loop the bottom over the top so it looks sort of like a Breast Cancer Awareness shape, with a little hole in the middle. (The hole will probably close up when the cookie is baked.) Put looped dough pieces about an inch apart on a greased cookie sheet.

Bake at 350º F for 10-12 minutes.

For the frosting:

1 box powdered sugar
1 stick butter
2 tablespoons vanilla
1/3 bottle anise flavoring (the rest of the bottle)
Colored sprinkles

Microwave the stick of butter until melted. Add powdered sugar, vanilla and anise. Mix until smooth and creamy. Frost cookies when still warm, and immediately put sprinkles on top.

There comes a time in every woman's life when she needs more.

Sometimes finding what you want means leaving everything you love. Big-hearted, warm and funny, Flying Lessons is a story of love and courage as Beth Holt Martin sets out to change her life and her marriage, for better or for worse.

Flying Lessons

by

Peggy Webb

REQUEST YOUR FREE BOOKS!

2 FREE NOVELS TO INTRODUCE YOU TO OUR BRAND-NEW LINE!

There's the life you planned. And there's what comes next.

A Boca Babe
on a Harley?

Harriet's former life as a Boca Babe—where only
looks, money and a husband count—left her
struggling for freedom. Finally gaining control
of her path, she's leaving that life behind as she
takes off on her Harley. When she drives straight
into a mystery that is connected to her past, will
she be able to stay true to her future?

Dirty Harriet
by Miriam Auerbach

HN40

Available April 2006
TheNextNovel.com

HARLEQUIN®
Next™

There are things inside us
we don't know how to express,
but that doesn't mean
they're not there.

A poignant story about a woman
coming to terms with her relationship
with her father and learning to open up
to the other men in her life.

The Birdman's Daughter

by Cindi Myers

HARLEQUIN®

Next™

Life is full of hope.

Facing a family crisis, Melinda and
her husband are forced to look
at their lives and end up learning
what is really important.

Falling Out
of Bed

by
Mary Schramski

It's a dating jungle out there!

Four thirtysomething women with a fear of dating form a network of support to empower each other as they face the trials and travails of modern matchmaking in Los Angeles.

The I Hate To Date Club

by
Elda Minger